THE STEIGER SURVEY OF MYSTICAL EXPERIENCES

Since 1967, our questionnaire of mystical experiences has been distributed to nearly 30,000 men and women worldwide, and we continue to hear from individuals who have knocked on Heaven's gate and even, in some remarkable instances, been allowed to visit loved ones and receive teachings from holy figures. Statistics from our questionnaire reveal the following percentages:

***76% report their soul leaving the physical body during an accident, a serious illness, a surgical procedure, or some other near-death experience (NDE)**

***57% claim to have visited a heavenly realm or dimension during their NDE**

***60% state that they received an inspirational communication from a Higher intelligence during their experience**

***50% are aware of their guardian angel or guide**

***35% feel that they have been blessed by the appearance of a holy figure**

***58% report an intense religious experience**

***72% claim an illumination experience**

***44% have communicated with the spirit of a departed loved one**

In other words, thousands of individuals need not simply believe in Heaven on faith alone. They've been there to experience firsthand what they consider to be their true home beyond our realm.

Also by Brad and Sherry Hansen Steiger

HE WALKS WITH ME

MOTHER MARY SPEAKS TO US

RETURNING FROM THE LIGHT

CHILDREN OF THE LIGHT

ONE WITH THE LIGHT

Touched by Heaven's Light

Brad Steiger and Sherry Hansen Steiger

A SIGNET VISIONS BOOK

SIGNET
Published by the Penguin Group
Penguin Putnam Inc., 375 Hudson Street,
New York, New York 10014, U.S.A.
Penguin Books Ltd, 27 Wrights Lane,
London W8 5TZ, England
Penguin Books Australia Ltd, Ringwood,
Victoria, Australia
Penguin Books Canada Ltd, 10 Alcorn Avenue,
Toronto, Ontario, Canada M4V 3B2
Penguin Books (N.Z.) Ltd, 182–190 Wairau Road,
Auckland 10, New Zealand

Penguin Books Ltd, Registered Offices:
Harmondsworth, Middlesex, England

First published by Signet, an imprint of Dutton NAL,
a member of Penguin Putnam Inc.

First Printing, May 1999
10 9 8 7 6 5 4 3 2 1

Printed in the United States of America

Although the events and experiences recounted in this book are true and happened to real people, the names of most individuals have been changed to protect their privacy.

Contents

CHAPTER ONE

Heaven Is Our Home

Jesus' warning regarding how difficult it could be for the rich to enter the gates of Heaven is apparently being heeded by the wealthiest families in the United States. According to a poll taken in October 1997, the one thing that the rich would most be willing to pay for was "a place in Heaven."[1]

The results of a December 21, 1994, *USA Today*/CNN/Gallup Poll showed that the United States is a land of believers. Not only do 96 percent of Americans believe in God, 90 percent believe in Heaven, 79 percent accept the reality of miracles, and 72 percent recognize the existence of angels.

"Americans have a tendency to take their religion straight," said Conrad Cherry, of the Center for the Study of Religion and Culture at Indiana University and Purdue University, Indianapolis. "That means don't water it down with an awful lot of intellectualism."

Jeffrey S. Levin, of the Eastern Virginia Medical School, Norfolk, has found that "mystical" beliefs in the United States appear "more common with each successive generation." Currently, he states, more than two-thirds of Americans say that they have had at least one mystical experience. As many as 64.8 percent believe that they have experienced some facet of extrasensory perception—telepathy, clairvoyance, prophecy—and nearly 40 percent are convinced that they have made contact with a family member or friend who has died.

Levin's extensive analysis is based on the most recent comprehensive data available on the individual religious experience, derived from the General Social Survey, a random national sociological survey of nearly 1,500 people conducted in 1988 for the National Opinion Research Center, University of Chicago.[2]

Time Questions the Existence of Heaven

With more people than ever before believing in God, angels, miracles, mystical experiences, and heaven, it seems quite easy to answer the question "Does Heaven Exist?" posed on the cover of the March 24, 1997, issue of *Time* magazine with a resounding *"Yes, it does!"* Millions of us acknowledge Heaven as our true spiritual home, a sanctuary that exists forever awaiting our return in a timeless dimension of the Eternal Now.

Within the text of *Time*'s cover story, a telephone

survey taken by Yankelovich Partners for TIME/CNN on March 11–12, 1997, indicated a much stronger hope for Heaven than the magazine's cover blurb seemed to suggest. Among the statistics acquired for the article were such percentages as the following:

- Do you believe in the existence of Heaven, where people live forever with God after they die? *Yes: 81 percent No: 13 percent*
- Do people get into Heaven based mostly on the good things they do or on their faith in God or both? *Good things they do: 6 percent; Faith in God: 34 percent; Both: 57 percent*
- Which of the following do you believe are in Heaven? *Angels: 93 percent; St. Peter: 79 percent; Harps: 43 percent; Halos: 36 percent*
- Is Heaven a perfect version of the life we know on earth, or is it totally different? *Perfect version: 11 percent; Totally different: 85 percent*
- Do you believe you will meet friends and family members in Heaven when you die? *Yes: 88 percent; No: 5 percent*

HEAVENLY CONCEPTS

Even the simplest of ancient societies espoused the concept of a continuation of life after death that placed the spirit among more advanced beings in a supernatural environment of perfect happiness. The Heaven of most polytheistic religions was considered a place where mortals might continue the pleasures of earthly life.

The Greeks and the Romans incorporated the necessity for the balance of divine justice into their beliefs and portrayed a distinction between Elysium (a place of reward for the virtuous) and Tartarus (a place where the wicked would be punished).

The various depths of Sheol (the abode of the dead) were perceived by later Jewish mystics as seven-layered, and they found in the Persian doctrine of resurrection a hope of release into a new life on Earth or in the heavens.

A general Christian belief holds that since the resurrection of Christ the souls of the just are admitted into Heaven immediately after death. Certain Roman Catholic theologians maintain that before entering Heaven souls must first pass through a state of purification called purgatory.

Islam generally adopts the concept of the seven heavens of the firmament, differing in degrees of glory from the abode of the Most High downward to the first, or most earthly, Paradise.

Many Eastern religions, such as Buddhism, conceive of nirvana as a state of extinction of all desire and of union with the Brahma, the creator god, achieved by the soul as it perfects itself through the course of successive incarnations.

Descriptions of Heaven's Environment

In 1987, *Parapsychology Review* published the results of an interesting experiment in which one hundred college students were asked to take "an imaginary tour of Heaven." In 40 percent of the accounts, the environment of Heaven was described as "cosmic"—as being both everywhere and nowhere at all.

Other descriptions included "a place of soft, diffused light," 32 percent; a "lush, pastoral setting," 30 percent; a place of only "being" without shapes or forms, 29 percent; and, lastly, a walled city with "golden or pearly gates," 7 percent.

Dr. Melvin Morse, clinical associate professor of pediatrics at the University of Washington, conducted a study of four hundred adults who'd nearly died and found that all of them reported leaving their bodies and entering another world. One described herself standing "high on top of a ridge overlooking a beautiful valley. The colors were extremely vivid, and I was filled with joy."

Dr. Tom Harpur, past professor of New Testament studies at the University of Toronto, surveyed nearly two hundred people who said that they had died and actually saw Heaven before being revived.

"We're going to have a spiritual body that resembles the way we were at the peak of our earthly lives," Dr. Harpur said. "We'll be able to see and talk with our loved ones in a beautiful spirit world—and we'll even be joined by our pets. The afterlife will be similar to a university setting where we will continue to learn and to grow spiritually and come to understand the mysteries of the universe. Heaven's not going to be a place where we float around on clouds all day. It'll be far more interesting."

Heavenly Music

According to a university study conducted by Dr. Joel Funk, professor of psychology at Plymouth State College in New Hampshire, many people who have near-death experiences (NDEs) hear the same heavenly music.

"The music that people hear during a near-death experience has a beautiful, floating sound," Dr. Funk stated. "It evokes feelings of overwhelming bliss, and whenever they hear music like that again, it gives them a wonderful feeling of total peace."

Dr. Funk researched sixty people who underwent NDEs and obtained a glimpse of the afterlife after their hearts had stopped. He played various instrumental recordings for them to determine which sounded most like the music that they had heard during their "deaths."

"The hands-down winner was New Age–style synthesizer music," he reported. "About fifty percent of people who have had an NDE recall the sound and are deeply touched by hearing it again. Some people burst into tears when they hear the music of their NDEs."

The Steiger Questionnaire of Mystical Experiences

Our own research tells us that belief in Heaven, angels, and the afterlife has never been stronger than it is today. Since 1967 our questionnaire asking about mystical experiences has been distributed to nearly thirty thousand men and women worldwide. Our questionnaire encourages respondents to share their inspirational accounts of their own near-death experiences, dreams, visions, and meditations, and we continue to receive dramatic personal stories from individuals who have knocked on Heaven's gate and even, in some remarkable instances, been allowed to visit loved ones and receive teachings from holy figures.

In other words, thousands of individuals need not simply *believe* in Heaven based on faith alone. They've been there, and have looked around in what they believe to be their true home beyond the stars.

Statistics from our questionnaire reveal the following percentages:

- 76 percent report their soul leaving the physical body during an accident, a serious illness, a surgical procedure, or some other near-death experience
- 57 percent claim to have visited a heavenly realm or dimension during their NDE
- 60 percent state that they received an inspirational communication from a Higher Intelligence during their experience
- 50 percent are aware of their guardian angel or guide
- 35 percent feel that they have been blessed by the appearance of a holy figure
- 58 percent report an intense religious experience
- 72 percent claim an illumination or enlightenment experience
- 44 percent have communicated with the spirit of a departed loved one

HEAVEN IS MY HOME

Whenever it was Brad Steiger's turn to request the hymn for daily religion class in elementary school, he always asked for "Heaven Is My Home."

> I'm but a stranger here—Heaven is my home. Earth is a desert drear—Heaven is my home. Danger and sorrow stand, 'round me on every hand; Heaven is my Fatherland, Heaven is my home.

There were other verses, but it was these simple lyrics that carried the greatest impact for him. He had often felt as though he were a stranger in a strange land and that "Heaven up above" must really be his true home.

Then, one August day in 1947, when he was eleven years old, the Iowa farm boy returned "home" for a visit.

In a blur of motion, he lost his balance and fell off the farm tractor that he had been driving, and landed in the path of the machine's whirling blades.

There was pain as the machine's left tire mashed his upper body and broke his collarbone.

And then there was no pain at all as the metal blades ripped at his head and tore open his scalp. He had left the body, and was now floating many feet above the grisly scene.

He had a sense of identification with the mangled boy that he saw lying bleeding beneath him on the hay stubble below, but he was growing increasingly aware that that unfortunate kid was not who he really was. The *real* him now appeared to be an orangish-colored ball that seemed intent only on moving steadily toward a brilliant light.

At first, because of his religious orientation, he believed the illumination to be Jesus coming to receive him. But he could distinguish no forms or shapes within the bright emanation of light. All he felt was an urgency to become one with the magnificent light.

When he understood that he was dying, he had a brief moment of panic. He did not want to leave his mother, father, sister, friends.

And then the beautiful light was very near to him, and he perceived a calming intelligence, a being composed of pure light that projected before him a peculiar, three-dimensional geometric design that somehow instantly permeated Brad's very essence with the *knowing* that everything would be all right. The very sight of that geometric design somehow transmitted to the boy the awareness that there was a pattern to the universe and a meaning, a Divine Plan to life.

His panic and fear left him, and he experienced only a blissful euphoria, an incredible sense of Oneness with All That Is. He was ready to die and to become one with the Light.

Instead, he was taken to what appeared to be a peaceful little village nestled at the foot of a mountain. The people there were very kind to him, and there were horses and cattle and dogs and other animals to play with. It was just the kind of place that would especially delight an eleven-year-old farm boy. And the village also had a beautiful park, complete with a bandstand, ice cream vendors, and men and women so kind that they just seemed to shine with an inner light.

And then there were words forming inside him that told him he would soon leave the peaceful valley village and return to his home in Iowa. He was being sent on a kind of mission, a mission to testify to others that there is an essential part of all humans that survives physical death.

Just a few days later, as he lay swathed in bandages in a hospital room, he gave his first testimonial of the world beyond death to the parents of his roommate, a baby girl who had just died. The Roman Catholic sisters who were caring for him had sensed that he had been *somewhere* with the angels and had seen beyond, and they had asked him to speak words of comfort to the bereaved parents, to tell them about the place where the angels had just taken their daughter.

His mission to speak about the heavenly home had begun.

Sherry Visits the New Jerusalem

In 1985, Sherry Hansen Steiger, who had practiced meditation for many years and had the ability to go very deeply into altered states of consciousness, traveled in another dimension and visited what she believes may have been the New Jerusalem.

Sherry, who comes from a very fundamentalist Christian family and who is herself an ordained Protestant minister, has found great strength and guidance from her times of deep meditation. On this particular occasion, she remained in an extremely intense meditative state for nearly five hours.

After praying and relaxing, she remembered leaving her body in a sudden *poof.* As she left for *somewhere,* she was met by a Light Being who would serve as her escort through the most mystically beautiful experience of her life.

In her own words, here is what Sherry experienced:

> As audacious as this may sound, I truly felt as though in some way I saw or touched the Divine Force. The Light Being was so loving and caring

and showed me so many things. It seemed as though we traveled through galaxies, making stops along the way.

There was one place—maybe it was the New Jerusalem—where the beauty was far above anything I've ever dreamed possible. It was like a crystal/diamond planet, reflecting and refracting the purest, most brilliant colors. The light all around was effervescent.

As a "living crystal" I became fused with the Light. I *became* the Light.

Blissful elation permeated every cell of my beingness. How I wished that others might be able to experience this powerful love . . . this perfect love.

Not long after that—or so it seemed—the Light Being told me that I had to go back. I was told that I would only remember a small part of what I had seen. More would be revealed to my conscious mind as I shared and used the experience to help others. Additional glimpses of the vision have gradually come back to me.

I *know* there is an absolute reality, a life beyond, a continuation of life, a perfect place of all-encompassing love, peace, order, and law. This absolute reality is the love we are to be, it's the love we were, it's the love we are.

George Asks, "What Does America Believe?"

Just a few months before the *Time* cover story, *George,* the magazine of political and societal commentary, ran the results of their poll "What Does America Believe?" in their December 1996 issue.

Among their findings regarding contemporary beliefs in the United States were the following:

- 86 percent believe in God
- 75 percent believe in life after death
- 86 percent believe in Heaven
- 77 percent believe in Hell
- 78 percent believe in angels

Father Greeley's Poll of Mystical Experiences

Father Andrew M. Greeley, who holds a Ph.D. in sociology and is a best-selling novelist, has been keeping tabs on the mystical experiences of Americans since 1973. Together with colleagues at the University of Chicago, Dr. Greeley, a professor of sociology at the University of Arizona in Tucson, released the following data in the January/February 1987 issue of *American Health:*

- 73 percent of the adult population in the United States believe in life after death
- 68 percent perceive the afterlife to be Paradise
- 74 percent expect to be reunited with their loved ones after death

"We are born with two incurable diseases," Father Greeley has said, "life, from which we die, and hope, which says maybe death isn't the end."[3]

The Lutherans Examine Heaven and Hell

The church publications *The Lutheran* and *Lutheran Women Today* polled 13,000 of its readers regarding their beliefs about Heaven and Hell. In July 1993 they published the results, with commentary by Pastor Martin E. Marty, a distinguished professor of the history of modern Christianity at the University of Chicago.

Dr. Marty readily acknowledges that in parables and proclamations, Jesus spoke of a "mansion with many rooms" awaiting us. "But we find him backing off when people want to get literal about a reality that cannot be grasped by human minds—in their time or ours."

One has a sense when reading Dr. Marty's analysis of the survey that each human heart creates its own Heaven within the heart of God.

As the British cleric Charles Stanford phrased it, "Heaven must be in me before I can be in Heaven."

Some theorists have suggested that after physical death the soul will find itself in a heaven that will be in harmony with its own ideals. Others have put forth the view that the whole point of our life on Earth might be to provide us with a stockpile of memories out of which we might construct an image world at the time of our death. Such a world would be a spiritual world, not a physical one, although it might seem a physical world to those experiencing it.

But now back to Dr. Marty's commentary:

> A minority [of Lutheran survey respondents] picks up on some literal biblical pictures: 20.6 per-

cent say hell is "down"; 26 percent have it as "a blazing inferno" for others. But 93 percent of those polled fully expect to go to heaven . . . 92.5 percent . . . say that hell is "separation from God" and, 73.4 percent, "beyond our ability to imagine," or 72.6 percent, that it is "a state of despair, hopelessness."

Better Homes and Gardens Surveys Spiritual Life

In the fall of 1988, the editors at *Better Homes and Gardens* decided to present a subject that they had never before explored: their readers' spiritual lives. They were amazed at both the quantity and the substance of the response to their survey.

Editor-in-Chief David Jordan was moved to comment:

"We reach thirty-six million readers each month. Usually, about twenty-five thousand respond to surveys we publish. But this subject drew more than eighty thousand responses—and more than ten thousand people attached thoughtful letters expressing remarkable strength of feeling. It's clearly a subject that strikes deeply at this time in our history."

Among the survey findings of *Better Homes and Gardens* were that:

- 89 percent believe in eternal life
- 87 percent envision a heaven; only 80 percent believe in a hell
- 86 percent believe in miracles
- 73 percent believe that it is possible to receive direct communication from God

- 13 percent accept the possibility of receiving messages from the spirit world
- 80 percent accept that prayer and meditation can lead to miraculous cures for diseases

Death Is Not to Be Feared

Our friend and colleague Dr. Bruce Goldberg, president of the Los Angeles Academy of Clinical Hypnosis, has compiled a kind of "newcomers' guide to heaven," which correlates precisely with our own findings. It states:

> Death is not an end, but a birth to a larger, fuller, and more meaningful life—one that is quite beautiful. At first, you may not even accept that you have died, because you really won't feel much different. You quickly realize that you have a body, but it is subject to very different physical laws and capable of doing many other things that the physical body cannot do. And your new environment will be far less limiting than that of the physical plane that you have just left. For example, you can move through walls and doors and travel thousands of miles in a matter of seconds.
>
> You will possess complete knowledge of the former life experience and can even read the minds of other people who were involved in that life.
>
> You will quickly be joined by Masters and Guides—angellike entities who will help you to adjust to the astral plane. They will guide you into a gradual realization that you have died, and it's time to move on.
>
> You may find yourself in the presence of dead

relatives or friends. Since everyone will communicate by telepathy, your true feelings toward those you encounter will be known—and vice versa.

Arrival in Heaven, the culmination of the death experience, is an almost blinding, yet peaceful, aura of pure light.

Not everyone chooses to enter the white light immediately, and some may wander around the lower astral plane for many years or even centuries before they finally do enter.

Heaven is an ultimate state—a state of happiness and pure joy.

And based on all the supporting evidence of extensive research, **we know that it really does exist.**

Rabbi David J. Wolpe, a professor at the Jewish Theological Seminary of America, recalls in his book *Teaching Your Children about God* an ancient Jewish parable about twin fetuses lying together in their mother's womb. One of the twins believes that there is life beyond the womb, a world where people walk upright, where there exist mountains, oceans, trees, stars. The other mocks his brother for cherishing such foolish notions.

Then, suddenly, the "believer" is forced through the birth canal, leaving behind him his twin and the only existence that he has ever known. The remaining fetus is distressed, saddened that his companion has been taken away by a great catastrophe.

Outside the womb, however, parents are rejoicing, for what the brother left behind has just witnessed is not death but birth—a process that he himself shall soon undergo.

And this, Rabbi Wolpe reminds his readers, is a

classic view of the afterlife—a birth into a world that those of us left behind on Earth can only hope to imagine.[4]

Throughout this book, you shall encounter the inspirational stories of many souls who achieved their birth into another, more glorious existence—the world beyond physical death that we call Heaven—and reached back to Earth to share the truth of an afterlife with friends and family. In addition, you shall travel with those who have returned to the earthplane after visiting Paradise through the near-death experience or the gift of revelatory visions.

CHAPTER TWO

Out-of-Body Visits to the Other Side

When Tom Purcell was twelve years old, he suffered a severe attack of bronchial asthma. Before his parents could summon their family doctor, the boy felt himself slipping into unconsciousness.

"All at once I felt peaceful and completely relaxed," Tom wrote in personal correspondence to us. "I remember clearly feeling that the *real* part of me, I guess you would say my soul, just seemed to float above that poor wheezing body on the bed. You know, I was concerned that the physical me couldn't breathe, but on the other hand, I had never experienced such a wonderful sense of freedom."

Although nearly fifty years have passed since Tom's near-death experience, he remembers it as vividly as if it had just occurred last week. "I felt myself drifting, floating, upward. I seemed to pass through the ceiling of my room, and I was soon looking down on our neighborhood.

"Then everything became rather surreal, and I felt as though I were drifting into another dimension of time and space. Ahead, I could see what looked like a tunnel through which I knew that I must pass. As I drew nearer to the opening, there seemed to be a force which began to tug and pull at me. That was the first time I felt anything at all like fear. I became concerned that it might not be a good thing to be pulled into the tunnel."

During those first moments of anxiety, Tom recalled that he was suddenly surrounded by a bright light. "It just seemed to appear, then wrap itself around me. I had the distinct feeling that it was some form of intelligence that had materialized to calm me or to protect me."

To Tom's recollection, the tunnel was a place of swirling darkness, and he was relieved when both he and the light emerged into a place of bright sunlight and green, rolling hills. "In the distance I could see a city that seemed to be made of crystal. The sunlight reflected off roofs and towers, and it seemed all in all like a magnificent place. I knew with all my heart that I wanted to enter the city. Even from that distance I could feel love, perfect love, emanating from its walls."

Suddenly finding himself in that heavenly environment, Tom began to take a few steps on a pathway that ostensibly led to the crystal city. "That's when the beautiful light that had enveloped me suddenly swirled into the form of a very commanding angel."

The heavenly being, attired in a brilliant white

robe, appeared somewhat stern in its facial expression, yet Tom could feel its very presence projecting feelings of unconditional love. Although it did not have the familiar wings that angels bore in Tom's Sunday School books, the angel still looked exactly the way he somehow knew that angels should.

"You're not ready to go there," the angel said in a voice that seemed to vibrate within Tom's soul body.

"But I feel that I belong there," Tom protested. "I feel as though it is my true home."

The angel only smiled, then indicated that Tom should look into a crystal that the angel held in an outstretched hand.

"Within the crystal the angel held before me, I could see Dr. Mueller come puffing into my room back in the Earth dimension," Tom said. "The *real* me in my soul body in Heaven thought, 'Oh, no, now he will make me breathe again, and I'll have to go back to that clumsy, awkward, imperfect, chubby body."

Tom watched as Dr. Mueller injected something into his arm. "The moment that he gave me a shot, I began to feel myself being pulled away from the angel and from the sight of the crystal city in Heaven. The angel only smiled and nodded."

Tom remembered that at first he tried his best to resist being pulled back into that lump of clay that was so susceptible to disease and physical ailments. "Then the angel brought the crystal up to my eyes once again and I saw Mom and Dad and they were both crying. I didn't want to hurt them, so I stopped struggling and let myself be sucked back into my physical body."

He opened his eyes, took a deep breath, and was at once conscious of terrible pain in his chest and back.

"That was nearly fifty years ago," Tom reminded us, "and I have valued every day of my life here on this physical plane. I have a wonderful wife, three grown kids who are doing very well for themselves, and five grandkids who are my little Earth angels. But I knew from that day on that to die is to enter a free, spiritual state, and I have never feared death. It is only a doorway that will return us to our true home in Heaven."

The Near-Death Experience as a Revelatory Experience

In *Life at Death,* Dr. Kenneth Ring, professor of psychology at the University of Connecticut, states that he considers the near-death experience (NDE) to be a teaching, revelatory experience. In his view, the NDE is an expression of "an intuitive sense of the transcendent aspect of creation." Dr. Ring feels that NDEs "clearly imply that there is something more, something beyond the physical world of the senses."

Dr. Ring's research has led him to isolate five elements that constitute what he has labeled the "core" of the near-death experience:

1. Peace and a sense of well-being
2. Separation from the body
3. Entering the darkness
4. Seeing the light
5. Entering the world of light

Dr. Ring concludes his book by admitting that he believes that humankind has a "conscious existence after our physical death and that the core experience does represent its beginning, a glimpse of things to come."

Testimonies from Those Who Have Glimpsed the World to Come

The following accounts—and many others throughout the book—come from two basic sources: the thousands of individuals who have returned their questionnaires to our office, and those men and women who have spontaneously sent us written reports of their mystical experiences after reading our books, attending our lectures or workshops, or hearing us during one of our media appearances. Our respondents and correspondents are all ages and come from all walks of life, representing a remarkable cross-section of educational backgrounds, ethnic groups, income brackets, and spiritual expressions. We have used initials rather than full names to protect the anonymity of those who have shared their inspirational stories.

F.C.W.: "Fifty years ago I had a near-death experience, but I was discouraged from giving it any credibility by my doctor. I remember going through a tunnel, meeting someone in a bright light. It was the most momentous experience, and I never forgot it. I was never afraid of death after that. I seemed to be aware that we are all one. I do remember a figure who talked to me and who sent me back. And I clearly recall the dreamy sense of calm, peace, and acceptance."

J.R.T.: "I was sitting beside my foxhole in Vietnam when an 82 mm mortar round hit within arm's reach of me. It blew my dog tags off from around my neck. My field gear next to me was completely demolished and turned to ashes. I didn't feel the ground when I hit it, because I was in the brightest, most beautiful, clearest light that seemed a million times brighter than the sun. This beautiful light also had a density and a texture to it. I felt bliss, ecstasy, contentment, and love as I had never felt before. I didn't really feel as if I was *in* the light. I felt as though I was a *part* of the light, because it totally consumed my soul.

"Then a newsreel of my entire life rolled in front of me. . . . I don't know for how long, because time and space no longer existed. Then I opened my eyes and the medic was shooting morphine into me."

Dr. P.B.C.: "After my friend had accidentally struck me in the throat, I couldn't breathe, and I started gasping for breath. I felt myself starting to spin . . . like I was falling a long, endless fall. Then I was no longer spinning, no longer gasping for breath. Everything around me was the deepest, darkest black that I had ever seen. . . . I felt no fear at all. I felt . . . a sense of peace that I have never felt before. . . .

"And then there was a light in front of me. . . . As I looked, I realized that there was no ground beneath my feet. I still continued to feel the sense of peace about me. I felt that it was so pure, so good, and so understanding, not condemning or judging. I saw the light come to a stop far below me. Where it rested it formed a perfect circle. . . . Then I noticed there was a figure in the circle of light. . . . I don't know how, but I knew that it was my body. As I looked down on it, I still continued to feel the same sense of peace. . . . Then I realized . . . that I was no longer in any kind of physical form, that I was now in the immortal form which we call 'spirit.'

"Suddenly the light was gone. . . . I heard a loud, indistinguishable sound from all around me. Then I felt something forcing its way into my chest, and I felt a slight pain throughout my body. I opened my eyes to find myself lying on the ground. . . . My friend told me that I had only been on the ground for a second or two before opening my eyes."

D. M.: "My experience came about when I was shot with a sawed-off 12 gauge shotgun by three kids out on a joyride looking for trouble. I am the only survivor out of at least four people whom they shot within a one-year period.

"In my NDE, I first found myself briefly in Hell before two angels took me to Heaven. I stood with them at the River of Life, staring at a great city. I wanted to go there, but I was not allowed to cross the river. The next thing I knew is that I was standing before God. I can only judge this by the intensity of the bright light all around me. I was in complete fear beyond all words—and yet there was such a feeling of peace that I wanted to stay there. But I was told that it was not my time, that I must return to Earth.

"Ever since then, I have been searching for that peace, but I know in my heart that I will not find it again until it is my time to return to Heaven."

R.J.B.: "I was in surgery for approximately three hours when my heart ceased to beat for the third time. This time, though, it didn't start back up after a moment or two. This was when my soul was separated from my physical body.

"An entity with a beard said that he was to be my guide. No words were needed to feel the warm, calm presence of peace eternal. . . . I had left the physical plane of existence, but I was still aware of Self. . . .

"The entity and I moved through what might resemble a time/space cylinder. It opened into what could be described as an electrically charged, highly lighted area with no containment. The light seemed to come from everywhere, and yet there was a focus ahead of me. I was ushered by a voice that could only be described as 'absolute' to go through the light. Not being one to disobey when a sense of superiority is present, I proceeded. . . . My questions were all answered, although I was not aware of such at that time. Information was given to me that I would not be able to understand until time had passed. It was decided that I needed to return and complete the divine mission that had been given to me. . . .

"Within a thought I found myself back in the hospital room surrounded in a beam of irradiating light and goodness. My soul lay down within my physical body, and for the next seventy-two hours, I was in a coma."

During Her NDE, She Visited Her Parents in Heaven

Norma Armand's doctor had not been completely honest with her. As she writhed in pain on the gurney headed toward the operating room, she knew that she was much sicker than he had led her to believe.

And then she was suddenly spinning around and around, and she heard a strange kind of crackling noise, as if stiff paper were being crunched up into a ball. "Then I . . . or my consciousness . . . or my soul was bobbing around like a balloon on a string," she recalled. "That's the best comparison I can make. I was like a shining balloon attached to my physical body by a thin, silver string. I could clearly see my body below me, and the two interns were chattering about their plans for the evening. I thought how wonderful it was to be young and to be able to plan for the future. I assumed that I was either dead or in the process of dying. Which I guess I was."

From her new perspective, Norma could see her doctor walking hurriedly down the hall. Dr. Mandel took a last puff of a cigarette, then put it out in an ashtray filled with sand.

Within seconds, he stood beside Norma's body. He looked at her carefully, then became very angry. He swore at the two interns as if they were schoolboys. He shouted down the hallway and two nurses came running. Norma was quickly wheeled into the operating room.

"It seemed obvious that something had gone terribly wrong," Norma said, vividly recalling her near-death experience. "It was equally obvious that my soul had left my body or I wouldn't be up above everything looking down. My face was contorted in pain, and I was ashen, as if all the blood had left my body. I thought of leaving my husband, Jack, and my two children, Deb and Louis, and I felt a moment of sadness—not for me, but for them."

As if from very far away, Norma heard Dr. Mandel shouting at the staff, but she didn't really want to observe what was going on in the operating room, so she thought of her bedroom at home, a place where she had always felt comfortable and secure—and suddenly she was there.

Then she heard bells tolling, as they do after funerals, and she thought that she must surely be dead.

"But suddenly a deep voice told me, 'Not yet!' And I felt myself being pulled upward and upward, like an arrow being shot into the sky," Norma said.

The next thing of which Norma was aware was that she was no longer a kind of shining balloon, but she seemed once again to be a replica of her familiar physical self. And standing before her were a number of figures in bright, glowing robes.

To Norma, they seemed to glow with an inner radiance, and they looked exactly the way she'd imagined angels should look. One of them stepped forward and told her that she could stay there with them in Heaven for a little while, but she would have to go back.

"That's when I understood what the 'not yet' statement was all about," Norma explained. "I certainly assumed that I had died, being in Heaven and all, but now I had received a second declaration that I was not to stay there long."

When Norma recalled the experience a few years later, she was certain that she had seen green fields, magnificent towering trees, brooks and streams, and lush meadows dense with lovely flowers. At the same moment that she was admiring the vivid beauty of Heaven, it also occurred to her that since she was there she should be able to see her parents.

"In a twinkling, Mom and Dad were standing there beside me," Norma said, "and the three of us were weeping tears of joy at our reunion. I was surprised to see that neither of them looked as old as they had when they died. Dad had passed when he was seventy-six, and Mom had gone when she was nearly eighty, but both of them now appeared as I remembered them from my childhood."

Norma said that she talked with her parents on a bench in what appeared to be a lakeside park. She remembered seeing ducks swimming about, and a number of deer drinking at the lake's edge. After a time, Norma and her parents were joined by her maternal grandparents, Alf and Marta Swensen, and by her paternal grandparents, Sal and Benedette Marino, as well.

"I had never met Dad's parents, since they were killed in a train accident before I was born," Norma said. "It was all so incredible. Like the best kind of family reunion."

As they spoke, Norma saw a small crowd of men and women gathering and encircling them. When she asked her mother who the other people were, she was told that those were relatives from many other previous generations of her father's and mother's families, but she would not have time to meet them before she had to leave.

"I remember feeling waves of love coming from my ancestors crowding around us," Norma said, "and it was as if I was somehow made up of bits and pieces of the soul energy of all of them. I had always kind of made fun of some cultures with their beliefs about their ancestors' ghosts hanging around, but maybe we really are the sum total of all those who have gone before us and had their own branches on the family tree."

Norma and her parents walked along a lakeside path for what seemed like hours, then one of the white-robed angels came for her and informed her that it was time for her to return.

"No sooner had he told me this than I was bobbing around in that shining balloon near the ceiling of a hospital room," Norma recalled. "I was shocked to hear Father Dupre giving the last rites to my poor old body on the bed below. Jack was crying, and I had an impression of my younger sister Nancy outside in the hall with my children. A nurse had been standing at the left side of the bed with her fingers on my pulse, but all of a sudden, she walked out of the room."

Norma heard the same deep voice telling her that it was not yet her time—and then she heard that same crackling noise, like paper being wadded into a ball. "I had a weird feeling, like I had been light as a feather and I was now heavy as an elephant. I had a sensation of red, the color red, all around me. And then I began to realize that I was somehow back inside my physical body."

Norma remembered moaning with the pain of her illness and the just-completed surgery. When she opened her eyes, her husband and Father Dupre were smiling, and the nurse was just returning with their family doctor.

Norma's first words were to whisper that she had been to Heaven.

Father Dupre chuckled and said that she'd had them all very worried that she might well be knocking at St. Peter's gate. Dr. Mandel said that he had given her only a few minutes to pass the crisis point or to die. Father Dupre had been called to administer the last rites, because her chances of living had really seemed almost nonexistent.

Norma firmly believes that her experience was genuine. "When I was alone with my sister, I told her that I had seen Mom and Dad in Heaven and I know that Nancy believed me."

The Silver Cord and the Golden Bowl

Many men and women who have undergone near-death experiences or out-of-body experiences (OBEs) have reported seeing themselves as "golden bowls" or balloon-like globular spheres of some sort, and just as many have seen a "silver cord" or shiny string of great elasticity that somehow connects the spirit body to the physical body. Although the spirit body may sometimes assume a form that exactly duplicates the physical body, numerous metaphysicians, who have been speaking about spirit bodies for centuries, and those individuals who have had a one-time spontaneous NDE or OBE describe the spirit body as being more or less egg-shaped with an orangish glow until a thought transforms the "egg" into the familiar body structure of the physical personality.

Verses from the book of *Ecclesiastes* in the Old Testament are often cited as evidence of the everlasting verity of the soul and the out-of-body experience:

> Also, when they shall be afraid of that which is high, and fears shall be in the way, and the almond tree shall flourish and the grasshopper shall be a burden, and desire shall fail; because man goeth to his *long home* [Heaven] and the mourners go about the streets. Or ever the *silver cord* be loosed, or the *golden bowl* be broken, or the pitcher be broken at the fountain, or the wheel be broken at the cistern. Then shall the *dust* [physical body] return to the earth as it was: and the spirit shall return unto God who gave it.
>
> —*Ecclesiastes*, 12:5–7;
> italics and brackets added by the authors.

The great psychical researcher Frederic W.H. Myers once referred to accounts of out-of-body experience as the most extraordinary achievement of the human will or soul. In his *Human Personality and Its Survival of Bodily Death,* he wrote:

> What can lie further outside any known capacity than the power to cause a semblance of oneself to appear at a distance? What can be more a central action—more manifestly the outcome of whatever is deepest and most unitary in man's whole being? Of all vital phenomena, I say this is the most significant; this self-projection is the one definite act which it seems as though a man might perform equally well before and after bodily death.

We heartily agree that accounts of out-of-body and near-death experiences offer most convincing proof that we each have within us a spirit body that exists as our essential vehicle of individual expression both before and after bodily death—and we also maintain that such near-death travels can provide the experiencer with a remarkable preview of Heaven.

She Returned from Heaven's Beautiful Garden for Children

Registered nurse Margery Cosentino was assisting Dr. J. P. Pesek in the pediatrics section of a county hospital in a northeastern state when she was called to the bedside of a nine-year-old girl who had developed complications following relatively minor surgery.

"Wendy's fever had just shot up during the night," Margery said. "About three o'clock in the morning, she seemed to lapse into a comatose state, and I spent some very anxious moments in the company of the girl's mother and Dr. Pesek."

It was just at dawn when the girl's fever broke and her eyes flickered open. She asked for a drink, and Nurse Consentino squeezed some water from a soaked cotton ball onto her parched lips.

Dr. Pesek scolded Wendy in a mock gruff voice about giving them all a scare. "Are you going to be a good girl now, Wendy, so your mommy can get some sleep?"

Wendy's eyes studied her mother's drawn features. "Oh, Mommy, you look so tired. I'm sorry if I worried you."

Mrs. Rundle told her daughter that Mommy was just fine now that she didn't have to worry about her baby. Then, no longer able to hold back the tears of relief, she began to cry as she bent over to hug her daughter.

"Oh, Mommy, you really didn't have to worry about me," Wendy said after receiving her mother's embrace. "I was just playing in the garden with the other boys and girls."

"A garden, eh?" Dr. Pesek smiled, winking at Nurse Consentino. "Seems to me it would have been a bit cold to be playing in a garden in December."

"Oh, no, it was nice and sunny," Wendy said. "And all the flowers and bushes were so pretty. The other boys and girls stay there all the time, but Alisa told me that I would soon have to go back."

"I hadn't really been paying that much attention to Wendy until she mentioned the name 'Alisa,' "

Margery Consentino said. "I had lost a sister by that name—and the name isn't that common."

Mrs. Rundle gently pushed aside a lock of her daughter's sweat-soaked hair to kiss her forehead. "Mommy is so glad that you did come back, Precious."

Margery Consentino said that her pulse began to race when little Wendy suddenly directed her attention to her. "Alisa said to tell you that she is fine. She really misses you, but she is fine."

"I was stunned," the nurse told us. "I could not help feeling a sudden twinge in my inner self. My sister, Alisa, had died of influenza when she was eight years old . . . nearly twenty years ago. Wendy had never seen me before, and she surely could know nothing about me or any member of my family."

Before Nurse Consentino could respond, Wendy added: "Oh, and she also said to tell you that your daddy is feeling much better now. I didn't see him, but Alisa said that he lives in another garden with some other grown-ups."

"I was feeling very strange at that point," Margery Consentino admitted. "My father had died just three months ago, and he had very much been in my thoughts."

Wendy had one more postscript to add: "And Alisa said to give your mother a big kiss from both your daddy and her."

Dr. Pesek still bore the same bemused smile. "Well, that's enough talk about the garden," he said. "Little Miss Wendy, you'd better get some rest now."

Nurse Consentino knew that she risked incurring the doctor's wrath, but at this point she couldn't help herself. "Please, Wendy, could you tell me a little more about Alisa? I mean, like, how she looked?"

Both Dr. Pesek and Mrs. Rundle looked surprised at the nurse's interest in the little girl's fevered dream. But Wendy pursed her lips in thought and did her best to oblige Nurse Consentino: "Well, she was a pretty girl. And, let's see, she wore pigtails with yellow ribbons. And her hair was real black."

Margery Consentino ignored Dr. Pesek's frown and nodded enthusiastically. Her sister Alisa had often tied her black pigtails with yellow ribbons.

"There's more that she said." Wendy smiled, crinkling her nose and scrunching her head down on the pillow. "But it's kind of grown-up."

Dr. Pesek cleared his throat peremptorily. "Wendy needs her rest, Nurse," he reminded her. It was apparent that he wanted to know why she was pursuing an examination of the kind of nonsensical prattle that was so common in a child after surgery.

"Please, just a moment more," the nurse requested. "And please, Wendy, tell me the 'grown-up' part."

"Well," Wendy began, feeling obviously ill at ease to be discussing a personal area, "Alisa said that you shouldn't be afraid to have babies. You shouldn't be afraid that they will die just because she did. She says that it is so beautiful in Heaven's gardens that she doesn't mind staying there for a while longer. She said that your daddy wants you to have babies, too. He was sad that you didn't have any while he was around."

Margery Consentino could no longer remain in Wendy's room, and she knew that she had taxed Dr. Pesek's patience and piqued Mrs. Rundle's curiosity, and that she had better justify her tiring the little girl after she had just regained consciousness.

Holding back her tears, she told Dr. Pesek and Mrs. Rundle about the death of her only sibling,

Alisa, at the age of eight. She went on to explain how her father had died only months before and how he had always complained about not having any grandchildren around. And, although she had been married for over nine years, her memories of Alisa's childhood death had been so intense and so terrible that she had refused to have children.

Nurse Margery Consentino concluded her account by stating, "I believe with all my being that Wendy Rundle somehow traveled to another dimension of reality, a world after physical death, where she met the spirit of another little girl, my sister, Alisa, who had made her transition to that beautiful garden in Heaven nearly twenty years ago."

What Is Heaven Like?

One of the principal criticisms of the validity of near-death experiences cited by scientific materialists is that they simply reflect the beliefs that individuals already have concerning Heaven and the afterlife. The January-February 1987 *Parapsychology Review* ran the results of an experiment during which one hundred college students were asked to travel on an imaginary tour through Heaven. The findings of the experiment were as follows:

- 40 percent described the environment of Heaven as "cosmic"—both everywhere and nowhere at all
- 32 percent, a place of soft, diffused light
- 30 percent, a lush pastoral setting
- 29 percent, a place of only "being" without shapes or forms

- 7 percent, a magnificent walled city with golden or pearly gates

When queried about their sources for their imaginings, the students who participated in the experiment named the Bible, interactions with other people, the media, and their own meditations and reflections. Only eight of the one hundred participants cited near-death experience reference material.

What Kind of World Awaits You in Heaven?

If you are one who believes in an existence after physical death and who takes the concept of Heaven seriously, you are quite likely more concerned with the rather mundane aspects of life after death than you are with the scientific and religio-philosophical implications. You are probably more interested in knowing what kind of world you can expect to be awaiting you. Is it really possible to live another existence, walking about in lovely gardens, interacting with other spirits, and welcoming those new to the Next World as in the account of Nurse Consentino's long-deceased sister?

Some of those who claim communication with the spirit of a deceased loved one or claim to have visited Heaven during a near-death experience express their belief that the world beyond death is a material one composed of some sort of higher matter. Moreover, the next world is a spatial one, having size, shape, and an environment roughly analogous to our own. These experiencers speak of various planes of existence in which the soul leaves the body at the time of physical death and advances to another plane, or level, of life. Thus, the promised New Jerusalem is a substantially real place with a higher concept of geometry and physics than that which we practice on the earthplane of existence.

Other theorists have speculated that the soul of the departed will find itself in a world that will be in harmony with its own ideals. "The real hell," suggested one clergyman to us, "would be to live in a purely carnal world until it becomes a perpetual torment, and the soul realizes its infinite mistakes."

Each Soul May Create Its Own Concept of Heaven

H. H. Price, who once served as the president of the Society for Psychical Research, London, put forth the view that the whole point of our life on Earth might be to provide us with a stockpile of memories out of which we might construct an image world at the time of our death. In other words, we each create our own concept of Heaven.

Such a world, Price emphasized, would be a psychic world, not a physical one, even though it might seem very physical to those entities experiencing it. The psychic world might, in fact, seem so tangible that the deceased, at first, might find it difficult to believe that he or she is dead.

The causal laws that these image-objects would obey would not be the three-dimensional laws of physics that control our physical reality, but would be laws more like those explored through dreams, archetypes, and symbols by psychotherapist C. G. Jung. Such a dream world of the disembodied would be incoherent only when judged by the nonapplicable laws of conventional physics, for the dream objects would not be physical objects as we would perceive them on the earth plane.

Price went on to theorize that such individually created afterlife existences would be the manifestation in image form of the memories and desires of its occupants, including their repressed or unconscious memories or desires. The soul-created world beyond death would then be every bit as detailed, as vivid, and as complex as is the present three-dimensional world that we now experience.

Three Modern-Day Mystics Share Their View of Heavenly Realms of Light

Lori Jean Flory, coauthor of *The Wisdom Teachings of Archangel Michael*, is a modern-day mystic who has received angelic communication since she was a child. When asked if it is true that after death we go to live in a Heaven created according to our prior thoughts about life after death, Lori Jean received the following information from her guide Daephrenocles:

"Beloved ones, it is your own perceptions and thoughts, beliefs, and awarenesses that will create the reality that you will experience in the heavenly realms of light. With the higher realms, the mode of communication and manifestation is through the process of thought, and the results are immediate, depending upon what one needs. Those who have passed over can create homes for themselves or any environment that is comfortable to them in their continued experience of light, love, and peace."

Leia Stinnet, a minister in the Universal Life Church and the author of fifteen *Little Angel* books for children, said:

> "As we enter the world of spirit we are absent from the concept of the definition of life and death. We know that whatever we want to create in the world of spirit—by desiring to create, by projecting our thought of creating, giving it energy—so it is. Instantly, as we think in a different way, we are there. There are no limitations or boundaries as to what we can create."

Diane Tessman, head of the Starlite Mystic Center and author of *Earth Changes Bible* and *Seven Rays of the Healing Millennium*, said that in her spiritual and psychic education her guides have shown her that each mind/soul makes its own reality, both while here on earth and also in the afterlife:

"Your mind waves are unique unto themselves and they do create the reality which you see around you. Your reality is a hologram created by your mind/soul. Therefore, when you die, you also create the reality to which you will go.

"Yes, [Heaven] exists on its own, as well, but your mind/soul cannot find its frequency unless it is attuned. It is very much like being tuned in to a radio station: You simply cannot hear it unless you hit the right spot on the frequency dial. Therefore, you tune in to a reality as you leave this corporeal life. It is basically your choice!"

"Death Is a Transition to Higher Consciousness"

Dr. Elisabeth Kübler-Ross, who has gained worldwide fame for her work with death and the dying, has said that the turning point in her work occurred in a Chicago hospital in 1969 when a deceased patient appeared before her in fully materialized form. Kübler-Ross had been feeling discouraged about her research with the dying because of the opposition that she had encountered among her colleagues. But the apparition of her former patient appeared before her to tell her not to abandon her work—life after death was a reality.

"Death is simply a shedding of the physical body, like the butterfly coming out of a cocoon," Dr. Kübler-Ross has often said in our personal conversations and in her lectures. "It is a transition into a higher state of consciousness, where you continue to perceive, to understand, to laugh, to be able to grow— and the only thing you lose is something you don't need anymore, and that is your physical body."

What is more, Dr. Kübler-Ross and other researchers have stressed, there is always some spirit entity there to help in the transition from life to death. In the next chapter, we shall read the inspiring accounts of those who experienced the loving arms of angels assisting them to ascend to the heavenly realms.

CHAPTER THREE

Angelic Beings Who Guide Spirits Home

There is a very old spiritual tradition that says that at the time of our birth each of us receives a guardian angel who stays with us throughout our life and who ushers us into Heaven at the time of our physical death. Over the years many respondents to our questionnaire and numerous attendees at our lectures and seminars have shared their moving stories of seeing angels interacting with loved ones at the time of their passing to a higher dimension or told of their own preview of Heaven in the company of an angelic escort.

Four Angels Materialized to Escort Her to the Heavenly Home

Reverend G.M.E. and his wife said that they were present in the hospital room of a dying woman when an angel appeared to stand at her bedside. Everyone in the room at that time—a nurse and four family members in addition to the minister and his wife—heard the angel say that it had come to take the woman home.

According to the minister and his wife, three other angels appeared and a number of other images of human beings manifested, which members of the dying woman's family identified as friends and relatives who had already gone home to Heaven. As the witnesses to the astonishing event observed, a white, hazy mist rose above the woman, hovered there for a few moments, then eventually congealed to take on perfect human form.

"The image we then perceived, according to the family members assembled, was of the dying woman in an earlier time, when she was healthy and robust," the minister said.

After the soul body had been fully released from its physical shell, the woman's spirit left in the joyful company of the angels and the dear ones who had already become citizens of the heavenly realm and who had come to escort their beloved to her true home.

An Angel Made Up of "Golden Sparks" Brought Her Back to the Body

K.K.C. told us that when she was five years old, she "died" from collapsed lungs.

"There was a clock in my room which in my mind I can still see. It was one-thirty in the morning. At that time my guardian angel came and identified itself to me. This angel was neither male nor female and seemed to be made up of thousands of golden sparks.

"My angel told me that I had to go back to Earth because it would make my parents very sad if I died then. I remember re-entering my body through the top of my head and feeling searing pain in my lungs.

"The angel touched me and stayed with me while I was returning to the physical state, then it disappeared. I have seen this angelic being from time to time and felt its presence ever since."

An Angel Got Him Out of the Wrecked Car before It Exploded

C.L.S. was trapped in the crushed wreckage of his overturned automobile and felt that he was doomed to die. Then he felt a warm and gentle hand clasp his own and guide it through the darkness to the seat belt release button.

In the next moment, he unexplainably found himself outside of his car, surrounded by a brilliant white light that had seemingly come from nowhere—and a voice was telling him to run away as fast as he could. He had only run a few yards when his automobile exploded.

C.L.S. is convinced that an angel saved his life. Although his car was demolished even before it exploded into flames, he suffered only minor cuts and bruises. A devoutly religious young man, C.L.S. gives credit for the miracle to an angel that was looking out for him.

The Angel of Death Called Twice

An interesting account of angelic interaction at the moment of death, with just a bit of a twist, was provided by Edna Carney.

"When I was eleven years old, my parents adopted Michael, a baby boy whom all the family loved very much," she said. "His mother was a young waitress in a village not far from ours whose husband had died in a factory accident. The young mother had become very ill, and since neither she nor her husband had any family in the area, she simply could not afford to keep the baby. Mom was a nurse in the local clinic, and she had come to know the woman and her situation. Since my parents were unable to have any children after my difficult birth, it seemed ordained that they should take baby Michael."

From the beginning, though, Edna recalled, they had all been concerned about the baby's waxen pallor. For a time, the infant seemed to improve, but both her mother and their family doctor were worried that Michael might have inherited his mother's ill health.

"One night when Mom and I were about to go to bed around ten-thirty, we heard a firm knock on the door," Edna said. "Dad had a small trucking business and was out of town for a couple nights, so we got a little nervous about who could be at our door so late at night."

Edna and her mother stood facing the door, so they were startled when they heard the latch of the locked door click, and they watched the door swing slowly open.

"An angelic figure in shining white robes entered the room and closed the door slowly behind it," Edna said. "Without a word, this incredible being crossed the room to where Michael lay sleeping."

Edna heard her mother cry out: "Dear God, it's the Angel of Death come to take Michael! Please, dear Lord, don't take our baby boy!"

Edna remembered clearly that the angel reached out as if to lift the baby from its crib, then lowered its arms and turned to walk away.

"I don't know if it was Mom's supplication that caused the angel to reconsider taking Michael, but the angel left him in his crib that night," Edna said. "Halfway to the door, though, the angel stopped and turned to face Mom and me. I will never forget that moment and that angelic countenance."

Edna recalled that she was so frightened that her teeth were chattering. "Mom finally broke the silence by questioning me whether or not the experience had been real and whether or not I, too, had seen the angel. I told her that I had most certainly seen the angel and that it had seemed to want to take Michael away, then changed its mind."

Her mother wiped tears away from her eyes. "I think that the angel has given us another chance to keep Michael," she told Edna.

At that moment, the baby began to moan and to toss restlessly in its crib. For three days, two doctors sought to save little Michael's life.

"Then, on a Sunday evening, while Mom was sleeping and I was keeping watch over the baby, the angel came again and stood beside the crib," Edna said. "I saw Michael smile up at the angel. Then he let out a long sigh, and I knew that he had died. Mom came out of her bedroom at that moment, just in time to see the angel rise through the ceiling with Michael's spirit body in its arms."

For more than twenty years now, Edna has remained convinced that the angel's initial visit was intended to prepare the family for the sad event that was soon to come. She also stated that the experience had deepened her family's faith in the higher worlds.

Dr. Elisabeth Kübler-Ross Identifies Four Phases of Life after Death

Dr. Elisabeth Kübler-Ross, in her autobiography, *The Wheel of Life,* draws upon her work with more than 20,000 dying patients to describe the four stages of life after death.

First, she says, the spirit leaves the physical body and experiences a wholeness.

Secondly, the spirit meets angels or guides and is able to travel anywhere with the speed of thought. The angels or guides comfort the spirit lovingly and may provide it with a cheerful reunion with friends and relatives who have already gone home. This phase, Dr. Kübler-Ross believes, is especially comforting to those who almost died suddenly.

The third phase of the afterlife is the entering of the tunnel or crossing some other transitional structure—a bridge, a mountain, a body of water. A bright light that radiates unconditional love awaits the spirit at the end of this transitional journey, and those who have returned from NDEs report having felt great peace and tranquility and the sense that they have come home.

The fourth phase that Dr. Kübler-Ross describes is when the spirit arrives in the presence of a higher source, which some call God. At this level the entity leaves its ethereal existence and becomes pure spiritual energy.

The Inspirational Research of Rev. W. Bennett Palmer

During the course of his many years of research into reports of angelic visitations and deathbed visions, Rev. W. Bennett Palmer, a retired Methodist minister, says that in the typical account, a bedside witness sees a mist or a cloudlike vapor emerging from the mouth or head of the dying man or woman. The vaporous substance soon takes on a human form that is generally a duplicate of the living person—only in most cases any present deformity or injury are partially or wholly absent. Angels or spirits of deceased loved ones are often reported standing ready to accompany the newly freed spirit to higher dimensions of light.

In numerous reports, the immediate process of death is not witnessed, but the deceased is seen leaving the earth plane for the higher world, most often accompanied by angelic beings. Frequently, such spirit and angel leave-taking is witnessed occurring in the sky, but this seems to be a mode of disappearance rather than an indication that Heaven is in any particular spatial area.

The environment and the scenery described in

near-death voyages to Heaven is said to be very much like the scenery on Earth, only it becomes more beautiful as the spirit progresses. Eventually the heavenly environment becomes ineffable, incapable of description in human terms or in earthly comprehension.

In instances wherein it appears that one has truly achieved a glimpse into Heaven, angels are very often described in the company of deceased loved ones. The angels may come to sing heavenly music, to summon the soul from the dying physical body, or to accompany the newly released spirit to the other world. Most of the men and women who have perceived the angelic beings are able to describe them in every detail, including their eyes, hair, wearing apparel, and other attributes and accouterments.

His Wife's Spirit Bade Him Join Her in Heaven with the Angels

In Rev. Palmer's church in New Port, Richey, Florida, two longtime members of the congregation, Mr. and Mrs. Symington, who were very ill, had been placed in separate rooms in their home to insure periods of peace and uninterrupted sleep for both of them.

One afternoon, as Mr. Symington lay back against the pillows of his bed, he saw the form of his wife pass through the wall of his room, wave her hand in farewell, and rise upward in the company of an angel.

In two or three minutes, the nurse came into his room and informed him that his wife had passed away. "I know," he said, blinking back the tears.

Later, when Rev. Palmer called upon him, Mr. Symington told him that his wife had had enough of the desperate struggle to maintain life. "She came to me to say goodbye with an angel by her side," he said. "She asked me to come join her soon and be with the angels in Heaven."

Mr. Symington died two days later.

Three Beautiful Angels at His Dying Wife's Bedside

"I saw three separate clouds float through the doorway into the room where my wife lay dying," M. G. told Rev. Palmer. "The clouds enveloped the bed."

As he gazed through the mist, M. G. saw a woman's form take shape. It was transparent and had a golden sheen. "It was a figure so glorious in appearance that no words can describe it."

The beautiful entity was dressed in a long, flowing robe, and there was a brilliant tiara on her head. "The angel remained motionless with its hands uplifted over the form of my wife, seemingly engaged in prayer. Then I noticed two other beautiful angels kneeling by my wife's bedside. In a few moments, there appeared above the physical form of my wife a spirit duplicate floating horizontally above it. It seemed to be connected to her body by a cord."

The whole experience, M. G. said, lasted for five hours. "As soon as my dear wife had taken her last breath, the three angels and the spirit form of my wife vanished."

She Watched Her Husband's Angel Come to Take Him Home

When Mrs. Ernestine Tamayo entered her husband's sickroom to bring him his evening newspaper, she saw a large, oval light emerging from the top of his head. The illuminated oval floated toward the window, hovered there a moment, then was met by a lovely angelic figure. Within seconds, both the illuminated oval and the angel had vanished.

"I knew that Miles was dead even before I reached my husband's bedside," she told Rev. Palmer. "I had seen his angel guide come to take him home."

The Rising Spirit Clapped Its Hands with Joy as the Angel Joined It

Bill Winstowne told Rev. Palmer that he saw the spirit of his brother as it was disengaging itself from the physical body. The cloudlike vapor took on human shape, clapped its hands with joy, then was joined by an angel.

Within another few moments, his brother's spirit and its angelic guide passed through the ceiling.

An Angel Guided His Son's Spirit through Heaven's Gates

Jerry Caldwell said that at the time of death of his ten-year-old son, he saw the child's spirit leaving the body as a luminous cloud. And then, he told Rev. Palmer, as the spirit was rising toward the ceiling, an angel appeared to take its hand.

"I felt an overwhelming sense of peace penetrate my grief," Caldwell said, "for I knew that my son was now in the company of a guiding angel who would see him safely inside Heaven's gates."

She Was Given an Angelic Tour of a Heavenly Abode

Seventy-year-old Millie Dorrance lay dying, and she felt her spirit leaving her body. As her consciousness seemed to ascend somewhere between dimensions of reality, she saw a beautiful light descending toward her.

She was drawn toward the light, and as she came nearer, she perceived that the source of the illumination was the aura or radiance around an angelic being. Later, she would say that the angel was lovelier than she would ever be able to put into words.

The angelic being carried a cross in one hand and a wandlike instrument in the other.

"The beautiful angel touched me with the wand," she said, "and I felt a warm vibration of holy love spread throughout my entire consciousness."

As she listened in rapt attention, the angel explained that the cross was the symbol of sacrificial love, without which there could be no Heaven.

While she was out of her body, Millie Dorrance said that the angel took her on a brief tour of an ethereal abode.

"I saw a beautiful angel instructing children who had died so young that they knew little or nothing of the earthly life of Jesus," she told Rev. Palmer. The instruction, to her perspective, appeared to be given in what might be called "spiritual moving pictures."

The story of Jesus, she said, was presented very much like it is in the New Testament, "but it was depicted from a more heavenly point of view. In the pictures, I saw Jesus before his resurrection walking among the tombs and speaking of the dead which he had redeemed. I saw the picture-teachings depict Jesus re-entering his body. And I heard God's voice say, 'This is my beloved son, the hope of Israel, the bright morning star. Peace to the world.' "

After she had observed the "spiritual moving pictures" portrayal of the earthly life of Jesus, Millie Dorrance was informed that she must return to Earth to share her heavenly experiences with others.

"I was extremely disappointed to learn that I was not yet deemed ready for my graduation to the higher world," she said, "but I was presented with a golden goblet from which I was told to drink. The angels promised me that the liquid would provide me with the necessary strength to endure the separation from Heaven and to perform my earthly ministry."

She was also given a definite time that she would stay on Earth—after which she was promised that she would return to Heaven.

"The angel who had been my guide in the ethereal world was my escort back to Earth," she said. "And I re-entered my physical body so that I might begin my true mission."

Rev. W. Bennett Palmer testified that Mrs. Millie Dorrance served as an inspiration to all who knew her. "And she never wavered in her account of her marvelous sojourn in Heaven," he said. "She truly inspired all those who heard her beautiful story of her time in Paradise."

Before she died for the *second* time at the age of eighty-four, Millie told her family and friends, "I will praise my Heavenly Father, for my hope in Jesus is worth more to me than ten thousand earthly worlds."

Then, having been fully appraised of her allotted time by her guiding angel, Millie Dorrance sang her favorite hymn and lay back against her pillow to complete her final transition to her heavenly home.

An Angel Permitted Him to Visit His Son's New Home in Heaven

Richard Mortonsen was sitting beside his son's bed in the hospital room, trying to read a newspaper to get his mind off the impending sorrow that he knew would soon devastate the lives of his wife and himself. Joseph, their beautiful ten-year-old son, lay dying. They had only recently admitted to themselves that it was unlikely that he would survive the fall from the apartment house rooftop that had crushed his spine, fractured his skull, and broken nearly every bone in his body. They knew that they must now face reality. There was no longer any need to place blame or to torture themselves with such questions as why they had permitted him to raise pigeons in the first place or why they weren't keeping a closer eye on him. What had happened had happened. And what would be would be.

Richard said that he had just set the newspaper down and was rubbing his eyes. He had worked a full shift at the plant that day and felt drained and exhausted. But it was only fair that he take his turn at the bedside vigil and allow Janeann, his wife, to get some sleep if it were possible for her to do so. The hospital staff had really been kind and thoughtful. Janeann had been permitted to lie down in a room just a few doors away.

"I became aware of a presence in the room," he said in his account of the incident. "At first I thought it might be Janeann, unable to sleep after all. The night nurse had already been in on rounds and checked Joey, so I didn't think she would be back for many hours."

When Richard turned around, he was astonished to see an angel standing behind him. "Both the angel and its white robe were glowing. He—and I say 'he' because he seemed very masculine to me—smiled at me, and I felt a wonderful peace moving over me. I knew in my heart that he was there for Joey, but I wasn't ready to let my son go yet."

Richard said that he pleaded with the angel not to take his son. "Please, just a few more days. Joey hasn't even regained consciousness. We want to be able to say goodbye. At least grant us that."

When the angel spoke, Richard recalled that it was as if the entire hospital room were vibrating at a peculiar kind of frequency. "His voice was gentle, yet authoritative. He told me that such matters weren't up to him. He was there to take Joey's spirit to Heaven. He had no power to grant any wishes of any kind."

Richard beseeched the being to have compassion, to show some understanding. "What kind of world is Joey going to?" Richard wanted to know. "How will we know if he will be happy there?"

The angel's eyes looked directly into Richard's. "A

strange kind of light seemed to shine in the angel's eyes, and it seemed to pass into mine. He seemed to be full of love, but when he moved toward me, I was afraid that he was going to hit me for trying to argue with him."

The next thing that Richard knew, the hospital room seemed to be spinning around. He felt faint and dizzy. He knew he was losing consciousness.

"Then it seemed as though I was under one arm of the angel and Joey was under the other," Richard said. "Joey was smiling at me as we moved up toward the ceiling. I started to reach out to take his hand, but the next thing I knew was that we seemed to be moving through space. I thought that I saw the night sky and stars all around us. All kinds of colors and lights seemed to be flashing past us."

And then Richard, Joey, and the angel were standing in what appeared to be a tranquil forest clearing surrounded by magnificent, towering trees. There were deer grazing nearby, and rabbits gamboled among thick stands of clover. Birds sang melodically from the trees, and squirrels perched on lower branches to study the newcomers to their world.

"Joey always loved the out-of-doors," Richard said. "He always begged to get out of the concrete canyons of the city as often as possible. If this was Heaven, he would love this part of it."

Joey took him by the hand and started tugging him toward a lazily moving brook. "Dad, come look! I'll bet there are trout in that stream!"

Although Richard hadn't noticed them at first, he was suddenly aware of a number of boys and girls about Joey's age engaged in various activities around the clearing and the stream. And here and there, angelic beings walked among the children, as if they were concerned shepherds seeing to their lively flocks.

"I was joyful and sorrowful at the same time," Richard remembered. "I saw how beautiful Heaven was and how attentive the angels were, but I also knew that we would be losing Joey forever."

And then a familiar voice echoed his thoughts: "Not 'forever,' Richard. One day you'll be with him again. We'll all be together again."

Richard turned, and came face to face with his father. "Pop! I can't believe it!"

His father scowled. "You can't believe I'm in Heaven?"

Richard shook his head, indicating the angel guide standing nearby. "Of course I would expect you to be in Heaven, Pop. What I can't believe is that God would bless me so!"

Joey hugged his grandfather. "I had a big fall, Gramps," he told him. "I got too close to the edge of the roof when Peachy, my favorite pigeon, was coming home."

Grandfather Mortensen nodded. "Yes, I saw you fall. I wanted to catch you, but you went right through me. I guess it was your time. None of us can know when it is our time or the time of our beloved ones. Not even the angels know."

Richard asked the angelic being who had brought them to Heaven if this were so.

"Yes," he replied, "it is so. Sometimes we are told that we may intervene and preserve a human's life so that his or her soul may continue on its earthly mission. Sometimes we wish that we could rescue some human, but we are told that we must not interfere. There are even times when we become advocates for a particular human and request that we may intervene. Even then we may be forbidden to interfere with that soul's destiny."

Richard was about to resume his argument that Joey's life was too short and plead that he should be allowed to recover from his terrible accident. "But suddenly I was given to understand that everything—even my son's death—was part of a much larger Divine Plan. The angel said something to me that triggered this great awareness and brought a peace that passes all understanding, but I cannot remember now a word of what he said that so enlightened me. I do remember that the angel, Joey, and I walked beside the little stream, talking, for what seemed like hours and hours."

And then Richard was opening his eyes. He was lying on a bed and Janeann and a husky male nurse were standing at its side.

"Oh, honey," Janeann said. "You've been so exhausted. You've been working full shifts, then relieving me at the hospital. I shouldn't have left you alone."

Richard wanted to know what had happened to him.

"You conked out, buddy." The nurse grinned. "We found you on the floor out cold. You've been out for five hours or more."

And then a older female nurse came into the room and told Richard and Janeann that Joey had opened his eyes. He had regained consciousness at last.

The compassionate angel had granted both of Richard's wishes. He had been shown the kind of loving place in Heaven that awaited their son, and he and Janeanne were able to say good-bye to Joey before he lapsed once again into unconsciousness.

"We were able to tell him how much we loved him," Richard said. "And we heard him whisper how much he loved us. Then he closed his eyes again. Within the hour, he had passed from this world into the next.

"I waited until after the funeral before I told Jane-ann about the wonderful blessing that the angel had granted me and how beautiful would be our son's new home in Heaven. She said that such knowledge of Joey's lovely place in Paradise brought her a great sense of peace."

Angels Are Always There during the Spirit's Transitional Period

"Just as there are helpers who came with us into life," said Lori Jean Flory, a channel for angelic intelligence, "so are there helpers who help us to translate our knowing and experience into yet higher levels of frequency. The level one ascends to depends upon the level of one's spiritual awareness, consciousness, frequency vibration, and love. Many who pass over are amazed and surprised to find that there are so many helpers of loving light there to help at the time of passing. Know it to be a truth that no one upon the Earth is alone or ever does anything alone. There are always helpers present—seen or unseen, they are present. It matters not if someone believes or not, they are still present and helping, loving, guiding, protecting."

Kay L. Barrett, an ordained minister and the director/founder of the Waking Spirit Foundation, commented that the angels who have looked after us throughout our entire lifetimes will certainly be there for us when we die. "Why would they desert us when we need them the most? They will take us to the light where we will be reborn in the light energy. They are with us to calm our fears and answer our questions about the experience we are having after death. They will fill us with peace and love, so there is no fear in leaving the physical plane."

He Met His True Love in "Angel School" after a Near-Death Experience

Although some readers may find the following story difficult to assimilate with more conventional religious or mystical experiences concerning Heaven, from our perspective it is but a representative account of similar reports that we have received from many respondents to our questionnaire. Who can say with utter certainty exactly where it is that we first meet our soulmates?

When Jason S. was thirteen years old, he had a near-death experience after being struck by an automobile. In his account of his remarkable experience, he said that he remembered traveling to higher dimensions.

"There I met a beautiful angel who told me that he was my guardian who would always be with me. I was told that it was not yet my time to remain in the heavenly realms, so I was returned to my battered body in the hospital, and to my very happy parents."

As sometimes occurs in such incidents, young

Jason was returned to life with accelerated paranormal abilities—and it wasn't long before he noticed that he could "hear" the unspoken thoughts of others.

"When I realized what I was doing, I became really frightened. At thirteen, I was really becoming aware of how important it was to fit in and to be like everyone else. I didn't want to be some kind of freak."

Next, Jason discovered that he also had the ability to pick up the emotional vibrations of others. "This really proved to be difficult for me, because, once again, it took me quite a while to truly understand what was taking place."

Jason vividly recalled the night when he was alone in his room praying for guidance and understanding to help him deal with what was happening to him. "My angel guide appeared before me in a glowing envelope of light. He told me that I was to serve as an emissary of peace and love. He said that while others around me might be spinning around in emotional and mental turmoil, I was to transmit a loving energy of tranquility."

His guardian angel went on to warn him that it would not be an easy mission to accomplish on the physical earthplane.

"He said that I would have to practice diligently to achieve mental and emotional harmony. He certainly was correct, for I failed often in my attempts to be a kind of emotional balancer. Especially during those turbulent early teenage years."

One night when his angel guide appeared before him, Jason began to weep. "I was beginning to feel so alone. When my angel asked what was troubling me so, I replied that I felt as though I was condemned to be a loner, to live life apart from others. I said that I would probably never marry, because I would never find anyone who would want to live with someone so different from everyone else. My angel just smiled and told me not to worry. He said that everything followed a Divine Plan that had already been worked out. Everything would be taken care of in the fullness of time."

When he was fourteen, Jason remembers being taken by his angel in a dreamstate to a beautiful golden temple on some higher dimension of reality. "I was taught many remarkable things in this temple. My teacher was a hooded being who never quite revealed all of his face. I was aware of other students seated near me, but I couldn't really see any of them clearly. I sensed, however, that they were young people of about my age.

"Everything was explained to me in terms of energy and vibrational patterns. I was told that there were many levels of reality. As a human, I could only see one level at a time. As a multidimensional being, I could perceive many different levels at the same time."

One night a year later, as he tried his best to absorb the higher-level teachings in some other dimension, he was suddenly able to see more of the celestial environment than ever before, and he could clearly see the other students seated around him. Almost all of the class members were indeed teenagers, like himself.

Jason awakened the next morning in a state of excitement and joy. "I was not alone! There were others like me!"

He remembered one student in particular—a

lovely girl about his age who had reddish-brown hair and bright blue-green eyes. He vowed that one day he would find her on Earth!

It was when he was seventeen that Jason no longer began to feel so lonely and isolated in the physical world among his family, friends, and schoolmates. In fact, he discovered that he was becoming increasingly popular. He overheard teachers and students alike talking about his "charisma," his "optimistic nature," and his "positive energy."

Jason became active in as many sports and extracurricular activities as his time would permit. He was better at some pursuits than others, of course, but that never seemed to bother him. He advised his friends not to be afraid to try different projects and activities, because there was really no such thing as failure.

Jason dated only when it seemed appropriate to do so to fulfill social obligations at special events on the high school calendar, but he had no real feelings for any of the girls that he escorted to those special occasions. He believed with all his heart that somewhere his beautiful fellow classmate in the Angel's Dream School was waiting for him—and he vowed to remain true to her.

"I admit that for a while there, I was beginning to wonder if she ever really would show up," Jason said in his account. "And then one day when I was nineteen and attending college in Boston, something caused me to turn around to face the person behind me at a bus stop—and there she was. Reddish-brown hair, bright blue-green eyes, the same intense look that I remembered from all those night classes in Angelic Dream School."

Although Jason was normally a reserved, self-contained sort of fellow, he knew that this was the time to put all that behind him and to seize the moment.

"Excuse me, miss, but I know you from somewhere," he said. "Somewhere almost heavenly, you could say."

She snapped out of her reverie, startled by the stranger who had suddenly begun to speak to her. Jason could read her expressions easily. Her initial response was to be prepared to deal with some jerk, but after she had actually taken a focused look at him, she offered a friendly smile.

"Why . . . why, yes," she said with a laugh. "I believe that I do know you from . . . somewhere. . . . I . . . think we took a class together, didn't we?"

Jason nodded. He was beginning to feel a bit queasy. She seemed to recognize him, but what if only he had the ability to notice others in the heavenly classroom?

Jason introduced himself properly. "Shouldn't we get off the street corner and go someplace nice, have a cup of coffee, maybe a little lunch, and talk about it?"

She said that her name was Tracey, and she agreed that they should do exactly that.

When he helped her off with her coat at the small, quiet restaurant that he'd selected for its lack of customers at that particular hour of the day, Jason noticed that she wore a small, gold angel on a chain around her neck.

"Do you believe in angels?" he asked. Then before she could answer, he asked her if she had ever seen one.

Tracey looked into his eyes for a long, silent moment as they were being seated at a small table in the back. "Yes," she answered. "As a matter of fact, I have. Several, in fact."

She sat quietly for a moment, then folded her napkin neatly in her lap. "I had a near-death experience when I was ten. I left my body and was drawn toward a beautiful light. That's when I saw angels. And then, afterward . . ."

Tracey looked down at the gold angel on the chain she wore around her neck. When she looked up again, she had tears in her eyes. "And you've seen them, too, haven't you, Jason?"

He knew then that a memory of having seen him at their angelic classroom had suddenly returned to her.

Tracey reached for his hand, and Jason clasped it warmly in his own. "I've been waiting for you . . . hoping for you . . . looking for you since I was fifteen," he told her.

"And I for you," she said softly, blinking back new tears. "I even took a vow that I would wait for you."

Jason felt tears welling up in his own eyes. "And I did the same for you. My guardian angel promised me that there would be a special someone for me so I would not feel so alone in my mission on Earth. I prayed that it would be you."

Jason concluded his report by stating that Tracey and he adjusted their life patterns to accommodate each other. They married as soon as possible, developed their own small business, and on weekends teach awareness-raising seminars that they hope will help transform the planet from a world of chaos to a planet of harmony.

CHAPTER FOUR

Loved Ones Who Left Heaven for a Final Farewell

Images of deceased loved ones who have come to bid a fond farewell or to deliver messages to those whom they have left behind constitute dramatic evidence of the soul's continued existence after physical death. Skeptical materialists may attempt to explain away such manifestations as the product of an hallucination caused by sorrow and loneliness, but those who have received such visits from the other side will always consider themselves to have been blessed with their personal proof of survival.

From the Steiger Questionnaire of Mystical Experiences:

M. C.: "In 1991, my mother passed away with cancer. The night of her funeral, I was standing outside the house when she appeared to me in a kind of vision. She wanted me to know that she was all right and she asked me to tell the other members of the family.

"Since that day, I have communicated with her on many occasions. I have also communicated with other deceased friends and relatives."

Y.M.W.: "I have experienced communication with deceased loved ones throughout my life.

"A week after a classmate died, I saw him sitting among us in class. When I graduated from high school, my dead grandmother appeared and kissed me on the cheek. After my cousin passed away, I clearly saw her standing in my bedroom looking at my book collection."

B. C.: "Ten days before our marriage, my fiancée was shot and killed. She died in my arms on a street corner.

"I was devastated. I even tried to commit suicide. Then one night she appeared and told me not to kill myself.

"Over the next several years, she would manifest each day on the anniversary of her murder. Then, for a time, she no longer appeared.

"After I got out of firefighting school, I became a firefighter/rescue specialist, and during one terrible fire, I got caught up in it. I thought I was dead, but the next thing I knew, I was with my fiancée in a bright hall. She told me that I must go back, because God needed me to protect and help his children. Then she said that I had to go.

"When I asked her if I would see her again, she

answered that she would be there for me whenever I truly needed her.

"Ever since that time, I see her every time I'm in a desperate situation on a fire call, and she has always guided me to safety. This has gone on for nine years now."

Proof of Her Sister's Joy in Heaven Removed Her Suicidal Depression

Claudia Epstein lost all her desire to go on living when her twenty-four-year-old sister, Ruth, and her sister's husband, Daniel Moore, were killed in an airplane crash in September 1988.

"It happened during the takeoff of their honeymoon flight to Tahiti," Claudia said. "They were on a small commuter plane that was supposed to take them to a larger airport for the longest leg of their flight. The commuter plane rose just high enough to take Ruth and Danny and seven other passengers to their deaths."

Their mother had died when Claudia was nine and Ruth was only four. "I guess that I became her surrogate mother," Claudia said, "and our relationship had always been closer than most sisters I knew."

Their father didn't remarry until Claudia was in her second year of college, so she had a lot of years of looking out for Ruth.

"I was delighted when Ruthie and Danny had begun dating during their sophomore year in high school," she said. "Dan was a decent guy from a good family. His older brothers were hard-working guys who treated their wives and families well, so I really hoped that this would be one of those high school romances that would last forever."

Ruth and Dan both got jobs right out of school and began to save for their marriage. Dan went to night school at a local junior college, and he was determined to better himself.

Because he could only attend college on a part-time basis, it took him six years to graduate, but he had done so with honors that May. Ruth had worked steadily at a local bank all those years, and though she had helped with Dan's education expenses, she had managed to save quite a nest egg. Two weeks after his graduation, they were married on a bright June afternoon—but the always practical young couple put off their honeymoon until September so they would better be able to afford it.

"And then, so quickly, their lives ended," Claudia said. "I was still waving good-bye when the commuter plane began to falter in midair. Before my mind could even deal with what was happening, the plane was nosedived into the runway. All their work, their plans, their dreams, their lives were snuffed out in a matter of seconds."

Claudia entered a period of deep depression after the fatal accident. For a time, she sincerely felt that she could not go on living. Her sister had been the central focus of her life for so long. Claudia's own plans for marriage had been dashed three years before when her fiancé was involved in a serious automobile accident and had been left mentally impaired. She had compensated for the loss of her own future by lavishing even more emotional energy on Ruth and Dan.

Although she had sought help from her rabbi, her

father and stepmother, her doctor, and her friends, Claudia could find no respite from her sorrow. She barely slept, for her dreams were haunted with scenes of the terrible crash and her deep sense of loss. What was the purpose of life and making plans if everything could be obliterated in a matter of minutes? Where was justice if two hard-working kids like Ruth and Dan could be killed at the very moment when they should have been happiest? And where was God in all of this? Could there truly be a God who would permit such a thing to happen to two beautiful young people at the advent of their marriage and what should have been a long life together?

Claudia is now ashamed to admit that she had often considered suicide. In her moments of deepest depression she would reason that since Ruth and Dan had been taken from her, she would join them on the other side. Thankfully, she had confessed her grim plan to her rabbi, and he had managed to convince her that such a drastic deed would not produce the desired results.

Three months after the tragedy, shortly before the Hanukkah/Christmas season, Claudia left her home in New Jersey to seek rest and seclusion in a small ski resort in northern Colorado. She knew that there was no way that she could deal with the holidays in the old familiar places in their hometown where Ruth and she had spent the previous two decades, so she had managed to find a little out-of-the-way lodge where she hoped that she might find solace of spirit.

One night as she sat reading near the fireplace, Claudia could no longer hold back her grief and depression. She dropped the book and reached for the bottle of rum that she had bought in town. At the same time, she saw the bottle of sleeping pills that her doctor had prescribed to help calm her restless nights.

"I had just begun to contemplate how easy it would be to wash down the bottle of sleeping pills with the rum and just drift away into oblivion, when I unmistakably felt a physical presence behind me," Claudia said. "I turned to see Ruth and Dan standing behind me in the center of the room. I saw them as solidly as I had ever seen them. They were smiling and holding hands. For the first time in months, I smiled also.

" 'Please, please do not continue to grieve so for us, dear one,' Ruth said in her familiar, soft, lilting voice. 'Dan and I are now happier than ever. Our love is even stronger here than it was on earth.'

"Dan put his arm around Ruth and added: 'It is so beautiful here, Claudia. And so filled with love. Don't grieve for us. We truly are in a better place.' "

Claudia could not hold back the tears. "Why did you have to leave me? It just isn't fair."

"You consider such a concept as 'fair' from a human point of view, Sis," Ruth replied. "Although it is difficult to understand, all things are part of God's larger plan. And this is our true home. We were only strangers in a strange land on Earth."

Claudia remained unconvinced. "It just isn't fair for God to take you from me. I can't go on without you. I want to join you. If you are truly in a better place, our true home, then I want to go where you are."

Ruth frowned as she followed Claudia's thoughts as they once again were directed toward the sleeping pills. "You forget about such thoughts, Sis," Ruth admonished her. "The rabbi was right. That's not the best way to get here. It's not good at all to be thinking along such lines."

The tears flowed unchecked down Claudia's cheeks. "But I really don't think I can live without you."

"Of course you can, Sis," Ruth told her. "When I was just a little girl, sometimes you would have to leave me—and I didn't think I could live without you. But you always came back home, just as you promised me that you would, and then I was so happy that we were together again. One day, when it is your time, you will join us here, and the three of us will be together again—with Mom, too. Until that day, dear, be happy and live a life of joy and fulfillment."

Before Claudia could speak again, Ruth and Dan faded from sight. But the impact of her sister's words have never left her.

The proof of Ruth's immortality freed Claudia from her deep depression, and the fact that Ruth and Dan appeared to be happy permitted her to be positive about life once again.

"All of my family members and friends were pleased to notice my new attitude when I came home after the holidays," Claudia said. "To all who would listen, I told the story of a sister's love that had been able to push aside the dark curtain of physical death long enough to restore the faith of one who had felt left behind, doomed to survive only in bitterness and despair. To all who would listen, I declared that love is the greatest power in the universe."

Basing the Hope of Heaven on a Visit from a Deceased Loved One

It is now the custom in these modern times to scoff at accounts of love that conquered the grave. But the cynics among us must remember that there are many stricken hearts whose wounds have been healed by the conviction that they have, in truth, communicated with the spirits of loved ones who have gone before.

Sadly, we do hear from time to time from people who have known with all of their heart that they perceived the surviving spirit of a deceased loved one only to have a friend or family member, a "proud regular churchgoer," insist that they had seen an "evil spirit" disguised as the loved one.

It has always puzzled us how members of most of the major religions believe, hope, or fear that they will survive death, but deny accounts of men and women who say that they have received personal proof that the promises of everlasting life are true. Why is it that certain members of orthodox religions say that it is *right* to hope for survival after death, but *wrong* to have Heaven proved to you?

We have always counseled our readers and our lecture and seminar audiences to exercise caution in accepting too soon that which might, indeed, be the ministrations of a masquerading entity or a deceptive lower-dimensional being. But we also know that through the ages hundreds of thousands of men and women have had the question of whether or not the soul survives physical death answered in the affirmative by their own personal interaction with loved ones who returned from the sepulchre to impart loving words that lifted their spirits. For those who have been so blessed, organized religion's promise of a life to come has been transformed from an ethereal covenant to a demonstrable guarantee.

Comforting Notes from Piano Practice in Heaven

Sixty-one-year-old Owen Martin remembered clearly that terrible January of his fourteenth year when the family lost their talented little Denise, a virtual child prodigy at the piano. Owen's little sister was only seven, but she was already a featured soloist at church socials, Sunday band concerts in the park, and every musical event at the school. In the small Wisconsin town where the Martin family resided, Denise was one of its most popular superstars.

"Every night Denise would practice and practice, perfecting her craft, improving her talent," Owen said. "Sometimes Rachael, my older sister, who was sixteen at the time, would sing along. Both of the girls liked to play and sing 'My Blue Heaven,' which was really popular that year."

For many years afterward, Owen blamed himself for what occurred that winter. Late one afternoon as he was shoveling snow for a neighbor to pick up some extra spending money, Denise insisted on helping him so he could get home sooner, for it was already after dark and several degrees below zero.

"I will never forget how that cold wind sliced through our parkas," he said. "I always kept a scarf over my mouth and nose so I could breathe without the wind pushing freezing air down my lungs. Denise had forgotten to bring a scarf. I will always wish that I had given her mine."

A few nights later, when Denise was practicing the piano, Owen heard her begin to cough. She had just begun to play "My Blue Heaven" when she once again coughed, pressed a hand to her chest, and cried out for their mother, complaining that she had a terrible pain.

Their mother and Rachael rushed to Denise, and Owen heard his older sister cry out that Denise was burning with fever. Mother shouted at his father to call Dr. Larsen at once.

Because it was a stormy night, Dr. Larsen was unable to reach them until it was very late. Owen recalled that when the doctor walked through their kitchen door, he had frost on his mustache and his eyeglasses were glazed with a thin layer of ice. The frozen tufts of matted hair on his heavy black fur coat began to steam as soon as he hung it to dry in front of the coal stove.

Owen, Rachael, and their father listened outside the bedroom door as the doctor examined their little sister. They heard their mother's stifled cry of fear when Dr. Larsen cautiously diagnosed pneumonia.

"For ten days and nights, we all did whatever we could to save our brilliant and talented little Denise," Owen said. "None of us would permit any other member of the family even to think that she would not get well."

Denise herself, although trembling with terrible fever and chills, would say over and over that she would get well. And she would plead with her mother or with Rachael to help her to walk downstairs so she could practice the piano. "You know I have my big recital in March," she would cry. "I have to practice my new pieces."

One night Owen heard Rachael attempt to pacify Denise by singing the words to "My Blue Heaven" and telling her to move her fingers on the covers as if she were playing the piano. "You can 'play' the stripes on the covers like they were piano keys," she told Denise.

It simply was not the energetic Denise's nature to lie idle in bed, regardless of how ill she might be. One night she somehow managed to get downstairs so she could practice. However, she had barely got herself seated on the piano stool when she fainted and fell to the floor.

It was after that incident that Denise took a sad and pronounced turn for the worst. On that cold and awful winter's night, they could all hear her fighting for every breath of air that she could force into her lungs. In spite of her determination to live and to play her beloved piano, before morning Dr. Larsen moved the blankets over Denise's forever silenced body.

The night after the funeral, the Martin family was seated in the front room at the table, trying their best to appreciate the chicken dinner that Grandmother Jorgensen had brought.

"Grandma had just asked the blessing when we heard the first notes come from the piano," Owen remembered. "Everyone was startled, and we all turned in our chairs to look at the keyboard. Again the notes sounded. Clearly, without question, we were all hearing a few bars from 'My Blue Heaven.' "

Owen's father reached out to take his wife's hand firmly in his own. "It's Denise," he said softly. "She's here with us, playing the piano."

Rachael nodded in agreement, tears streaming unchecked down her cheeks. "It's exactly the way she would play it."

Owen recalled his mother questioning Grandmother Jorgensen. "Is it possible, Mama?"

"Grandma answered Mom very solemnly," Owen said. "She reminded us all that our Lord promised that we will be joined together with all our loved ones one day in Heaven."

Once again the notes sounded from "My Blue Heaven."

"Listen," Rachael said. "Listen to the part that plays over and over. It's the part where the lyrics say how happy we will all be in our blue heaven."

Owen's mother cried out from the depths of her being. "Is . . . is it really you, Denise, my darling baby?"

The refrain sounded louder than before, then once again, just a bit fainter.

"Thank the blessed Lord." His mother smiled, her eyes brimming with tears. "Our beloved Denise is free of the terrible illness . . . and she can now practice the piano all she wants in Heaven."

Owen Martin concluded his account by stating that although the family never again heard any spectral notes emanating from the piano, Denise had provided each one of them with indisputable proof of the survival of the spirit after physical death. "We were all able to lead stronger, more focused lives because of our certainty that the soul lives on and that one day, once again, we will all be listening to Denise play the piano for us—this time in Heaven."

Camille Flammarion's Sixty Years of Research into the Mysteries of Death

In 1922, French astronomer and psychical researcher Camille Flammarion completed his sixty-year research project of exploring death and its mysteries. Quoting a sorrowful stanza from a poem by the Countess of Noailles—"Never to see you again, O radiance of the sky!/Alas, I was not made to die!"—the scientist himself waxes poetic: "No, poets, your vibrant souls were not made to die; no soul was made to die, and the light of the heavens is not extinguished."

Reflecting upon the project that he began in 1861, Flammarion optimistically concludes that those readers "who have had the time and the inclination to read the 1,265 pages of the three volumes of this work must, like me, have reached the conviction that there is in a human being an element not yet understood in the recognized scientific theories: a thinking soul, endowed with special faculties. And they must know, also, that this soul does not undergo dissolution, like the body; that it survives the body. It was our object to prove this survival by positive occurrences. That is the chief result of this work."

Flammarion reminds his readers that the instances reported in his massive study are "actual occurrences, as real as all the happenings which make up daily life."

The appearance of images and forms of those who have died indicate most clearly that there exists something within each human being that is unknown, and that this something "survives the disintegration of the earthly body and the transformation of our material molecules; these, as a matter of fact, cannot from the strictly scientific point of view, be said to be destroyed, either."

After sixty years of research, Flammarion felt justified in putting forth certain conclusions as "statements resting upon unshakable foundations." Among those statements are the following:

- Human beings who have died . . . still live on after the dissolution of the material organism.
- They exist in the form of invisible, intangible substances [of which our normal five senses] do not perceive under ordinary circumstances.
- In general, they do not manifest themselves. Their mode of existence is entirely different from ours. They act on our consciousness and, in certain circumstances, may prove their existence.
- When they act upon our souls and, through these, upon our brains, we see them . . . as we have known them, with their clothing . . . their habitual movements, their individualities. It is our inner eye which sees them. One soul can perceive another soul.
- Apparitions and manifestations occur with relative frequency during the hours which follow immediately upon [death]; their number diminishes as time passes. . . .[1]

Spirits of Their Loved Ones Guided Them from Beyond the Grave

Recently, Barbra Streisand, the famous songstress, actor, and director, told of the indecision that was troubling her about whether or not to direct the 1983 film *Yentl.* As she was internally debating the matter, she went to visit her father's grave for the first time. She admitted that she had not done so before "because I was angry, probably, that he died on me."

Later that same day, she invited a medium, "a nice Jewish woman who had a spiritual guide," to her older brother's home. When the table began to move, Ms. Streisand confessed that she became so frightened that she ran into the bathroom.

Later, when she had regrouped her courage, she observed the leg of the table raise and lower itself to the floor to spell out M-A-N-N-Y, which was her father Emanuel's nickname, and the messages, "S-O-R-R-Y" and "S-I-N-G P-R-O-U-D." Ms. Streisand said that the messages tapped out by the table leg under the direction of the medium's guide seemed to comprise a definite signal to her that she would direct the movie.

Of all the films that she has made, she said, she is most proud of *Yentl*, because it was dedicated to her father.[2]

When Jaclyn Smith first achieved success as one of the trio of *Charlie's Angels*, she was both fascinated and frightened when she awoke to see a "set of stairs from Heaven" materialize at her bedside. Standing at the bottom of the shimmering, golden staircase, she recognized the features of her beloved grandfather, who had died almost twenty years before at the age of 101. In Ms. Smith's opinion, her grandfather had been a saintly figure, "untarnished by worldliness." So when he told her that her success on television was a superficial achievement, she listened as he further advised her to begin doing some charity work.

Ms. Smith said that the spirit of her grandfather has since appeared to her on many occasions, and he has guided her in her work with underprivileged and handicapped children.[3]

* * *

Famed superlawyer Melvin Belli revealed that the spirit of his deceased father saved his life when he took a turn too wide and lost control of his car.

The car skidded, flipped, and began to roll, as the forty-four-year-old attorney was thrown clear. Belli watched the automobile wheel up an embankment, then begin to slide back down. It looked as though it would come down directly on him, so Belli prepared to dive out of the way to a spot where he was certain the car would miss him.

That was when he saw an apparition of his father, who had been dead for about ten years. The spirit told him not to move, to sit still.

"So instead of diving to safety, I froze right where I was," Belli said. "The car rolled over and crashed down—right on the spot I would have moved to if my father hadn't saved me!"[4]

Popular actress Susan Lucci, the conniving Erica Kane on the TV soap *All My Children*, has freely admitted that she has regular communication with her grandmother, who has been dead for more than thirty years.

Ms. Lucci insists that she is not just dreaming. She is always wide awake when she achieves contact with her grandmother: "I've never lost touch with her, and I'm sure she's a source of my guidance."[5]

Spirit Messages Regarding the Appearances of Deceased Loved Ones

Liz Smith Anderson (also known as Liberty), author of *A Journey of Ascension*, seeks to serve the Creator of All and the Christ Consciousness by allowing spirit to work through her and by channeling such messages as this one by the entity Zadkiel:

> Oftentimes, in the case of what one of Earth would call sudden death or accidental death, the spirit is given the opportunity to communicate with those loved ones left behind. Many people have experienced this in the form of spirit manifestations, rappings, lights going off and on, voices, and other forms. This is performed in conjunction with Universal Law and enabled by the departed spirit's level of evolvement.
>
> An evolved spirit who has transmuted to the higher realms will instantly be reconnected with the collective consciousness of which you are a part. The spirit immediately knows of its options and can see which of its family and friends is most likely to accept and respond to spirit communication.
>
> This does not mean that the spirit does not see or visit everyone involved: It means that the spirit will be drawn according to the brightness of the life force surrounding a person, thus communicating with the person the spirit feels will most likely accept and understand when communication commences.
>
> A spirit is always accompanied by its guardian and gatekeeper spirits/angels. These beings are with you from conception to death and beyond. They are oftentimes beings with whom you have soul agreements, and many times the departed goes on to become a guardian or a gatekeeper for one of these souls.[6]

Daephrenocles, the spirit entity who communicates with the modern mystic Lori Jean Flory, spoke to the matter of those incidents in which a loved one who has died returns from the other side in the spirit body:

> Love is eternal, infinite, continuous, and lives on forever. The love and the desire to comfort and soothe those who have been left behind is strong. The desire to let others who are loved know that one is all right and at peace is to bring that same peace to the loved ones.
>
> Excessive grief, however, can hold back the departed soul from progressing as it needs into the Light, for [the deceased may wish] to watch over and care for those who are still upon the Earth. . . .
>
> Celebrate the life, the love, and the blessings of that one who has made the transition and know that love lives forever within the heart.
>
> One's angels and guides are always present and accompany the departed one and care for the departed one during life in this dimension from the time of transition and ever onward. Love is always present. Help is always present.[7]

He Brought Her a Loving Kiss from Heaven

One of our favorite stories regarding a friend or loved one who returned from the grave to give testimony to a life beyond came to us from one of our readers, Mrs. Helen Murad. Now a fifty-five-year-old grandmother, Mrs. Murad sent us a detailed account of an incident in her adolescence during which she swears that she kissed a ghost!

When Helen was fifteen, her parents moved to the country, thus placing her in a rural school district and separating her from her friends in the city. At first it was quite difficult to adjust to village life and a much smaller school, but every week or so, her mother would drive in to the city to shop and to permit the children—Helen and her two younger brothers—to check out books at the large municipal library. Helen always looked forward to these trips as an occasion to meet with old school friends among the quiet stacks of the library.

About a year after her family moved to the country, Helen was sitting on the library steps awaiting her mother's return when she saw a familiar figure approaching her. It was Jeff, a boy with whom she had gone to school before they moved. He was a grade ahead of her, a handsome boy, a fine athlete, and all of the girls made a fuss over him.

Jeff spotted her sitting on the steps and called out to her. "Hey, Helen! Boy, you're even prettier than I remembered."

Helen felt herself blushing. "I offered no resistance when he asked me to walk across the street to the little park and sit on a bench with him. He put his arm around me, and I thought I would fall off the bench when he bent down and kissed me on the cheek."

Jeff told her that he had always liked her. Helen said that she had missed him—and all of her other friends. "I sure would love it if you would drive out to see me sometime." She blushed again at her sudden boldness.

But rather than returning her flirtation with a smile, Jeff suddenly became rather serious. "Helen," he began in a soft voice that was almost a whisper, "I don't live here anymore."

"Where do you live?" Helen wanted to know. It didn't matter where he had moved. They could write letters back and forth. He could still come driving down their lane in his old car.

Jeff sighed and tightened his arm around her shoulder. "I moved far, far away from here, Helen. I'm just back in town for a little visit."

Regardless of how far away Jeff had moved, she didn't see why they couldn't write to each other. "Can I have your address?" she asked.

Jeff chuckled. "There's no mail delivery where I live."

"What a terrible place," Helen frowned.

Jeff shook his head. "Oh, no, it's a beautiful place, absolutely wonderful."

Helen asked the unthinkable. "Is . . . is it just that you don't want to write to me?"

Jeff firmly denied such a charge. "No, it's like I told you, there's no mail delivery where I live. But maybe I can keep in touch with you. Maybe I can visit you again someday."

Helen said that it would be wonderful to see him anytime.

Jeff suddenly seemed very anxious. "I've got to go. I'm out of time. How about another kiss?" he asked gently. "A nice good-bye kiss."

This time Jeff kissed her full on the lips, and Helen thought she surely would faint.

When he let her go, Helen was looking up into her mother's scowling face. Helen barely had time to shout goodbye to Jeff over her shoulder before her mother dragged her off to the car. Her last image of Jeff was the sight of him returning her farewell wave.

Helen talked to her mother all the way home, trying to make her not be angry with her. When she explained that Jeff had moved away and that she would probably never see him again, her mother began to lighten up.

"But she really let me know that she did not approve of any daughter of hers smooching and necking on a bench in a public park. And I knew that my two kid brothers would probably tease me about being 'caught in the act' until I was sixty years old."

It was nearly three weeks before Helen got back to the city library. Illness had prevented their mother from taking them into town any sooner, and they knew that all the books would have overdue fines on them.

Jill, one of Helen's former classmates, was working at the library desk, and as Helen doled out the fine she could not resist telling her friend how she and Jeff had kissed in the park a few weeks previously.

Jill rolled her eyes and sniffed disdainfully. "That's really bad taste, Helen."

Jill was obviously very jealous, and she wasn't finished with Helen, either, momentarily forgetting about the large sign over her desk that advised extreme quiet in the library. "You're awful, you know that? You are just plain crude and vulgar to say such a thing about you and Jeff!"

The head librarian came to shush the girls, and Helen's former classmate turned to walk away from her.

"Don't go, please," Helen whispered, catching Jill's

arm. "We were always such good friends. Why am I crude and vulgar because I let Jeff kiss me? Are you jealous or what?"

Her friend fixed her with a cold glare. Then something within Helen's own eyes seemed to cause Jill to thaw just a bit. "Look, Helen," she began, "it was in really bad taste for you to say that Jeff kissed you a couple of weeks ago. If you were just trying to be funny, you weren't. So knock it off about Jeff."

Helen shook her head. "But Jeff did kiss me. He said it would be a good-bye kiss because he no longer lived here."

Tears began to form in Jill's eyes. "What's wrong with you, Helen? You're just plain sick and terrible! You disgust me!"

Helen was left standing with her mouth open in utter confusion and amazement as her friend ran sobbing from the library. Confused and hurt, Helen was soon in tears herself. The head librarian had overheard the girls' heated conversation, and she came over to confront Helen.

"She said that she had always known me to be a decent girl, so she was going to give me the benefit of the doubt in case I really did not know that Jeff had been killed in an automobile accident shortly after we had moved," Helen said.

"I was stunned, literally struck dumb with shock upon hearing that Jeff had been killed. I knew that I had seen him just a few weeks ago. I knew that I had walked with him, talked with him—and kissed him. When my senses and my voice returned, I began denying what the librarian had told me. It simply could not be true."

Because Helen and Jill and now the head librarian

had created a disturbance that many people could no longer overlook, a number of former classmates came over to Helen and confirmed the startling news that Jeff was dead.

"I remember that I cried and that my body began to tremble as if I were about to have convulsions," Helen said. "I had to sit down and the librarian had to bring me a glass of water. I knew I wasn't crazy. I knew that I had really seen Jeff. But all these people were telling me that he had been dead for a year."

To this day, Helen Murad can provide no explanation of the experience that she'd had with an affectionate ghost when she was a teenager. But, she emphasizes, she knows as certain as she knows anything that she sat on that park bench and received a warm kiss from a boy who had been dead for a year—and she can offer the additional testimony of her mother and two younger brothers, who saw Jeff as unmistakably as she did.

"I don't know why Jeff chose to come to me that day," Helen said, concluding her account. "We had never been that close while he was alive. Perhaps we had some soul link that I still don't understand. What his appearance did for me was to remove all fear of death and dying, for Jeff proved to me that life continues after the grave.

"As the years have gone by, though, I have sometimes wondered if, in some way, he might have returned for my mother's benefit and learning as much as for my own. Her mother, Grandma Constable, was dying of cancer at that time, and Mom was taking it very hard. After the experience with Jeff, her faith in God and in Heaven was wonderfully renewed and elevated, and she came to accept Grandma's passing with courage and with much more peace of mind and spirit."

His Best Friend Returned from Heaven to Remove His Fear of Death

Dan Fowler stated in his account that Peter Fowler was not only his first cousin, but he was also his best friend. They lived about three blocks apart, just the right distance to warm up their bikes for an excursion around the middle-sized Nebraska town that their family had called home for three generations.

One Sunday afternoon after the two fourteen-year-olds had taken in a matinee at the larger of the town's two movie theaters, Dan found himself extremely depressed. At the end of the feature, a teen-aged boy about their age died in the arms of his weeping mother, and the scene had shaken Dan to the very core of his youthful existence. He had never before realized that he had such a great fear of death and dying.

"Pete tried to comfort me as we sat around the kitchen table after the movie and spooned into the generous bowls of chocolate swirl ice cream that my mother had set before us. 'Come on, Danny,' he said with a strange kind of conviction. 'Dying isn't such a bad thing, you know.' "

Dan wanted to know the source of Pete's cheerful optimism.

Pete shrugged. "I just know that when we die we are all going to go to a better place. I know that Heaven is going to be a wonderful, beautiful place."

Dan said he would always remember that Pete's

face seemed almost to be glowing as he spoke about the afterlife. "I have no idea where Pete received his special knowledge of Heaven. Neither of our families were very faithful churchgoers."

Once, when the two boys were camping out down by the creek, Dan set forth his argument that once you quit breathing and your heart stops, you are stone-cold dead and that's it.

Pete had laughed at his pessimism. "I'll tell you what. When I die, I'll come back from Heaven and say a special good-bye to you."

Dan didn't like such talk. He couldn't imagine life without his best friend and first cousin.

At first Pete made a joke about graveyards and people dying to get in, then he suddenly became very serious. "Danny, here's one more thing. When I die, I'll come back and give you a special farewell. And you know where it will be? Right in the old Ford Hotel!"

The Ford Hotel had a lot of history connected with it. It had been built back in the 1880s, and local folklore had it that Buffalo Bill and Annie Oakley had stayed there once when they were touring with their wild west show. Pete had always loved the old hotel, and the two boys used to spend hours there, guessing the life stories of the people who checked in.

"Yessir," Pete repeated with emphasis. "When I'm dead and gone, I'll get a pass from St. Peter to leave Heaven for a while—then I'll pop up right in front of you right there in the old Ford Hotel."

Then, even though he was upset with the nature of such talk, Dan had to laugh at the imagined spectre of Pete as a spook scaring the hotel guests.

On that summer night by the creek, they both

knew that they would each live at least a hundred years or more. They counted shooting stars until they fell asleep in their sleeping bags.

Two months later, just a few days after school had resumed in September, Pete was struck by a feed truck from the farmers' grain elevator in the south end of town. He had been riding his bike en route to junior high baseball practice. An elderly woman had stepped down from her front steps directly into his path, and Pete swerved out into the street to avoid hitting her. The truck threw the teenager for thirty feet or more. He died on the way to the hospital in Lincoln.

Somehow Dan managed to get through the funeral. He has almost no memories of the next several days. "I would wake up in the morning and start to call Pete. Then I would remember that he was dead, and the sorrow would hit me again. Sometimes I would dream at night that Pete was still alive, but he was hiding out, playing a big joke on everyone but me, his best friend."

A few months after Pete's funeral and just a few days before his fifteenth birthday, Dan was invited to have lunch at the Ford Hotel's dining room by his uncle, George Cook.

"Uncle George couldn't have given me a better birthday gift," Dan remembered. "For all the hours that Pete and I had spent there, I had never eaten in the dining room. Also, I felt that I would somehow be closer to Pete, since he loved the old hotel so much."

Everyone knew that Dan had taken his cousin's death very hard, and since Uncle George had once studied to be a preacher before he went back to farming, Dan figured that the family had elected him to provide some counseling.

During the course of eating lunch, Dan told his uncle that Pete had once promised that if he died his spirit would return to the Ford Hotel. Dan started to cry a little thinking about Pete. At first he felt embarrassed, unmanly, but he knew that Uncle George was a kind and understanding man.

Uncle George smiled and said that he didn't rightly know if he believed in ghosts and stuff like that, but he did know for certain that the Savior promised folks that they would see their loved ones again if they kept on the straight and narrow pathway to Heaven.

"I hope that is true, Uncle George," Dan said. "I surely do."

"Be of faith, boy," Uncle George promised. "It is most certainly true."

After lunch, Dan walked slowly out into the lobby, his mind flooded with a hundred memories of the times that he had walked around the Ford Hotel with Pete.

"As I walked down the hall, I saw the elevator doors slide open for a boy about my age who was waiting to step inside," Dan recalled. "The kid stepped in, then turned to face me. *It was Pete!*

"He grinned at me, winked, then gave me that strange kind of salute the way he always did when we said good-bye to each other. Then the doors closed.

"I started bawling right there in front of the elevators, and I didn't care who saw me or if they thought that I was the biggest sissy in the whole state of

Nebraska. Pete had come back to spook me in the Ford Hotel, just as he had promised. He came back to say a final good-bye and to prove to me that life is eternal and that I shouldn't have such a terrible fear of dying.

"From that day onward, I never again had a fear of death, and I knew that Pete and all my loved ones wait for me in Heaven. I have a great certainty that one day we shall all be reunited in the firm bonds of love. Like Uncle George said, you have to have faith that Heaven and the afterlife exists. But it is even better when you have proof."

CHAPTER FIVE

The Mystery of Mediumship: Talking to Heaven's Inhabitants

The idea that certain humans have the ability to communicate with the deceased, to be able, as medium James Van Praagh phrases it, to "talk to Heaven," is perhaps one of the oldest surviving aspects of shamanism. In Cro-Magnon cave paintings we can clearly see depictions of the entranced shaman making contact with the spirit world. One of the most essential attributes of the traditional practitioner of Native American Medicine is the ability to make contact with the grandfathers and grandmothers who have passed to the world beyond death. We should in no way be surprised that we continue to have mediums among us in the 1990s, and doubtless their number will increase as we approach the new millennium.

As children of Christian fundamentalist orthodoxy, we were reared in that peculiar religious paradox that entreats its members to pray earnestly for life everlasting, but to shun those who claim to communicate with the spirit world as if they were demons incarnate. We still urge caution when it comes to heedlessly consorting with just any old spirit who manifests in either our front parlor or the séance room, but if it could be proved to a reasonable degree that sincere and honest mediums are able to make contact with the deceased, then the survival question would be answered and millions and millions of people would find their fears of what lies beyond death immediately transformed to peaceful acceptance.

Why are we so reluctant to accept the communications provided us by sincere mediums as "proof" of life after death?

For one thing, our modern materialistic and mechanistic science has done much to obliterate the concept of a soul and the duality of mind and body. The notion of the mind/soul has been replaced by an emphasis on brain cells, conditioned responses, and memory patterns.

Scientists such as the parapsychologists and psychical researchers contend that we humans are something other than physical things, and their extensive studies have demonstrated the enormous reach and abilities of the human psyche. Parapsychologists have garnered evidence indicating that the human mind is capable of projecting a segment of its psyche unhampered by time and space, that one level of the mind may be able to "birth" new personalities, that one level of the subconscious may telepathically gain knowledge from the minds of others. However, the more the parapsychologists learn about the remarkable range and power of the living human mind, the less credence they are likely to grant to the medium's proof of survival.

Another important factor that has long contributed to the general skepticism toward the survival evidence offered by mediums is the unfortunate fact that no area of human relationships is so open to cruel deception as that which exploits the grieving process. It has taken no great amount of scientific training to have been able to expose a great many so-called mediums as charlatans, spiritual vultures preying upon human emotions.

That being said, it must also be acknowledged that no area of human endeavor is without its weaker members—and that would include certain clerics who horde the widow's mite from the collection plate in secret bank accounts and certain scientists who falsify the results of an experiment to ensure continued grant money. To suggest that all mediums are fraudulent would be to employ the same kind of distorted logic that maintains that all bank tellers abscond with funds, all policemen accept bribes, all lawyers are unscrupulous ambulance chasers, and all doctors are money-hungry quacks.

The Insights and Mediumship of Deon Frey

Some years ago, the highly respected Chicago spirit medium Deon Frey told us about a woman who had come to her because she was in great distress and in need of money. The woman's husband had passed on suddenly, and since he had no insurance policies and a number of debts, he had left his wife and four children virtually penniless. It was a cold fall, and the winter would be even colder. The children needed new heavy clothing, and she needed some money until she could find suitable employment.

Deon met her for lunch, and although they were seated in a crowded restaurant and she did not enter a trance state, she could see distinctly a clear image of the woman's husband building up behind her. "I described the man that I was seeing, and the woman verified that I must be seeing her husband," Deon said. "She began to cry, but I paid little attention to her. The entity who was in spirit was telling me something very important.

"He said to tell his wife that he loved her and that he would cherish the memory of her and their children forever. He also insisted that he had not left her destitute. If she would go down into their basement and look behind the cabinet of old fruit jars, she would find several loose bricks. If she were to pry them out, she would find three paid-up insurance policies in a tin box. There would be more than enough money there to provide for the children's education and to keep the family functioning comfortably until she would be able to find an adequate job or otherwise reestablish her life."

The woman was shocked and extremely skeptical. She knew of no such hiding place, and she knew of no insurance policies. And if such policies did exist, why hadn't she been contacted by agents from the insurance companies?

"I've never gone to a medium before," the woman told Deon. "I just don't know about all this. I mean, my sister recommended you, but if my priest ever found out . . ."

Deon was not unfamiliar with the situation. Someone desperately wanted help from the spirit world, but almost as desperately attempted to reject spiritual assistance when it was offered.

But then the man in spirit was speaking to Deon once again. "Your husband says that he was wrong to have kept the papers and the hiding place a secret," the spirit medium relayed. "He knows that now. He had been paying the premiums on them for many years, and he regarded them as a nest egg for his old age and as a comfortable sum for you and the children if he should die before his retirement. He admits that he was wrong not to have told you about the insurance policies, but he died so suddenly that he had no time to give you this information. He is so glad that your sister convinced you to come to see a spirit medium. Oh, and he adds that no agents have called you because he first acquired these policies when he was a young man just out of college back in Milwaukee. The companies have not been notified of his death."

When the woman left the spirit medium, she was pale, shaken, and uncertain whether she had had lunch with an angel or one of the devil's daughters.

But that night, Deon received a telephone call from the woman, stating that she must truly have communicated with the spirit of her husband. She had looked behind the cabinet of old fruit jars, found the loose bricks, and discovered the insurance policies in a tin box. True to her husband's promise, it appeared as though she and their children would be comfortably situated.

Deon firmly reiterated the facts of the spirit communication: "Number one, I had never met this woman before in my life. I knew nothing about her except that a mutual friend knew her sister. Number two, I had never known her husband or what he looked like on the earthplane. Number three, I provided the woman with information which no living person knew—information which only the dead man could have provided. Good Lord, is that proof of survival after death or what?"

Deon Frey experienced her first conscious trance when she was fifteen years old and a student librarian at the high school. One day she walked out of the school in a trance state, continued across the street to her home, and entered the room where her father lay dead. Her cousin had gone to the school, entering by a side door, and told Deon's teacher to send her home because her father had just passed away. Her cousin was amazed when she learned that Deon had already left the building.

"Eternal life was proved to me that very night," Deon said. "I was awakened by my father scratching on a screen beside my bed. My father had not been a churchgoer and had not believed in life after death, but he told me, 'You were right, Deon. If I live, all these people live.' "

Her father said that he was sorry he'd had to leave her so abruptly, especially since because of his death family financial stresses would not permit her to continue to attend public school. "But he did say that he would see to it that I received a different kind of education."

A year later Deon moved to Chicago, and her sister introduced her to Eleanor Dunne, a spiritual medium. During their meeting, an image of Deon's father appeared to her and she understood at once what his spirit had meant when he spoke of her receiving a "different kind of education."

Deon became a member of the National Spiritualist Association and minister of the First Roseland Spiritualist Church. She became widely known as a medium and was selected for a number of impressive experiments by psychical research groups in the United States and in Great Britain. We met Deon in April 1969 and continued to study her mediumistic abilities until about 1976. On dozens of occasions, we witnessed firsthand her control over spirit communications and physical manifestations.

A Step-by-Step Description of the Process of Spirit Communication

During a séance she conducted in our home, we asked Deon if it were possible for her to step out of her trance state and, at the same time, describe the process of spirit communication step-by-step for our purposes of research. Here, edited and condensed for space requirements, is her running description of mediumistic spirit communication.

"Okay, I'll face east. I just lie down in the center [of the couch], place my hands at my side. My mind goes in about a thousand different directions.

"See? [*Her voice becomes hoarse*] They've [spirits] already started taking my voice, and I'm not even fully in trance yet. [*Addressing the group in attendance at the séance*] Be sure you're relaxed, too. They might want to use one or more of you. Now remember, even though I'm not in full trance, it is possible for me to walk, move, or whatever the spirits want me to do.

"If they move me around, I'll go anywhere without touching anything. From now on, you don't call me Deon. You call me 'the medium.' Call me that throughout the séance. Whoever [referring to spirit entities from the other side] you talk to will probably give you their names. However, if they don't, you just talk to them anyway and try to find out who they are. Give them the same courtesy you would if anyone entered your home and wanted to talk with you.

"My body usually gets cold. Sometimes it gets so cold, people think that I am dying or dead.

"I might act out the part of a spirit who wants to communicate with one of you. I never know what the spirits are going to want me to do. And I can't promise anything. All I do is lie here and see what happens.

"Right now, I feel my chest getting very heavy. At this point I can feel a terrible vibration in my hands and body.

"It is important to me that you do not keep silent. You must talk among yourselves and create energy for the voice of my spirit guide. It is important to him.

"If you are able to see something or feel something or are aware of something that is happening in the room, please talk about it."

[*After a few more moments, Dr. Richard Speidel,*

Deon's principal spirit guide, came through] "Good evening, friends. I am very happy to greet you tonight and work with you in this manner.

"As you sit in attendance, always be looking to see what may be taking place around the medium's face. And remember to keep working with me. I am Dr. Richard Speidel, and I work with the medium in this manner in order to open up the séance and to talk with you and others in the spirit world."

Although Deon accepted the reality of her spirit guide as an entity independent of herself, she had the ability to remain somewhat objective in regard to her mediumship. One night after we had completed a number of very successful experiments in spirit communication, she said, "I wonder sometimes if I am really picking up thought forms from sitters in the séance circle rather than seeing the actual etheric images of those who have passed over. Or could it be that in trance I somehow travel to Heaven—the other world, another plane of existence—and there communicate with spirits rather than that they come back to the earthplane? Can it be that I am only a glorified relay station for vibratory forces?"

Examining the Remarkable Career of Irene Hughes

We have now known the remarkable seeress and medium Irene Hughes for more than thirty years, and during those three decades, we have conducted a series of wide-ranging experiments utilizing her incredible psychic abilities. We have sat in numerous successful and productive séances under her control, and we have traveled to haunted sites throughout the Midwest to witness her astonishing ability to contact the restless spirits who remain earthbound and to direct them toward the light and eternal peace.

On one occasion, a Lutheran pastor who had heard Irene speak told us how surprised he was at how orthodox the medium's religious views were. Irene, herself an ordained Baptist minister, has always felt that her psychic talents are compatible with organized religion, but that they may also transcend certain orthodox beliefs. "It may seem a paradox to some," she has said, "but everything I do in life is based on eternal and immutable laws."

Irene Hughes feels that intuition is one of God's original gifts to all humankind. "I have had mystical communication with a Divine Intelligence whom I call God, and I also gain many of my talents through telepathic communication and through assistance from spirit intelligences, such as Kaygee, my Japanese spirit guide and teacher."

Irene's understanding of Heaven is that it is a state of consciousness both here on Earth and after physical death. "The afterlife is another experience in the evolution and growth of the soul as it reaches toward Christlike perfection."

Her perception of herself as a medium is that she is honest and extremely loyal to her beliefs. "I feel that I have a sincere spiritual love for all human beings. I respect all people because of my belief that the Christ consciousness is within each of us. I believe that each being is guided from within in moments of crisis. I would always act according to the guidance which was given to me at that crisis moment. I believe that such guidance would come from the original survival abilities instilled through, or within, the faculties of perception, which come from acknowledging God."

Although Irene often goes into a light trance state, she doesn't seem to employ her spirit guide in the manner in which the majority of mediums utilize their spirit helpers. Usually when a medium has entered trance, the personality of the spirit guide will temporarily "possess" the medium's body and assume control of the séance. The voice that one hears will no longer be that of the medium's, but will be altered to some degree indicative of another personality. It seems that Irene's mentor, Kaygee, the spirit of a prominent Japanese Christian leader, is more of a teacher than a guide; and he seldom manifests to control the voice, facial features, or mannerisms of Irene Hughes. In the dozens of times that we have conducted experiments with Irene, we have been present at only one séance when Kaygee "came through," and that was only for a brief time and specifically to deal with a matter of great importance to one of the sitters in attendance.

Irene Hughes's Tips for Successful Spirit Communication

Irene always encourages her sitters to take a tablet, spare pens or pencils, and if possible, a tape recorder to her séances. "Messages may come helter-skelter from several discarnate beings, and you cannot possibly trust your memory to unscramble what is uttered.

Accurate notes are essential if you are to check up on details."

In what she terms "daylight readings," the medium will not be in full trance and will, in his or her own personality, relay impressions and interpretations to the sitter. When the medium is in deep trance, a completely different personality—a guide or a gatekeeper—will be in control of his or her physical body. This personality, the guide, will identify itself and mediate the conversations between the medium and the sitters.

"Look at it like this," Irene explained, "it's kind of like communicating with a bunch of friends who telephone to speak to you, but catch you in the bathtub, and your husband or wife relays—mediates—what your friends say and what you say."

Irene agrees with other mediums that the importance of the sitters' attitudes toward the spirit personalities cannot be overstressed. "Be polite and friendly, even if the entity who murdered Grandpa seems to be there. Speak promptly when spoken to, just as you would if addressed by a guest in your home. Be positive and brief in your remarks, never negative, but never volunteering crucial information."

How does a sitter respond if the communicating entity seems to be an unknown personality? What if a spirit addresses you and says, "I'm Fred Chamberlain," and you don't have a clue as to his identity?

"Don't say you've never heard of him," Irene advised. "Say, instead, 'Can you describe yourself?' Or, 'Do you have a message for me?'

"You see, the catch is that Fred may have been in the first grade with you, but you have not seen him since. Or he may have retired from Smith and

Schmidt before you began your apprenticeship there. Of *nobody* can you really be certain that you have had no connection with him or her. If you do so assert, the spirit will hush."

Irene Hughes is always careful to admonish sitters that occasionally, just as a prank—or perhaps as a test—a discarnate spirit will pretend to be some friend or relative. The giveaway will always be in an extended conversation with the masquerading entity.

"If Aunt Constance had a Calvinist conscience," Irene pointed out, "you'll soon know if you are dealing with a masquerader if the spirit advises some shady or shabby manuever."

And just because your beloved one is now on the other side, the practical Irene cautions, the experience of death has not transformed him or her into an all-knowing wise one. "Although those in the spirit world do have sources of information denied you, they are still merely people, limited in knowledge, imperfect in judgment, human in motive. Weigh their advice as you would that given to you by intelligent friends on this plane—consider it seriously, but not slavishly."

In her many years of experience in dealing with the spirit world, Irene comments that "saucer-eyed naivete and trustful gullibility" lead only to tearful disillusionment.

"On the other hand," she promises, "if judicious investigation is able to bring through even one authentic evidential message from the other side, your world will never be so drab again."

Irene Hughes is frequently asked just how she is able to differentiate between a telepathic communication from a living mind on the earthplane and a direct impression from a discarnate entity on the other side. She responded,

> Here is a simplified description of how it happens: I am quiet, completely relaxed, deep in meditation. I may be alone at home or among friends in a prayer circle. A tingling sensation, similar to a chill, begins on my right ankle, then on my left. Slowly the tingling spreads to cover my entire body. It is as though a soft silken skin has been pulled over me, glove-tight—even over my face, changing its features—yet comfortable and protective. It is soothing, yet thrilling, and ethereally light.
>
> At this point, I am on my way to that golden flow of consciousness that we earthlings term the *spiritplane.* I am in semi-trance. Were I in full trance, I could not recall a single detail.

As her involvement with the spirit plane progresses, Irene's body becomes as icy cold as death. "Yet a delightful warmth engulfs my inner self," she said.

Soon Kaygee, her spirit teacher, appears, smiles, and bows to her, indicating approval of her incursion into the spirit world. By a slight waving of his hand, Kaygee ushers in those entities of the spiritplane who wish to speak through her.

Irene explained that she is bound to her spirit teacher by "ties that are ethereal, yet mighty as a coaxial cable."

> They give me energy. Every thought that flashes through my teacher's consciousness becomes crystal clear also in my consciousness.

The inhabitants of Heaven appear to Irene just as they did on Earth. "They do not appear as a cloud of ectoplasm when they appear to me," she said. "They have the same eyes, hair, dress, manner, and above all, the same personality that characterized them on the earthplane.

"Something they owned on Earth often identifies the spirit personalities to their loved ones waiting to hear from them. Whatever the calling or profession, some appropriate object will be shown."

Interestingly, Irene said that some things that are shown to her must not be told to persons on the earthplane. Her spirit mentor always warns her of such things, and such an admonition may take a moment or two to register on her consciousness.

Irene has said that she is able to distinguish whether a sudden impression originates from the earthplane or the spirit world by the state of insight known as *noesis.* The great psychologist William James wrote that the "noetic quality" gave illuminations and revelations a "curious sense of knowing." When a thought comes from someone on the earthplane, Irene commented, it has a different feeling:

> When the communicator is a living person, I am aware that this thought is his; that this deed is what he has done or what he will do; that he lives in a certain city or follows a specific calling. His personality, too, is analyzed for me; but often I am told to be cautious about translating the signs and symbols by which I am informed.

Irene Hughes suggested that a sitter might make believe that a spirit medium is a telephone. "When it rings, you answer. You must carry on the conversation with the entity that speaks to you on the other end of the line. The medium cannot speak for you. He or she acts as the wires of the instrument through which the vibrations flow, turning them into words and symbols."

The Mediums among Us

In 1967, we began a research project to identify the kind of person who was most likely to become a spirit medium. The skeptics immediately nominated the odd or poorly adjusted members of society as their candidates for the role of psychic sensitive or spirit medium. The cynics among our associates quickly added that the general level of intelligence among mediums must be very low.

The first thing we learned once we had gained a broad sampling of the mediumistic population—i.e., those men and women who freely admitted to being spirit mediums—is that mediums are people. They are nurses, accountants, ministers, schoolteachers, journalists, psychiatrists, advertising executives, real estate agents, housewives, farmers, police officers, military personnel—in short, we found as wide a range of occupations among mediums as we would find among lefthanded people or folks with red hair. Few mediums are full-time professionals.

As far as social adjustment is concerned, psychologists and psychical researchers have found that those people who score highest in ESP tests are well-adjusted socially and possessed of extroverted, rather than an introverted, personalities. Consistently, the more mediums we encountered, the more we met the enthusiastic extrovert rather than the moody, withdrawn, misanthropic introvert.

There is no conclusive evidence to indicate that high or low intelligence contributes to either ESP or mediumistic, shamanistic sensitivity. Once again, we tend to find generally average to high-average intelligence among spirit mediums, certainly not at all the low IQ dullards that some skeptical investigators would like to consider as being representative of someone who claims to talk to Heaven.

Seven Hundred Fifty Hours of Taped Spirit Communication through Rev. Homer Watkins

In the 1970s, we made the acquaintances of Emil and Edythe Gerdes, who had been seriously researching the mystery of life after death for more than forty years. Professing themselves to be "Christian survivalists," rather than Spiritualists, for eleven years the Gerdeses journeyed from their home in a suburb of Minneapolis to Detroit to sit in private séances with Rev. Homer Watkins until his death in 1972 at the age of seventy-eight. Each of those sessions was taped and subsequently transcribed and filed for easy access to specific information, thus amassing evidence that life is continuous and proceeds far beyond physical death.

There was little in the Gerdes home to indicate an interest in the spirit world until they opened their filing cabinets. There, in neat arrangement, were hundreds of tapes, professionally boxed and labeled, comprising a total of 750 hours of spirit communication through the mediumship of Rev. Watkins. Other filing cabinets contained the notes and transcriptions of other sessions with other mediums, dating back over forty years.

The Gerdeses began their research into the spiritual field as scoffers. A hard-nosed, direct, and tough-minded businessman, Emil was taken aback one day when one of his customers told him that his recently deceased daughter had returned in spirit to speak of her transition to the heavenly realms. Intrigued by such a revelation of the afterlife, Emil and Edythe arranged to attend a séance in St. Paul.

Although they witnessed some interesting and inspirational interactions between the medium and various sitters, Emil initially was too distracted by his search for hidden microphones and wires to be greatly impressed. And, since both of them came from strict German Baptist families, they were concerned that they might be trespassing into Satan's lair. In later sessions, however, when the manifestations continued to seem genuine, they became more interested in the information being received than the phenomena that produced it.

Then, too, they were impressed by their fellow sitters: a prominent educator, a highly respected doctor and wife, a dentist, a geologist, and a number of successful businessmen and women. If their minds could accept such communication with the deceased, then perhaps the Gerdeses ought to look a bit further into spiritual phenomena.

"Those early séances were meaningful to Edythe and me," Emil said. "Almost everything that came through was spiritual in nature. Because of our family backgrounds we were receptive to information that told of the beginnings of spiritual life. We both were uplifted by this information. This also gave us encouragement to continue our research."

Homer Watkins was a very unusual individual. He was well known as an actor with a tremendous singing voice. Even at the age of seventy-six, he was still very active on stage and was invited to give a concert in Amsterdam. Watkins was on a first-name basis with the Fords and the Hudsons, and many prominent people from the Detroit area came to him for psychic counseling.

"He was an ordained minister in the Spiritualist Church," Emil said, "But because of his money and position, he had no motivation to exploit his mediumship. This was another reason for us to be encouraged to continue our quest through his spiritual agency. And the sole purpose of our quest was to compile a full and complete documentation of the continuity of life."

Rev. Watkins would enter a deep trance state when spiritual information came through his mediumship. Afterward, according to Emil and Edythe, he was never able to recall one word that he said.

"After our first beginnings, we would receive direction from the spirits coming through in séance that would tell us how to proceed and develop our own spiritual consciousness," Emil said. "After learning these techniques, we could literally tune in to our own spiritual consciousness whenever we wanted to.

"We got a great deal of general information from political leaders like John F. Kennedy and Dwight D. Eisenhower," he continued. "In one of our recordings, Eisenhower says, 'This is the first time I have ever done this.' This was true also of Robert Kennedy. We received messages from business leaders, professors, personal friends, and family members.

"We heard from one of my friends, a research engineer for a major chemical company, who was killed in an airplane accident over Baltimore. He related some things we had done together that no one else knew about."

The Gerdeses soon discovered that Rev. Watkins transmitted information through the speaking voices of many spirit guides, the "Keepers of the Keys."

"Messages that came through Homer Watkins's mediumship were given by a number of spirit entities or guides who were tuned in to his wavelength and were attracted to him in some way," Emil explained. "His number one guide was a Dr. Richard Long. Dr. Long was very well known in medical circles because of his outstanding work during World War I. We learned that he was still operating in Detroit hospitals at the age of one hundred before he died.

"Rev. Watkins's second guide, Nelson Saunders, had been a railroad man whose mother had been an outstanding medium. His third guide was a Dr. White."

The research of Edythe and Emil Gerdes led them to theorize that the quality of the medium has a great deal to do with attracting the particular spirit entities that can bring forth the information that one needs.

"Homer Watkins's forces seemed to have had a faculty for attracting the best of the business leaders and the greatest of politicians," Emil said, "simply because, to some extent, he was that type of person and attracted that type of individual. However, if a particular guide could not answer our questions, he would say, 'I will get the answer for you.' Then he would go to the correct intelligence in the Heaven's World—the area in which the entity exists in spirit form until it reaches God's Kingdom—and come back with the answer."

The Gerdeses were informed of a certain hierarchy of spiritual realms. "We were told that we enter the spirit area when we first leave this physical world. We can remain there as long as we want. This is the condition that I call the 'Heaven's World.' Then if we want to go on to God's Kingdom, it is our own decision. But once we go there, we never return. No one has gone on to see God and returned to tell about it."

Edythe and Emil stated firmly that their interest in spiritual phenomena had added to their religious life, and they found many of the more orthodox church leaders to be very broadminded about mediumship. Because of their research, however, they tend to take exception to the present doctrines that the organized churches generally espouse in connection with the afterlife.

"I have a stock phrase," Emil said, "and that is: Death is manufactured by man. We make such a ceremony out of it. I think death is the golden key to eternal living.

"When the spirit leaves the body, there is nothing left but two or three dollars worth of chemicals that would fill a small vial. I think we must realize that we are all created by our Maker.

"The Creator places you within a physical body and says, 'Here, use this body.' You literally become a part of it with the free will to make decisions. All the information and knowledge that you will ever need is stored within you, but to get it you must dig for it. If you do—and properly use meditation—you will find that you are being your own 'real self.' And you will learn that your life will continue after your three-score-and-ten part is over. When you move into the other life, you can enjoy the things that await you."

Emil said that he and Edythe had received enough firsthand evidence to convince them that there is a continuity of life. "We only wish that we could convince larger numbers of people to accept the truths that we have witnessed. One of the greatest fears of living is the fear of death. If that could just be alleviated, people would see that their passing from the physical body should be a joyous occasion. They will pass into a new world and join their family and friends. It is a wonderful experience.

"If I have any comments to make about the dogma of many of our religious organizations it is that they indicate to people that they must repent or they will never see the Kingdom of God. In my opinion, Christ's spirit never left the world. He is still here. How can there be a Second Coming?

"If we could adhere to the full concept of what was originally taught by Christ, we would find life very simple, indeed. We would find death very simple, also."

When asked to attempt to define the essence of the material in the 750 hours of material taped at the séances conducted by Rev. Watkins, Emil said that the general information might be classified as a fundamental way of life that teaches conclusively that we do come from a spirit world and we do go back to it. "The material also tells us that we can secure all our power from the God within through meditation.

There is no judge and jury awaiting us—just a personal appraisal of what we have gone through in our lives."

Although they received a wealth of material through the agency of spirit mediums, the Gerdeses don't necessarily recommend that all people seek out mediums in order to obtain direction in their lives.

"It all depends, of course, on what people are seeking," Emil said. "Edythe and I were looking for a certain continuity, and we stayed with our research with mediumship for all these years. It was our destiny. It worked for us. But most people can get what they need if they seriously apply themselves to the practice of meditation for fifteen or twenty minutes every day."

Have Spirit Mediums Discovered the Doorway between Dimensions?

There is one aspect of mediumistic phenomena that both the psychical researchers and spirit mediums acknowledge: that there is an intelligence directing and controlling these manifestations.

Another point of agreement is that this intelligence seems to be a human intelligence, characterized by the limitations, imperfections, and psychological drives of *Homo sapiens.*

The area of dispute that remains after decades of debate is whether that intelligence issues from the living or from those who have crossed over to the other side.

Modern humanity seeks the answers to the mysteries of life and death as earnestly as did our ancestors.

The will to believe in the afterlife is as strong today as it has ever been.

One facet of spirit communication that has always struck us as intriguing throughout our nearly fifty years of research is that such communion still requires both a soul and a physical body—the soul of the discarnate entity and the physical body of the medium. If it is the temporary union of discarnate entity and human body that is necessary to produce spirit contact, then any sensitive and aware human should be able to accomplish spirit communication—especially when the undying energy of a deceased loved one wishes to make contact with those who have remained behind on the earthplane.

In the next chapter, we shall further explore the phenomenon of the spirit teachers that guide mediums in their avowed mission to communicate with those on the other side, and we shall also meet ordinary men and women whose spirit guides enabled them to establish communion with their loved ones in Heaven.

CHAPTER SIX

Guardian Angels and Spirit Guides: Heaven's Personal Messengers

Numerous parapsychologists have suggested that the spirit guide or guardian angel may be another as yet little known power of the mind, enabling one's subjective level of consciousness to dramatize another personality, complete with a full range of personal characteristics and its very own "voice." Such a theory sounds too much like schizophrenia to those men and women who are convinced beyond reasonable doubt that they were guided, directed, and protected by a spiritual being. Perhaps in certain cases there may be some parallels, but the spirit guide or teacher is so much more than any kind of psychological phenomena.

The idea of a spirit guide dates back to the furthest reaches of antiquity. It is unlikely that anthropologists have ever discovered a single aboriginal culture that did not include the concept of a spiritual guide in its theology. The great Socrates provides us with the most notable example in the classical period of a man whose subjective mind was stimulated by the voice of his *daemon,* a guardian spirit who kept constant vigil and warned the philosopher of any approaching danger.

And while many materialists may argue that such concepts as guiding spirits should remain cloistered in the ruins of ancient Greece, contemporary opinion polls consistently find that around 78 percent of Americans believe that a benevolent being watches out for them. Even among today's Internet-savvy, television-jaded, pseudo-sophisticated teenagers, a 1993 Gallup Poll found that 76 percent believe in angels—a percentage that has been steadily increasing since 1978 when only 64 percent admitted to their belief in angelic beings.

From an analysis of our questionnaire of mystical experiences, we have discovered thousands of men and women who have encountered spirit guides and spirits of the deceased since their earliest childhood. An even higher percentage of our respondents have commonly met their guardian angels and their spirit teachers during both deliberate and spontaneous out-of-body experiences. Some of those individuals who have completed our questionnaire maintain that such interactions with spirit guides and spirits of the deceased have served as an effective method of spiritual instruction.

Attending Night School with Spirit Guides

K. S.: "I used to project my soul consciousness often when I was a girl. At first, two spirit guides would come to me and lift me from my physical body, but soon I was able to slip out of the body without their assistance.

"As soon as I was out of the body, I would receive instruction from spirit teachers. I suppose you could say it was like going to night school. During the day, I went to junior high. At night, my soul body was taken up to a higher plane to attend a spirit school.

"I am often asked if such double schooling wasn't tiring. On the contrary, I used to awaken in the morning feeling completely refreshed.

"Now that I am in my thirties, I have developed my level of awareness so that I am aware of my guides' presence without leaving the physical body."

Regular Visits to Heaven Have Prepared Him for the Final Trip

G. B.: "I have been aware of my spirit guides and my ability to leave the physical body and travel to Heaven since I had a terrible bout of illness when I was only twelve.

"I regularly travel to the higher planes to meet with the spirits of friends who have passed on. I have been doing this for so long that it seems completely natural to me. When the time comes for me to make the final, ultimate projection to Heaven, I will already know my way around. I won't have to go through the period of adjustment that so many individuals have to go through when they leave their physical bodies behind in death."

A Spirit Guide's Appearance Transformed Her Life

T.K.H.: "I was going through a lot of emotional trauma; raising four sons alone, becoming financially desperate, beginning a new relationship that seemed uncertain. I was at the point where I was beginning to think that if there really was a God, He sure had a grudge against me for some reason.

"Then one spring night in 1991, just as I was drifting off to sleep, something made me open my eyes—and there he was! I can still see him standing there in his drab robe, the hood closely draped around his darkly shadowed face, a rope loosely knotted around his waist. He was about five feet eight, of slim to average build; and in the moonlight, his hand seemed olive complexioned.

"After an initial feeling of fear, I immediately became calm. He said nothing, but merely brought his hand very slowly close to mine so that the backs of our hands nearly touched. I think that our auras must have mingled somehow and that was the means of communication.

"I have a hard time finding words to describe all of this, but at that moment I was filled with a feeling of total and complete unconditional love. If there had been a gauge to measure my heart and spirit, I would have been at maximum capacity. The forgiveness and the absolute divine lovingness that he was conveying brought tears to my eyes, and I had the feeling that this was but one molecule of one grain of sand in an entire universe of love. I felt that if he were to turn up his love energy to full power, there could be no way in which my mind would ever be able to handle it. Then I fell asleep.

"This visitation brought me back to my senses spiritually, and it seemed to have been a turning point in my life. I was given the courage and emotional strength to face all my problems. In essence, I think I was being told to let go, and let God. I wish I could have seen my guide's face!"

Helping Two Troubled Spirits Make the Adjustment to Death

D. D.: "I have had mediumistic gifts since I was a young girl, and not long ago, I had to aid the recently deceased to make the adjustment to the afterlife.

"Two young men had just been killed in a terrible accident near my home. A couple of nights after the accident, I could sense their presence around me. This did not surprise or frighten me, for I suspected that they had been drawn by my psychic awareness and my proximity to the scene of their deaths.

"I went into a light trance state and saw that Cornelius, my angel guide, stood by my side to be of assistance. As soon as Cornelius had manifested solidly, I could clearly see the spirits of the two young men. They were moving about wildly in a state of panic. I was puzzled by the fact that their own spirit guides had not yet arrived to be with them.

"I tried to calm them and explained what had happened to them. I told them that they must accept what had taken place. But their thoughts were filled with earthly desires and frustrations. They were still very much of the earthplane, and I understood that was why I could not see their spirit guides manifesting near them. I understood also that the frightened spirits of these two young men had been directed to me by their spirit guides, who, in their wisdom, had known that these earthbound entities would not yet accept guidance from spirits.

"For the longest time I talked to them but they would not listen. They seemed unable to perceive Cornelius by my side, which was probably just as well at that point, and they made it very clear that they did not want to leave the earthplane. Their girlfriends would be waiting for them. They had big plans for their futures, and they felt cheated to have their lives cut so short. They were truly what is referred to as 'earthbound spirits.' They did not feel the peace that comes to most spirits when they are to leave the earthplane.

"At last, after what had been at least four to five hours, I must have calmed them enough for their spirit guides to be able to elevate them to another plane, for suddenly the two entities before me began to be pulled straight up. Such action on the part of their guides startled the spirits of the two young men, and they emitted horrible screams of fear. There would still be much work for their spirit guides to accomplish, but at least I had aided them in their transference. Cornelius patted my shoulder and told me that I had conducted myself well and done a great service to the spirits of the two young men.

"When I emerged from trance, I became aware that my front room was filled with neighbors. I lay on my couch, and one of my closest friends was bending over me and rubbing my wrists. My neighbors had heard the awful screams of the young men and had come to see if anything was wrong.

"I was amazed that they had been able to hear the screams of the spirit entities. I told my friends that I had just dozed off, and I tried to blame the screams on the television set, which had been left on in my front room. I don't know how many of my neighbors accepted this explanation, but they could certainly see that I was all alone in my little house."

Subjecting a Spirit Guide to Rigorous Testing Procedures

Eileen Garrett was a gifted medium who, throughout her long career, never ceased to study the phenomena of her mediumship in a manner that was remarkably detached. As a child she was ill a great deal, and at a very early age she began to experience visions and to see "people" who were not there.

She did not realize that she was developing as a trance medium until she was a good deal older and accidentally fell asleep one night while at a public meeting. When she awakened, she learned that the voices of deceased relatives of many of the people gathered there that night had spoken through her. One gentleman present explained to Eileen what had happened to her and informed her that he had communicated with an Oriental spirit named Uvani, who would thereafter be her spirit guide and work with her to prove the validity of the survival of the spirit after physical death.

Eileen Garrett was so horrified at the prospect of an Oriental spirit sharing her mind and body that for weeks she slept with the light burning in her room to ward off the advances of Uvani. Later, someone at a London spiritualist society did his best to explain away her misgivings about sharing her psyche with a spirit guide. He assured her that Uvani would not be at all interested in her daily and private life and that the spirit guide's entire purpose would be based on a sincere wish to be of service to humanity.

During the years in which she perfected her communication skills with Uvani, Eileen Garrett often expressed doubts about her spirit guide's psychic independence, and she frequently voiced her suspicions that he might only be a segment of her own subconscious mind. The respected psychical researcher Hereward Carrington administered an extensive battery of personality tests to both the medium and her spirit guide so that researchers might compare the two sets of responses. Eileen Garrett and Uvani sat through sessions of the Bernreuter Personality Inventory, the Thurstone Attitude Scale, the Woodworth Neurotic Inventory, the Rorschach test, and a seemingly endless number of word association tests.

Carrington concluded that in such cases of genuine mediumship as that expressed by Eileen Garrett, the spirit guide succeeded in bringing through a vast mass of supernormal information that could not be obtained through normal sensory means. The spirit guide, he theorized, appeared to act as some sort of "psychic catalyzer."

The psychical researcher went on to suggest that the function of a spirit guide seems to be that of an intermediary, and whether the entity is truly a spirit or a personification of the medium's subconscious, it is only through the cooperation of the guide that veridical messages are obtained. The essential and significant difference between the ordinary secondary personality as observed in pathological cases and the personality of the spirit guide in mediumistic expression is that the spirit entity brings forth supernormal information.

> In the pathological cases, we seem to have a *mere* splitting of the mind, while in the mediumistic cases we have to deal with a . . . personality which is . . . in touch or contact, in some mysterious way, with another [spiritual] world, from which it derives information and through which genuine messages often come.

During the course of extensive testing, Uvani emphasized the fact that although he controlled Eileen Garrett's underconsciousness, he had absolutely no control over her conscious mind—nor would he consider such control to be right. The spirit guide also clarified that he had no interest in the medium's normal thinking processes or in the activities of her conscious mind. The trance state was the only time when Uvani and other spirit entities could utilize Eileen Garrett's underconsciousness as a vehicle for their communication with humans.

When Carrington asked how Uvani would know when Eileen was ready for him to manifest, the spirit guide replied that he would receive a "telegraphed impression" that the mediumistic instrument was ready. "The moment that the conscious mind becomes very low, then the soul body becomes more vibrant," Uvani explained.

During the course of the experiments, Carrington also asked a question that we are certain has occurred to every psychic investigator who has ever sat with a medium. Why is it that spirit entities who claim foreign origins, such as Uvani purporting to be of Oriental derivation, are able to speak such good English through their mediums?

Uvani immediately replied that he did not speak English: "It is my instrument [Eileen Garrett] who speaks. I impress my thought upon her, on that 'figment' on which I must work upon, but no word of mine actually comes to you. The instrument is impressed by my personal contact." Thoughts, Uvani goes on to elaborate, are impressed and expressed automatically.

He Traveled to Heaven to Bid His Sister Farewell

Dr. T. is convinced that he has traveled to another plane of existence in the company of his spiritual guide and met with the spirits of his departed loved ones. It is his contention that the deceased of this earthly plane continue to exist in Heaven in much the same manner as they did in life.

"I first had the experience of visiting the heavenly realms when my dear sister passed away," he said in his report. "I had been practicing meditation for years, and more than once I had achieved astral projection, out-of-body experience. Because I missed my sister so much, it seemed logical to me that I might travel in my soul body to visit her in Heaven."

Dr. T. prayed, surrounded himself with light, and asked for angelic guidance. "Within a short time, my guide appeared. It was the strangest thing. It was as if I had always been aware of his existence on one level of my consciousness. He appeared to me in the robes of a priest, which would be consistent with my religious orientation. His countenance was magnificent. When he reached out and took my hand, I felt as though electricity was flowing through my spirit body."

In the next moment, Dr. T. and his spirit guide were standing in a lovely courtyard. "There were grape arbors, olive trees, and a host of other splendid trees, vines, and flowers. I knew this had to be my sister Virginia's idea of Heaven."

Dr. T.'s guide nodded approval at his deduction, and within a few moments, Virginia entered the courtyard. "She seemed surprised to see me, but she came immediately to embrace me. I was delighted to see that her arrival in Paradise had eliminated all traces of the ravages of her disease. " 'We had no time to say a proper good-bye, darling,' I told her. She agreed that this was so."

Dr. T. said that he was able to spend a few hours with his sister in Heaven before his guide indicated that it was time to return to his physical body on Earth.

"Since that time, I have traveled time and again to Heaven and talked with departed loved ones," he said. "I have also met the spirits of many individuals whom I did not know in life. In many instances, I have recorded their names and former addresses immediately upon returning to my body. In each case, my subsequent investigations have determined the reality of their lives on Earth, and whenever possible, I have contacted their living loved ones with their messages from Heaven."

An Angel Brought His Brother's Spirit to Receive a Solemn Vow

L. W., a lawyer, insisted to us that he had never had any spiritualist tendencies and that before his experience he had never really thought much about an afterlife. However, late one night while he was doing research for a particularly difficult case, he happened to glance up and see what at first appeared to be a shimmering light in the corner of his office. As he directed his attention to the strange light, he was astonished to see it take the form of his deceased younger brother, who had died three months before in a hunting accident.

"I know that I was wide awake," he said, "but suddenly it felt as if I were being pulled out of my body . . . as if my very soul were somehow being drawn out through the top of my skull. My brother reached out his hand to me, and suddenly I was at his side, clasping the hand that I had so often held in life. I looked back toward the desk and saw my physical body sitting slumped over my desk and staring at some papers. My eyes were open, but I seemed to be in some kind of trance."

L. W. said that he became very frightened. He had no idea how such things could be. Had the ghost of his kid brother come to claim his soul and take him with him into the grave?

"And then this big guy in a brilliant white suit was standing there with Arnie and me. There was no question in my mind that he was an angel. His eyes seemed to penetrate my very soul. You know, this is weird, but I can't remember if his mouth opened and closed when he spoke, but I surely heard his words inside my very essence. 'You must come with us for a little while,' the angel said to me."

L. W. felt his entire universe begin to spin and everything went black. "But it was only dark for a second or two, then the three of us were standing on the side of a mountain. It seemed like we were somewhere in Colorado, but I'm sure we were in some place even higher than the Rockies. Arnie was still holding on to my hand, and he squeezed it hard when he spoke to me. 'You got to promise me to look after Arnie, Jr.,' he told me. 'You got to spend a lot of time with him. He's only seven. He can't handle my dying and all.' "

L. W. told his brother that he was surprised that he would have to ask such a thing. "Arnie, you know I will take care of the kid like he was my own."

Arnie told him that was why he had brought an angel with him to record his brother's vow. "You're so busy building your law career you don't spend enough time with your own wife and kids. You certainly wouldn't find time for Arnie, Jr. You know that your wife is thinking about leaving you, man. You didn't even take the afternoon off when your baby girl was born last month. You probably don't even know the birthdays of your two other kids, 'cause you weren't at the hospital when they were born, either."

L. W. looked from the pleading eyes of his brother to the stern, unyielding eyes of the big angel. "Make your vow," the angelic being said in the voice that vibrated within L. W.'s soul. "Make your vow so your brother may enter Heaven in peace."

L. W. felt tears come to his eyes. "I promise, Arnie. I swear by all that's holy that I'll be like a father to your son. And I promise I'll be a better father to my own kids and a better husband to my wife."

Arnie kissed him on the cheek and gave him a bear hug. And for the first time since he joined them, the big angel smiled.

"There was a moment or two of that spinning sensation, and when I regained consciousness, I was resting my head on my arms folded across the top of the desk," L. W. said. "The whole episode couldn't have taken more than a minute or so, but it felt as though I had been somewhere else for a long time. I was very troubled after the experience. I left my office right away to head home to my wife and kids. I made another promise to Arnie and the big angel that I would keep my vow.

"That was ten years ago, and I've been making good on my promises. My wife and I are really close and deeply in love. I make the time to spend with my kids no matter what, and we include Arnie, Jr., and his mom in every family thing we do. The whole experience with Arnie and the angel is as vivid to me as if it had happened yesterday."

"I Am Your Control, Your Teacher, Your Friend"

It was on June 13, 1961, that Irene Hughes's spirit teacher first appeared to her. She was recovering from surgery, and when the turbaned Oriental materialized in her bedroom, she did not know at first if she were suffering from hallucinations or if she had died in surgery without realizing her passing.

The spirit entity permitted Irene to test it, and promised to make three desires come to pass. When the being, who called himself "Kaygee," had seen to the fulfillment of these wishes, he led Irene back through a dramatic recall of a prior existence in Egypt, and he predicted in what manner she would soon meet the other principals from her Egyptian life experience.

"I am your control, your teacher, and your friend," Kaygee told her. "You will learn many things unknown to others. You now have the key to all of life. Use it well, and it will grow. I will always be there to help you."

As their spiritual relationship progressed, Irene could see that the entity that she had at first assumed to be a turbaned Indian was quite obviously a Japanese gentleman.

Once he held out a hand of friendship, and when Irene accepted it, she was startled to find it solid, warm, filled with life—although the air surrounding Kaygee was chilled.

Kaygee explained that it had been necessary for him to leave the earthplane before Irene could fully achieve total development. "I had to go before you could come," he said.

On another occasion, Kaygee told her that he would teach her that love is truly the whole law of life, that "love is the mightiest power in the universe. You will learn this and teach this and lecture to people about this eternal truth. You will be given the power to see beyond the thin veil of the earthplane."

Irene Hughes wanted to know who Kaygee had been on the earthplane. In response, the spirit teacher provided the name of his daughter, who at that time was in the United States studying at Cornell University. "Write to her," he bade Irene. "She shall verify who I was on the earthplane."

Irene wrote down the name and address of the woman whom Kaygee claimed was his daughter. She decided that she had nothing to lose by writing such a letter of inquiry—although she felt that the envelope was likely to be returned marked "addressee unknown."

In five days, Irene received a reply from the woman, verifying that she was indeed Kaygee's daughter. She went on to declare that her father had been one of the greatest Japanese Christians who had ever lived and that he had died in April of that year, 1961.

"The fact that the name and the address were correct seemed to me to be most evidential of Kaygee's survival after death," Irene said. "I had to accept the fact that his spirit was coming to work through me. He had lived a life of poverty, and he had given his life to help others. Perhaps he felt that I was so physically, emotionally, and psychically constructed that he could work through me. I considered myself honored that he had chosen me as a channel by which he might continue certain facets of his work."

Shortly after the initial appearance of Kaygee, Irene Hughes had confided in two highly respectable members of the prestigious Spiritual Frontiers Fellowship and had relayed her experiences with the spirit entity. She later allowed them to read both the letter that she had written to Kaygee's daughter and the letter that she had received in reply from the young woman, confirming the evidence of survival which the spirit being had channeled through her mediumship.

Irene recalled the time when Kaygee spoke to her of his life and how he had fought for the living truth in the slums and along the highways. He had met with continued opposition in life, but now he was at peace.

"I know my work will go on through you and

others like you," Kaygee said. "You, Irene, are a prophet, so filled with the knowledge of love and life that you are my vibratory equal. I have chosen you to work through, as you will see."

Meeting Your Guardian or Guide through Creative Visualization

One must always exercise caution in exploring the spiritual realms, especially when offering invitations to entities who inhabit the worlds unseen that exist in other dimensions all around us. We always admonish our students that they must be spiritually disciplined and practice discernment on every step of their lifepath.

True achievement of higher states of consciousness and meaningful contact with the spirit guardian or guide is accomplished through many hours of serious and disciplined application to the study of certain principles of spiritual growth that have been repeatedly tested by masters and teachers since ancient times. There are few instances of instant success in the area of spiritual attunement. There are seldom any instances of "beginner's luck." Spiritual exercises may have to be practiced over and over again before any facet of enlightenment may be achieved.

Rather than consider the following exercise as presenting you with any kind of guarantee of achieving communion or oneness with your spiritual guide or guardian angel, it might be better to regard it simply as a creative visualization that will place you in a particular frame of mind that may allow an aspect of higher consciousness or self-revelation to manifest in your psyche. While we firmly believe that encounters with the guide or guardian are available for every sincere seeker of love, wisdom, and knowledge, we also believe that such experiences should never be forced.

First we will provide a relaxation technique that we have employed over many years at innumerable workshops and seminars. It will place you in a tranquil state of mind that will enable you to imagine a linkup with your spirit guide or guardian angel or with a more aware aspect of yourself. It may also provide a kind of spiritual blueprint whereby you may one day actually achieve a pure state of communion with your angels or guides and those deceased loved ones who have entered the higher plane known as Heaven.

It is possible for you to read this relaxation technique, pausing every now and then to permit its effectiveness to permeate your consciousness. Later, during the creative visualization itself, it is possible for you to read the technique of spirit contact, pausing now and then to contemplate the significance of your inner journey and to receive elevation to a higher state of consciousness. But perhaps a better method would be to read the techniques to another person or to have someone read the instructions to you. When reading the relaxation process, be certain to proceed in as soft and soothing a voice as you can. Read slowly, calmly, unhurried.

Many of our students have informed us that it is extremely effective to record one's own voice reading the relaxation technique and the spiritual exercise onto a cassette, thereby allowing your voice to guide you through the techniques.

Any of these methods may be effective. As with so many endeavors in life, your success will depend upon your willingness to permit such an experience to manifest within your psyche. We would also recommend the use of some musical background as a means of achieving excellent results. Just be careful that the music contains no lyrics to distract from the process. Instrumental symphonic scores and the category of music known as New Age, which utilizes electronic instruments and synthesizers, have been found to be especially effective.

The Relaxation Technique:

Imagine that you are lying on a blanket on a beautiful stretch of beach. You are alone. There is no one else near to distract or disturb you. You are lying in the warm sun or in the shade, whichever you prefer.

You are listening to the sounds of Mother Ocean, the rhythmic sound of the waves as they lap against the shore. You are listening to the same restful lullaby that Mother Ocean has been singing to men and to women for thousands and thousands of years.

As you relax, you know that nothing will disturb you, nothing will distress you, nothing will molest or bother you in any way. Even now, you are becoming aware of a golden light of love, wisdom, and knowledge that is moving over you, protecting you. You know this is the love of God that is being focused on you by your spirit guardian and guide.

You know that you have nothing to fear. Nothing can harm you. As you listen to the sound of the ocean waves, you feel all tension beginning to leave your body. The sound of the waves helps you to become more and more relaxed . . . more and more relaxed.

With every breath you take, you find yourself feeling better, more relaxed, more at peace. You know that you must permit your body to relax so that you may rise to higher states of consciousness.

Your body must relax so that the Real You, your Soul Body, may rise higher and higher to greater states of awareness.

You are feeling a beautiful energy of tranquility, peace, and love enter your *feet* . . . and you feel every muscle in your feet relaxing. That beautiful energy of tranquility, peace, and love moves up your *legs,* into your *ankles,* your *calves,* your *knees,* your *thighs*—and you feel every muscle in your feet, your ankles, your calves, your knees, your thighs, relaxing, relaxing, relaxing.

If you should hear any sound at all other than the sound of my voice that sound shall not disturb you in any way. A slamming door, a honking horn, a shouting voice—*that sound will help you to relax even more.*

And now that beautiful energy of tranquility, peace, and love is moving up your body to your *hips . . . stomach . . . back.* And you feel every muscle in your hips, your stomach, your back, relaxing, relaxing, relaxing.

With every breath you take, you find that your body is becoming more and more relaxed.

Now the beautiful energy of tranquility, peace, and love enters your *chest . . . shoulders . . . arms . . . even your fingers.* And you feel every muscle in your chest, your shoulders, your arms, and your fingers, relaxing, relaxing, relaxing.

And with every breath you take, you find that you are becoming more and more relaxed. Every part of your body is becoming completely free of tension.

Now that beautiful energy of tranquility, peace, and love moves into your *neck . . . face . . . the very top of your head.* And you feel every muscle in your neck, your face, and the very top of your head, relaxing, relaxing, relaxing.

Your body is now relaxed . . . completely relaxed and at peace. *But your mind, your spirit, your True Self, is very aware.*

The Spiritual Exercise: Meeting Your Spiritual Guide/Angel Guardian

And now a beautiful golden globe of light is moving toward you. You are not afraid, for you realize, you *know,* that within the golden globe of light is your angel guide, your guardian spirit, who has loved you since before you became you.

Feel the love as this presence comes closer. Feel the vibrations of love moving over you.

You know that within this golden globe of light is someone who has always loved you just as you are.

You know that you have been aware of this loving, guiding presence ever since you were a child, a very small child.

You have been aware that this beautiful being has always loved you just as you are . . . no masks, no pretenses, no facades. This spirit guardian has looked out for you, protected you, and loved you unconditionally with heavenly love, love that accepts the real you just as you are.

And now you feel that love moving all around you. And look! *Two eyes* are beginning to form in the midst of the golden light. The eyes of your angelic guide. Feel the love flowing to you from your guardian spirit.

Now a *face* is forming. Look at the loving smile on the lips of your spiritual guardian. Feel the love that flows from your angel guide to you.

Now a *body* is forming. Behold the beauty of form, structure, and stature of your spirit protector. Feel the love that flows to you from the very presence of your angel guide.

Your spirit guardian is now stretching forth a loving hand. Take that hand in yours. Feel the love flowing through you. Feel the love as you and your spirit guide blend and flow together.

Now, hand in hand, you feel yourself being lifted higher and higher. Your angel guide is taking you to that other dimension for which you have always longed.

You are moving into a higher vibration.

You are moving toward a place of higher awareness, of higher consciousness.

Now you have arrived in that place for which you have always yearned, your true home beyond the stars. Look around you. The trees, grass, sky, *everything* is more alive here. The colors are more vivid.

You, too, have been transformed. Even though you know that you must soon return to the earthplane, you temporarily have been granted a new nervous system, new eyes, new senses, to perceive once again those things that you have always remembered, those things that you have always known.

You are clothed in a robe of your favorite color. Sandals are on your feet.

And look ahead—the beautiful crystal city. See

sunbeams reflecting from every tower, every spire, every turret.

You know where you are. You've come home. You've come home to Heaven.

Look at the people coming to greet you. Look at their eyes. Feel the love. You recognize so many of them. Some are dear ones from the earth plane who have already come home.

They reach out to touch you, to embrace you, to kiss you. And you feel the love flowing all around you.

As you follow your angel guide through the streets of the crystal city, you feel love all around you. Love as you have never felt it on Earth. Love as you could never feel it on Earth. Love as you have yearned for all of your life. And you feel it now, all around you.

As you walk through these beautiful streets, you know where you are going. You know that your spiritual guide is leading you to the beautiful garden temple of love, wisdom, and knowledge. You remember the lovely garden where you spent so many hours in your spirit body learning great lessons from your angel teacher.

There is the garden ahead. See the trees heavy with fruit. See the incredible array of colorful flowers. Smell the sweet air.

There is the beautiful silver stream that runs at the foot of the nine golden steps that lead to the great door of the temple of love, wisdom, and knowledge. Now, taking your angel guide's hand, you begin to walk up the nine golden steps. Feel the steps beneath your sandals. Feel your spiritual guardian's hand in yours.

The great door opens, and you step inside. Look

at the tapestry that covers the wall to your left. This tapestry reminds you that you are but a single, though important, thread that runs throughout the great fabric of life.

Look at the altar! There must be thousands of little candles burning and glowing before the beautiful golden altar.

And now you clearly hear the voice of your angel guide, your spirit guardian, speak to you: "You may always call upon my name when you feel that you need guidance or protection. My name is [*pause for ten seconds to allow the name to come through*]."

And you clearly hear the name of your angel guide, your spirit guardian.

And you know that you may return to the crystal city, your true home, the golden temple, on those occasions when you need to feel its strength, its power, its unconditional love. You may return to receive the beautiful reinforcement of this love vibration as often as you desire it or require it.

And you will remember the name of your angel guide, your spirit guardian, forever.

And now with all these wonderful memories of your true home in Heaven and the unconditional love of your spirit guardian firmly in your mind and spirit, you feel yourself beginning to return to full consciousness on the earthplane. At the count of five, you will be fully awake, fully conscious, and feeling better than you have felt in weeks and weeks, months and months. *One,* coming awake. *Two,* more and more awake. *Three,* opening your eyes, taking a deep breath. *Four,* stretching out your arms. *Five,* wide awake—and feeling wonderful and full of love for all living things.

CHAPTER SEVEN

Station H-E-A-V-E-N Calling Earth: The Enigma of Electronic Voice Communication

What would it mean to you to know absolutely and without a doubt that you can survive physical death? Would you change and reorganize your life on the basis of this information?

Beyond the personal considerations, what effect would verified truth of our immortality have on our earthly societies, institutions, and governments? Would the scientific establishment accept the reality of an existant dimension that has lain previously uncharted by science and that has for centuries been ridiculed as the product of wishful thinking and desperate fantasies?

One of the main reasons why neither science nor society at large has seriously considered the immortality question is the lack of tangible physical evidence proving that there is anything other than a void waiting for us when we die. Skeptical scientists will remain untouched by the most moving and inspirational anecdotes of personal experience, and even the most open-minded of contemporary scientists are reluctant to get involved in the abstract and esoteric elements of faith and religion for fear of tarnishing their shields of objectivity.

All this may soon be changing thanks to the breakthroughs into the hidden reaches of immortality that have been made by modern technological instrumentation—most frequently by audio tape recorders. For quite a few years now, a number of serious-minded scientists have been recording spirit voices on tape and even communicating with these remarkable vocal manifestations. Perhaps for the first time in history, even the most materialistic of scientists will have something tangible with which to work to prove the reality of life after death.

Thomas Edison's "Dead Man's Gramophone"

The concept of contacting the dead through electronic means actually goes back to Thomas Alva Edison, the Genius of Menlo Park, who believed that the soul of a human being is composed of "swarms of billions of highly charged entities which live in the cells." Edison further maintained that when a person dies, "this swarm deserts the body and goes into space, but keeps on and enters another cycle of life and is immortal."

In the October 1920 issue of *Scientific American*, Edison revealed that he was in fact working on a device that would facilitate communication with the deceased. It was his intention to fashion an electronic instrument so sensitive that it would be able to detect even the slightest movements of discarnate entities. His fellow pioneers in electronic achievements, Charles Proteus Steinmetz and Nikola Tesla, agreed that it should be theoretically possible to communicate with other dimensions.

Notes in Thomas Edison's personal diary reveal such observations as the following:

> I believe [our bodies] are composed of myriads and myriads of infinitesimally small individuals, each in itself a unit of life, and that these units work in squads—or swarms as I prefer to call them—and that these infinitesimally small units live forever. When we "die" these swarms of units, like swarms of bees, so to speak, betake themselves *elsewhere*, and go on functioning in some other form of environment.
>
> I cannot believe . . . that life in the first instance originated on this insignificant little ball which we call Earth. The particles which combined to evolve living creatures on this planet of ours probably came from some other body elsewhere in the universe.[1]

Everyone knows that Edison's legacy to his fellow humans includes the electric light, the gramophone, motion pictures, and scores of other inventions that have made life easier, more productive, and more enjoyable in the twentieth century. But few people know that among the diagrams of unachieved creations lay the plans for a machine that would enable its user to speak to the dead.

And those who knew Edison best stated that he was reluctant to take any credit for his remarkable achievements. In his opinion, he was simply a vehicle or a channel for information from a higher source.

"I proclaim," Edison said, "that it is possible to construct an apparatus that will be so delicate that if there are personalities in another existence or sphere who wish to get in touch with us, this apparatus will give them the opportunity. Why should personalities in another existence spend their time working a triangular piece of wood over a board with lettering on it [referring to the common Ouija Board] when something much better can be devised?"[2]

During a period of six or seven months, Edison is said to have worked full time on his project of building a "dead man's gramophone," and he allowed few people entrance to his laboratory. Nobody knows for certain if his device for speaking with the dead was ever completed or if it was ever successful in its application, but it was the genius of Thomas Edison that lay the groundwork for the research in electronic voice communication that is being conducted today.

Dr. Konstantin Raudive's Breakthrough

In 1971, Taplinger Publishing Company sent us a review copy of *Breakthrough: An Amazing Experiment in Electronic Communication with the Dead* by Dr. Konstantin Raudive, a book that had created a sensation in Europe. The Latvian-born Raudive, a noted psychologist and philosopher, had lived in Sweden and Germany since the close of World War II and had become well known in both literary and scientific communities.

Sometime in the mid-1960s, Dr. Raudive discovered the work of Swedish author Friedrich Jurgenson, who had encountered the phenomenon of spirit voices quite by accident when he was out in the woods attempting to capture bird songs on his tape recorder. Jurgenson knew that the voices had somehow appeared on his recordings without the intervention of any human agency.

Further experiments demonstrated that the spirit voices did not appear at random, but seemed to respond to invitations to manifest themselves. The voices always identified themselves as specific deceased personalities, but all spoke much faster than normal speech.

In her book *A Psychic Explores the Unseen World,* Kay Sterner recounts a visit to Jurgenson in Sweden in 1972. During an experiment, Jurgenson invited his spirit guide and any other entities who wished to communicate to speak to them over the tape in the recorder. An hour and a half later, they replayed the recording. Kay writes that all this may have been a matter of routine to Jurgenson, who listened to a number of voices in Swedish responding to specific questions that he had asked, but she was excited and filled with anticipation.

"Then," she writes, "to my total amazement, we heard a female voice clearly singing a Negro spiritual in English. Mr. Jurgenson called out excitedly, 'It is unmistakably Mahalia Jackson's voice!' "

Kay Sterner continues in her book:

> You might be tempted to conclude that we had merely picked up a bit of radio broadcast. However, this was not the case at all since the voice had considerable psychic significance for me. A year previously, an apparition of a female Negro spiritual singer had appeared to me one night at 2:00 A.M. She conveyed to me that she was Mahalia Jackson and was lovingly assigned to me in order to assist me whenever I called out to her. [During the taping, Sterner had silently asked,] "Would the deceased Negro spiritual singer who psychically appeared to me one night a year ago in my home verify her appearance to me perhaps by singing?"[3]

Dr. Raudive had been investigating postmortem phenomena for twenty-five years before he learned of Jurgenson's experiments, and he vigorously embarked on a research program of his own, employing the strictest of professional standards and establishing firm documentation of his results. It wasn't long before Dr. Raudive was joined in his research by eminent European scientists, physicists, psychologists, and theologians.

And, as the dustjacket of the Taplinger edition declared, "before undertaking the publication of this English-language edition, the publishers have requested other respected scientists and scholars to verify the procedures and findings related in Dr. Raudive's book. The discovery of this phenomenon is a breakthrough of unquestionable importance."

The Astonishing Phenomenon of Recording Spirit Voices

What is meant by the phenomenon of recording spirit voices? Those who make such claims define the phenomenon as the unexplained manifestation of human voice–like sounds on recording tape. These sounds are in fact vocal sounds, and human language is employed, but it must be understood that the voices cannot be heard during the recording period. They can only be heard during the playback.

Once one becomes accustomed to the voices and has learned how to screen out any interference, anyone can understand that is being said. The voices are genuine and have been verified by respected scientists.

Where the voices originate and how they get on the recording tape, however, remain open questions.

When one is initially exposed to the electronic voice phenomenon, the thought which comes first to mind is that they might be random voices somehow picked up from a radio station or some other type of sound transmission. That objection leads to the most mystifying characteristic of the paranormal voices on tape: The operator of the tape recorder may actually enter into an intelligent conversation with the mysterious voices.

The spirit voices may be heard not only responding to specific questions, but in some instances, they volunteer information—and the unseen intelligences appear to be aware of all that is occuring at the site of the recording. In certain cases, the information volunteered by the spirits of the dead has been precognitive.

Quite frankly, it does take some diligence and determination to work with the electronic voice phenomenon. For one thing, it is hard on the ears. The voices are often faint, and the sentences and phrases may often be brief, rapid, and barely audible, even with maximum amplification. And sometimes the background noise and interference may be extremely difficult to penetrate.

When listening to tapes containing successfully recorded paranormal voices, one is immediately aware of their eerie nature. Some voices are mechanical sounding; others are whispered and echoing. Yet there can be no mistake, they are voices speaking in a human language. The voices captured by Dr. Raudive issue forth in German, Russian, English, French, Latvian, and many other languages.

The Research of Professor Walter Uphoff

Shortly after the publication of *Breakthrough* in the United States, we met Professor Walter Uphoff, who had taken as his mission the tracking of electronic voice phenomena in this country. Uphoff had first learned of Dr. Raudive's experiments during one of his frequent trips to Europe, where he had contacts with psychical researchers all over the continent.

Skeptical at first, he was invited to Dr. Raudive's laboratory at Bad Kronzingen, Germany to hear the voices for himself. The initial exposure to the exciting experiments being conducted by the respected scientist motivated Uphoff to explore the electronic voice phenomenon as thoroughly as possible.

At the time of our first meeting with Walter Uphoff and his wife, Mary Jo, he was working independently, and occasionally under the auspices of Harold Sherman and the ESP Research Associates Foundation of Little Rock, Arkansas, to check out the validity of spirit voices recorded on tape by the Lamoreaux family in White Salmon, Washington.

The first thing that we noticed about Uphoff was that he was a realist, a man of science and education. He was also a man accustomed to the tough infighting of labor and management. His book *Kohler on Strike* was cited by Robert F. Kennedy as being an extremely important study in the field of labor relations.

Later, we learned that Uphoff had found Michael Lamoreaux, a former teacher who had been doing graduate work at a college in the Northwest. Like so many others, Lamoreaux had become interested in the paranormal voice phenomenon after reading Dr. Raudive's book. He had tried unsuccessfully for two months to capture spirit voices on tape by following the procedures in *Breakthrough,* then during a visit to his two brothers, success was achieved on their first night of experimentation.

By June of 1973, the Lamoreaux brothers had accumulated hundreds of pages of transcribed paranormal voices that they had captured on tape.

Their technique was simplicity itself. They would turn on the tape recorder and ask whatever spirit might be listening some specific questions. They next allowed the machine to record for fifteen seconds.

After that brief time had elapsed, they would rewind the tape and play it back to see if they had picked up any spirit voices.

The Lamoreaux Brother's Learn about the Hierarchy of the Spirit World

Professor Uphoff soon ascertained that the Lamoreaux were especially interested in gaining information about life after death, and they had interrogated the spirits for specific details about the world that lies beyond the grave. The paranormal voices that came through on their tape recorder described the ethereal region from which they communicated as a frequency or vibrational level, a dimension, rather than a physical location.

Pareenah (phonetic spelling) was the name the spirit voices gave the Lamoreaux brothers for the earthplane of existence. *Deenah* was the designation applied to the main place or state where one goes after physical death. According to the spirit voices, although this state appears to be largely a subjective reality, it has some rather stringent rules. Most of the spirits coming through the tape recorder said that they now existed in *Deenah* and referred to themselves in that state as *Moozla.*

Those who disobeyed the rules and laws of *Deenah* are sent to *Nilow,* an apparent region of conditioning. Once one has been made more fit for spirit progress, he or she may return to *Deenah.* Those entities that must remain for a longer period of time are called *Nilowins.*

There was also described an area between *Deenah* and *Nilow* called *Ree,* a kind of therapeutic or hospital environment wherein the spirits are permitted only limited movement. Those beings who must remain in that area for a prolonged period are called *Moolit.*

There is more movement and freedom in a level known as *Montayloo,* which supports twelve levels of planned progression. The *Montaylooins* can advance to the levels of *Piloncentric* and *Sentra.* It seems that it is from the *Sentra* level that the spirits may influence those on Earth with what is commonly known as inspiration.

How to Record Spirit Voices

Tracking down spirit voices is not an esoteric science reserved for initiates or those with special training in electronics. Anyone with a tape recorder can take part in this form of psychical research.

It may be that there is an element of extrasensory perception or mediumistic ability involved, but this has not been determined as a necessary requirement for a successful recording of spirit voices.

Some researchers have suggested that Dr. Raudive had some abilities as a medium, but there are no published reports of his being aware of such talents before he seriously began to record paranormal voices. It is also known that Michael Lamoreaux once slipped into a trance state during a taping session. He had never done this before, and he did not at first realize that his "nap" of three or four minutes had actually lasted for well over half an hour.

Walter Uphoff prepared some guidelines for people who wish to conduct experiments in capturing spirit voices with their own tape recorders. There is no guarantee that anyone can duplicate the successful experiments that have been carried out around the world, but if a person is serious about recording the spirit voice phenomenon, he or she should resolve not to become discouraged if early attempts are unproductive.

A general consensus among electronic voice researchers indicated that they spent an average of two months before they got really impressive results. On the other hand, many researchers state that they were successful on their very first effort.

A point on which all electronic voice researchers agree is that it is very necessary to go back over their early tapes and review them. They have discovered that as their ability to hear and to understand paranormal voices improved, so are they able to hear voices that they had initially missed.

There is no absolute rule as to when and where recording should be attempted. Professor Uphoff advised experimenters to select a place that is as free as possible from all extraneous noises. The best time appears to be in the evening, especially around midnight.

Since the weather is always a factor in radio transmissions, it is advisable to avoid times when there is a large amount of static electricity in the air.

Very often, the spirit voices are heard in the pauses between words and sentences, so Professor Uphoff advised novice experimenters always to speak slowly and clearly.

"What must be guarded against is becoming an uncritical believer," he warned.

"Everyone I know who has devoted time to listening to the spirit tapes grants that something paranormal is happening. Some feel more comfortable, while others feel less so, if they can somehow credit the voices to the work of the experimenter's subconscious. But no one has come forward with an explanation of the dynamics or the forms of energy involved in producing the phenomenon.

"Tape recorders have become one more instrument

to push the frontiers of the unknown back and to bring us closer to the awareness that man is more than a mere combination of chemicals and electrical energy—and that what we know as human personality may not cease at death."

Sarah Estep's American Association for Electronic Voice Phenomena

Over the nearly twenty years that we have known of Sarah Wilson Estep and her fine work with the American Association for Electronic Voice Phenomena, we have been impressed with her tireless efforts to compile recordings of spirit voices that are of high quality and bound to impress the professional skeptics. And Sarah is the first to admit that she completely understands the position of those who doubt the validity of spirit recordings. As a long-time psychical researcher, Sarah recalled that her initial reaction to someone who claimed that they had recorded voices of the dead on tape was utter disbelief.

Today, after many years of recording spirit voices from other dimensions and after amassing well over 24,000 messages from beyond, she feels that she may safely say that she has learned a great deal about life on the other side.

In her book, *Voices of Eternity*, she writes that those spirits who have spoken to her via tape have expressed feelings of both joy and sadness.

> Most have been surprised at what they found. They contribute, on their own, totally unexpected yet meaningful comments. My direct questions are

> frequently answered. . . . Musical chords and notes have been played at my request. . . . I have been assured of their support, their protection, their help. They have asked me for help.[4]

Sarah has stated that one of the greatest rewards of her work has been her ability to assist those who are grief-stricken with the loss of a loved one and to give them hope and comfort in the knowledge that people they loved are continuing to live on the other side.

> As the one left behind tells the individual that he or she is missed and still loved, and the voice from the next dimension replies, *"I love you, too,"* one would have to be devoid of all compassion not to find the moment extremely moving.[5]

In her advice to novice experimenters, she has suggested that it is better to make one five-minute recording each day than to sit down once or twice a week to record for half an hour.

> Those on the other side soon learn when and where you will record and if you are dependable as well as persistent and they will start to speak to you. Each experimenter must work out his own way to record. I always start each recording with the date, time, and a welcome for those who come in love and peace. During a five-minute recording, I will ask three or four questions, allowing at least a minute between questions for the answer.[6]

Sarah Estep is frank in admitting that she has been searching since she was a child for evidence that humans survive death. The search has been long and frequently fraught with failure. She persevered, she says, until she finally found the answers in the "voices of eternity."

Electronic Spirit Communication in the 1990s

In the 1990s, spirit communication takes place via tape recorders, radio, television, telephone, and even computers.

Respected scientists around the world are making claims that they may well have doubted a few years ago. A veritable network of engineers, doctors, and mathematicians have devoted their energies to research in electronic spirit communication through the Center for the Study of Transcommunication in Luxembourg. What is more, these scientists who seek a permanent link between the earth and the Beyond claim that the spirits of such illustrious predecessors as Thomas Edison and Marie Curie have communicated with them.

Swedish parapsychologist Claude Thorin was able to capture the image of the late Friedrich Jurgenson with his Polaroid camera as Jurgenson, one of the fathers of electronic spirit recordings, appeared on the screen of his television set. Not long after that startling spirit manifestation, Jules and Maggy Harsch-Fischbach of Luxembourg managed to tune in a spirit image on their television set. It was that of Konstantin Raudive, the psychologist who recorded 70,000 voices from the spirit world before his own voyage to the Other Side.

Two of the most highly acclaimed researchers in ITC (Instrumental Transcommunication), the Harsch-Fischbachs said that they received a message left on their telephone answering machine by an entity who identified herself as Dr. Swejen Salter, a deceased scientist. Dr. Salter described the afterlife as a paradise where one can live anywhere one chooses, from an elegant mansion to a cabin in a forest. The spirit entity also provided details of a rejuvenation process that eliminates all symptoms of earthly diseases and which restores the elderly to a permanent age between twenty-five and thirty.

On November 10, 1993, a remarkable accomplishment occurred when the clear image of Anne De Guigne, a French girl who died in 1922 at the age of ten, came through the television set of a researcher in Germany and the Harsch-Fischbachs' computer scanning device in Luxembourg. In addition, Maggy found a letter in her computer from Anne that explained that she had been a little girl in Annecy, France, who "through spirit insight and prayer" had desired a transition to a multidimensional world, the same beautiful world that humans have always heard about from those who have gone to the other side.

The spirit Anne De Guigne went on to state that she was now in charge of a group of entities that sought to protect all newborn life. They were particularly concerned about the approximately 40,000 children who died daily on Earth.

> Be aware therefore that the wars and violent events caused by you, and from which particularly your innocent children suffer, are not sparing you. . . . Every debt you shoulder by sacrificing

> your own flesh and blood to wars is adding to the misery and suffering that awaits you. The more you create your own hell on Earth by your criminal deeds and negligence, the less it will be diminished for you here later. Therefore, consider carefully what you do. . . .[7]

The International Network for Instrumental Transcommunication

Mark Macy is the U.S. spokesman for the International Network for Instrumental Transcommunication (ITC), a group of researchers who endeavor to make available to the public the latest significant communications by residents of the spirit realms via electronic means. Macy has stated that spirit communication through television, radio, computer, or whatever depends upon some rather complex variables. In this regard, he reported that the group has received a message from Dr. Raudive, who made his own transition some years ago, who told them that "[Electronic spirit communication] can only work when the vibrations of those present are in complete harmony and when their aims and intentions are pure."

According to the "spirit colleagues" who work with the members of ITC, communication works best

> . . . when it involves a group of psychically sensitive people whose vibrations are in complete harmony and whose aims and intentions are pure.
>
> [It] does not work with a group of psychics who are jealous or resentful of each other, because jealousy, resentment, and other such feelings create

status that disrupts all communications across all dimensions. So does hostile skepticism.[8]

In the February 1997 issue of *Fate* magazine, Macy said that nearly any spirit could get involved in their experiments and create short, faint voices on audio-tape. "However, more elaborate contacts—television and computer images, telephone calls, and letters via computer—require a team of spirit beings and the intervention of higher beings."

Such technical breakthroughs, he stressed, were miracles made possible by "brilliant minds in ethereal realms."

> Earth technology is primitive compared to what our spirit colleagues use on their side. Unfortunately . . . they cannot simply hand over circuit diagrams of their equipment. We first have to be mentally receptive. . . . We must have a basic understanding of the technologies and principles they send to us before we can receive it through our equipment. Whether this catch-22 is because of spirit-world physics or the hands-off-rule of a spiritual heirarchy, we just don't know.[9]

The paranormal voices recorded on tape and other electronic means affirm that they are the surviving personalities of human beings who once lived on Earth. Whether these voices truly represent who they say they do has yet to be proved to the satisfaction of our material sciences.

The fact does remain, however, that the voices do exist and have been captured on tape.

For those who are convinced that research with

electronic spirit communication fulfills its promise, it is no longer necessary to seek out a medium in order to establish contact.

Those who wish and who have the patience may work with their own electronic equipment in order to establish the truth of personal survival and solve the age-old riddle about life after death to their own satisfaction.

In the next chapter, we shall meet men and women who have utilized the age-old, tried and tested instruments of body, mind, and spirit to receive meaningful messages from Heaven.

CHAPTER EIGHT

Receiving Messages from Those Spirits Who Dwell in Heaven's Harbor

During a discussion that we once enjoyed with the late Olof Jonsson, whom many regard as the greatest physical medium of our time, the topic turned to the spiritual essence of humans and the reality of the afterlife that awaits the spirit after physical death.

Olof believed that the life of the soul is interdimensional, dwelling within a fleshly domicile in our material dimension, then graduating to a higher plane upon the physical death of bone, blood, and tissue. "While we are alive and existing physically on Earth, our souls really belong to another dimension. In meditation and in dreams, this fact becomes quite apparent. It is quite simple for the transcendental element within us to rise to the higher plane of existence."

Because of this view, Olof said that one might, through proper techniques of meditation, achieve full consciousness of one's true potential before the transition of physical death.

"When one meditates properly, he or she learns to flow with the dimensional frequencies and to enter the higher planes of being while his soul still retains residence in the body," Olof said. "Of course, if one has allowed his or her psyche to become crystallized by an excessive interest in material possessions, proper meditation can become all but impossible to achieve. Material objects belong to the lower dimension, and if one cannot release his or her hold on them, the liberation of the psyche, both before and after physical death, will be very difficult to achieve."

In his view of reality, Olof repeatedly stressed the importance of meaningful and effective sessions of meditation in which the transcendent level of mind is allowed free reign to move through the higher dimensions. According to Olof, such meditative states are so valuable because "they help people to understand that this life really means almost nothing compared to what we can expect in the next life."

Contact with deceased loved ones attained through properly prayerful meditative techniques and one's own transcendent journeys to Heaven can help one gain insight into the next stage of existence and provide a valuable perspective that will aid one in living the present life on the material plane much more significantly.

"When we see what awaits us in the afterlife, we

will regard all the worries of this life to be but petty considerations," Olof said during our discussion.

What may we expect in the afterlife?

According to the transcendental travels of Olof Jonsson, we may expect to know more about the universe, because we will have more senses than we have now. We will be able to travel anywhere in the cosmos we desire in an instant.

Will the surroundings in Heaven be similar to our earthly environment?

"They will be similar," Olof answered, "but much more wonderful, more colorful, and richer in texture."

But we, ourselves, will be mind/soul, rather than physical body.

"Yes," Olof said. "Now we see our material world with five senses, and only occasionally do we utilize the transcendent level of consciousness which we commonly call our 'sixth sense.' In Heaven, the next world, all souls will have full control of this unknown faculty and their existence will be fuller, richer."

Olof Jonsson's perception of the afterlife is one of pure mind in which the processes of existence seem very much like the mechanics of a dream. One wishes a large castle and proceeds to construct it with the mind. Whatever one wishes, he or she will have but to think it and it will be there.

"But we will not long be interested in such things," Olof explained. "We will know many more of the secrets of life, the real meanings of existence, so that we will not long be satisfied in building dream castles. We will become more concerned with learning more of the great spiritual lessons in the Universe.

"It is my understanding that in the afterlife there will be another kind of transition that will graduate the soul to an even higher level of being. We will continue to evolve from plane to plane, on each level vibrating faster and faster, until we have become pure light, pure cosmic energy. At that time, we shall have achieved the highest of harmonious states."

At that highest of harmonious states, what will become of the individual personality, the specific personality, that we possessed as humans?

"I believe that we belong to a system of universal intelligence," Olof replied. "One can splinter off and become an individual anytime he or she likes, even after harmonizing with the Supermind."

While we have spoken of Heaven, what of Hell? Is there also a place or system of punishment in the afterlife?

"It is my philosophy that we have no bad people, only those who are born with abilities or disabilities that differ from others," Olof said. "I believe that we all belong to a Supermind that we may call God, a Supermind that must obey the same universal laws which it has established for the most minute and flawed atom of its whole. In the afterlife, there is no punishment, no suffering, no good or bad—there is only perfect Harmony."

Receiving Direct Communication with Loved Ones in Heaven

Since 1960, we have interviewed and corresponded with scores of mediums, psychical researchers, professional seers and clairvoyants, and ordinary men and women who have had extraordinary experiences in communicating with the spirits of their deceased loved ones. Beginning in 1967, various forms of the *Steiger Questionnaire of Mystical Experiences* have produced thousands of individual accounts of people who have received direct contact with spirits of those beloved who had already returned to Heaven, their true home beyond the stars.

Through a cautious and judicious study of the research that we have assembled over nearly forty years, it is possible to compile a kind of synthesis regarding certain aspects of existence in Heaven, the Next World.

At the moment of physical death, the spirits newly freed from their former confines of flesh are profoundly influenced by the belief constructs that they maintained while on Earth. Therefore, devout Roman Catholics will often perceive a saint or Mother Mary waiting to welcome their soul into Heaven. Practicing Jews may anticipate Moses or Father Abraham stretching forth a hand of greeting. Protestant Christians may perceive angels or even Jesus himself waiting to open the gates of Heaven for the newly arrived souls. After the spirit has had a period of time to adjust to existence in Heaven, however, once-vital matters of creeds and ecclesiasticisms seem to fade into matters of little or no importance.

As we have seen in earlier chapters of this book, as a kind of general rule, the moment people die, regardless of the kind of life that they have led, a spirit entity, an angel or friend or relative, arrives to meet the newly deceased and becomes a guide whose mission is to greet them, comfort them, and to acquaint them with their new surroundings. Without such guides, many recent arrivals to Heaven would feel desperately frightened, lonely, and confused.

"My wife, Ramona, told me that she was met by her grandparents and by her best friend Carmen, who had been killed in a car accident two years ago," J. S. told us. "I had grieved so terribly until the spirit form of my wife appeared and told me that she was not alone in Heaven. It brought me great peace, knowing that she had someone with her."

A particular consensus that we have derived from hundreds of spirit messages is that the more spiritually attuned people were during their lives on Earth, the less that their minds have been obsessed with the accumulation of wealth and the attainment of selfish goals, the more rapid will be their adjustment to life on the other side. The more spiritually minded the recently deceased, the greater will their spirit essences be focused on Heaven and its noble aims.

"From what the spirit of my husband has told me, Heaven seems to be the summation of perfect harmony and love," B. C. told us. "He says that it is a person's inner life that makes for righteousness and happiness. He says that he has met spirits from all religious persuasions. Things that he once believed in with such fervor don't seem to matter all that much in Heaven."

"Jackie has told me that the souls of all those in Heaven are filled with unimagined happiness," M. P. wrote in her account of the afterlife that she had received from her beloved sister. "She said that the divine energy of being, becoming, and loving permeate their essence with an intensity that we on Earth cannot comprehend. In Heaven, love is the great guiding star. Love fills all the spirit entities with the highest joy."

Here follow a number of excerpts from discussions,

interviews, and questionnaire reports that have centered around the survival question.

A Sojourn in Paradise

D. J.: "My wife, Georgia, told me that she at first found herself in a kind of gathering place for all newly arrived spirits. She said that the place had nothing to do with whether or not you had lived a good life or a bad life on Earth. Everyone goes there, regardless. It is something like a kind of resting place before the spirit moves on."

D. J. said that his wife's spirit mentioned the word "paradise" so often that he felt compelled to do some research on the matter.

"I discovered that the word 'paradise' comes from the Persian for a park or a garden. From what I can ascertain from Georgia's communications, it is only after the spirit has been deceased for a while that it begins to grow weary of the familiar scenes of life on Earth. I am certain that it all depends upon the individual entity and the personal circumstances of his or her passing, but it seems that the spirits must be willing to set aside their material interests before they are ready to progress more completely into the light of higher awarenesses."

The Beauty and Brilliance of Heaven Must Be Experienced for Oneself

P.A.L.: "I often felt as though the spirit of my husband, Patrick, really found it impossible to convey the beauty and the brilliance of Heaven in mere mortal words. Of course, I am not certain if Patrick is simply unable to describe the wonder of the afterlife or if my finite mind is simply unable to grasp it all.

"At first Patrick told me that everything in Heaven was so marvelously different from existence on Earth that he found it impossible to grasp. Now, after nearly a year of spirit communication, I fear that he has given up on the task of allowing me to perceive vicariously the glory of the afterlife. He has told me that I will just have to wait and see it all for myself."

Spirits Who Have Lived Gross, Materialistic Lives Evolve More Slowly

L.P.A.: "My sister Camille, who passed over five years ago, has learned that those souls who on Earth lived gross, material lives may remain unaware that they have passed over for many days, months, or even years.

"Very materialistic spirits may arrive in a kind of dreamlike state. This kind of spirit dreaming is very different from earthplane dreaming in that the dreamer will never again awaken to physical realities. When the spirit does awaken, it will do so in a world of new realities which are unknown to it. It will only be some time later that such materialistic entities will emerge from their stupor and gradually become convinced that they are no longer living in the physical world."

Heaven Is Filled with Spirit Duplicates of Earth

E.F.D.: "My wife, Donna, told me that they have spirit duplicates of everything that we have on Earth.

They have trees, flowers, animals, mountains, rivers, seas—everything.

"One time she told me, 'Darling, we have clouds and rainy days, storms and lightning. We have the thousand and one forms that make Mother Nature so beautiful. We have houses and books and clothes. Everything on Earth has its mental duplicates or counterparts in Heaven.' "

An Essential Key to the Universe: "Thoughts Are Things"

R. P.: "My wife, Sherrana, had been deceased for three years before she appeared to me and gave me the following message: 'My beloved, if you can grasp the concept that thoughts are things, you will be in a much better position to understand many of the essential mysteries of the universe, including life after death. Because of my more rapid ethereal vibration, I can appear before you in your more physically dense world. Likewise, I can easily walk through your doors and walls, because they are objects of the third dimension. I now exist in Heaven, which is beyond the fourth dimension.' "

The Etheric, Mental, and Spiritual Dimensions

L. A.: "My husband materialized to me to explain the three distinct realms or dimensions of spiritual expression. Floyd said that in the afterlife there is the Etheric, the Mental, and the Spiritual. Our plane is the world of Matter, wherein we have physical bodies that are controlled by our minds. On the other side, in Heaven, the beings manifest mentally formed etheric bodies that are controlled by their spirituality.

"The key to all this, Floyd said, is to interpret the physical in terms of the mental, and control the whole by means of the spiritual."

Limitations of Time and Space Do Not Apply in Heaven

T.M.T.: "According to the spirit of my husband, Norman, the principal difference between life on Earth and that of Heaven lies in the fact that we exist in a physical world wherein everything is governed by physical laws. In Heaven, the spirit beings live on a mental plane and thought replaces physical action and crude matter. Thoughts are things, and the limitations of time and space do not apply to them.

"Another main difference is that in Heaven, love is the principal energy that controls every thought, every deed, every vibration."

Spirits Can Travel Instantaneously

T.A.M.: "My husband, Al, had been confined to a wheelchair for eleven years before he passed on. When his spirit appeared to me, he told me that time and space do not have the same meaning in Heaven. He told me that he could travel from one spot to another, simply by thinking about it. He could appear on Earth if he wished, simply by visualizing me or our children or other loved ones.

"He said, 'Honey, I'm not welded to that darn

wheelchair any longer. Now I can travel all over the universe.' "

Like Attracts Like in Heaven

B. W.: "My daughter Kris's spirit essence communicated to me often. Once she told me our like-minded souls are attracted to one another. In Heaven, the happiness of the soul depends upon its own resources. They, of course, no longer have to work to earn money for the pleasures of existence. They are free to utilize their individual talents as they prefer. Because their thoughts and characters are completely open and naked for all to see, there is no attempt at pretense. Spirits of similar vibrational frequencies just naturally moved toward one another.

"Those souls who, for whatever reasons, are slower to adjust to the Next World may stay on the lower planes for years. Some entities exist for quite some time in a kind of mental darkness. That is quite sad, for the heavenly life is to be one of growth in wisdom, insight, and love."

Telepathy Is the Normal Means of Spirit Communication

G. C.: "My father's spirit told me that telepathy was the normal means of communication among spirits and between spirit beings and humans. He told me that telepathy dispenses with the clumsiness of language and renders sound superfluous.

"It is this mechanism of telepathy that permits spirit entities to communicate with the living in whatever country they may exist and regardless of which Earth language they may employ. Telepathy also allows spirits from ancient times to be able to be understood by men and women in the twentieth century."

His New Spiritual Sight Detected the Malignant Lump in Her Breast

S. A.: "The spirit of my husband, Philip, appeared to me and told me to go at once to my physician to have a lump in my left breast examined. A biopsy determined that the pea-sized lump was malignant, but because of Phil's early warning, the surgery was effective and the cancer was removed with very little trauma.

"Phil had been able to see inside my body, and he explained that a spirit's sense of color is vastly superior to ours. Their range of sight extends far beyond our small share of the spectrum. Their sight moves beyond even what we know as the ultraviolet range. He said that everything that was around me in my environment appeared totally different to him—and different from the way that he had remembered it.

"Phil surprised me when he said that there was no sunlight in Heaven, but that everything was intensely bright nonetheless. I guess that was why my physical body was more or less transparent to his spiritual eyes. His sight could penetrate between the molecules of my body, just like X rays do."

After Forty-six Years, She Still Feels the Spiritual Presence of Her Husband

M.K.R.: "Our children were all under six years of age when my husband, Larry, was killed in the Korean conflict in 1952. But even today, forty-six years later, I still feel the guiding and protecting influence, as well as the spiritual presence, of my husband.

"I have come to understand that when the spirits in Heaven develop spiritually, they pass to a higher spiritual sphere. Those spirits who graduate to that higher plane eventually lose all their interest in the mundane, the earthly, the material. The higher the spirits evolve, the less often they will be concerned with earthly considerations. In fact, the highly progressed entities will rarely come to anyone on Earth unless there should be such a strong bond of affection between the spirit and those left behind that the spirit will frequently return to monitor loved ones until the loved ones join him or her in Heaven. I know that Larry's spirit remains concerned about us and that he awaits our joining him on the other side."

Dr. George Lindsay Johnson's Analysis of Thousands of Spirit Messages

Among Dr. George Lindsay Johnson's conclusions after evaluating thousands of spirit communications was that whatever creed or religion one might believe in this world, on the other side such belief constructs were purely a matter of indifference.

"Whether we believe in one God or three Gods or no God at all—whether we are Christians, Mohammedans, Jews, Buddhists, or Free-thinkers without any religion except that of nature—will count for nothing on the other side; nor will our beliefs affect our happiness at all, except indirectly," Dr. Johnson wrote. "Our religion or nonreligion is merely an accident of our birth and bringing up, and we are in nowise responsible for it."

Dr. Johnson also learned that many spirits, especially if they had lived extremely materialistic lives on Earth, are unaware that they have passed over to the other side. "Such a state must be the exception rather than the rule," he said, "and I believe that it never takes place if the person who passes over has accustomed himself before his departure to higher objects in life than mere selfish gratification."

Thus Dr. Johnson maintained that the more spiritually minded a person is on Earth, the more his or her thoughts would be centered on new goals and aims on the other side.

Even after his extensive firsthand study of spirit communications and his analysis of the investigations of dozens of other psychical researchers, Dr. Johnson expressed no reluctance in admitting that we are "lamentably ignorant" concerning conditions on the other side.

At the same time, he insisted that certain well-established facts were worth recording and that if the reader could grasp the following passage, he or she would be in a better position to comprehend conditions in the next world:

> The Universe is a vast exhibition of intense activity, movement, and intelligence—a becoming through perpetual evolution. This consists of two systems—the natural or the physical, and the psychic or spiritual world, and each of them is governed by its own laws, which are entirely different in their action. These two-world systems are perpetually acting and reacting on each other; the

physical world being subservient to the spiritual world and controlled by it. Furthermore, the inhabitants of the spirit world are merely human beings freed from the limitations imposed upon them by their physical bodies.[1]

ACHIEVING SPIRIT COMMUNICATION

Those men and women who have been blessed by messages from their loved ones in Heaven have received them in many different ways—through dreams, visions, direct spirit communication and materialization, mediums, séances, automatic writing, and so on. Whether one should deliberately seek spirit communication is an age-old question that is certain to spark debate in many homes.

Surely, it is best if spirit contact and communication should be spontaneous—a true blessing beyond all human understanding that grants a temporary reprieve from the final sentence of death in order for loved ones to share a last farewell. However, we humans do have free will and the cosmic birthright to make our own spiritual decisions, and many of us have felt capable and qualified to seek our own transcendent pathways to Heaven.

There remain, of course, all those ancient and traditional warnings about spirit deceivers and masqueraders which must be taken seriously. On the other hand, one of the primary essences of personal shamanism and spiritual development is a strong belief in the partnership between our physical world and the world of the spirits.

Once again, we issue our cautions that if you should seek to explore any aspect of the spiritual world, you must learn to develop self-discipline, discernment, and discretion—and you must learn to exercise all three at the proper time. One must approach any level of spiritual development with a seriousness of purpose and a genuine commitment to the ultimate goal of achieving higher awareness.

Set a Regular Time for Your Development Exercises

Melinda K. of Oregon shared her advice that anyone seeking to establish contact with the spirit world should set a regular time for development exercises.

- Don't overdo this by becoming a slave to the clock or by sitting too often.
- Begin with ten- or fifteen-minute sessions every other day, or twice a week. Daily sessions are all right, too.
- Gradually increase your time allotment to half an hour a sitting. Don't go beyond that unless and until you reach the stage where manifestations occur regularly and may occasionally require longer periods.
- The time of day most suitable for your early exercises—and for that matter, perhaps for all psychic training and experimentation—is the latter part of the evening. This is usually the time of day when you are finished with your responsibilities, when your segment of the world has slowed down to a more serene pace.

- The room in which you sit should be quiet, not too large, and sufficiently remote to assure privacy and safety from interruptions.

You Don't Need to Sit in the Dark

Gina from Montana says that it is not necessary to sit in a completely darkened room.

The lighting should be subdued. One low wattage bulb in a wall socket or a desk lamp is more than adequate—and even that should be shaded, possibly with a blue or a purple scarf or some gauze of similar color.

When you are more accomplished, complete darkness will be fine. But at first, sitting alone late at night in total darkness, attempting to make spirit contact, is often a bit unnerving for the beginner. So don't let anyone tell you that absolute darkness is essential to spirit manifestations.

Beginning Your Sittings

Robert H., a lawyer from California with pronounced mediumistic abilities, set forth a procedure for the lone experimenter to follow that had proved successful for him.

- Place yourself in a comfortable chair and sit quietly.
- Divest your thoughts of all of your immediate worldly concerns and do your best to keep your mind blank.
- Place yourself in as receptive a mood as possible. Be alert, but don't expect anything particular to occur. Be patient and sit and wait.

- If there seem to be points of light darting about the room, understand that they *could* be caused by natural manifestations of eye strain.
- If you hear the creaking of floor boards, recognize that the sounds could be caused by changes in temperature, rather than the appearance of an unseen spirit.
- If your arms and legs become numb and cold, know that these sensations may be due to fatigue or rigidity, rather than the advent of the supernatural.
- In other words, remain calm and don't become panicky or credulous. You will know well enough when the real thing occurs.
- Adjourn your sitting after ten or fifteen minutes. Repeat it a day later—or two or three days later—up to a total of a dozen times or more.
- If genuine phenomena do occur, don't be surprised and don't be frightened. Such things merely indicate that you are on your way to establishing spirit contact and that you are gaining in spiritual strength.

How to Practice Automatic Writing

Automatic writing has been responsible for numerous classic works of inspiration, and according to its many advocates among the respondents to our questionnaire, it seems to be one of the most popular methods for communicating with the beyond. It is apparent that many serious seekers of spirit contact find this method very adaptable to their personal cosmologies and deem it preferable to other mediumistic techniques.

Donna J. of Manitoba explained her method of achieving spirit communication through automatic writing.

- Seat yourself comfortably at a table or desk.
- Place a piece of paper before you and hold a pen or a pencil in your normal writing hand in the manner in which you usually write. Let the writing instrument's tip rest lightly on the paper.
- Keep your wrist and arm loose, your wrist preferably in such a position that it does not touch the table at all.
- Wait quietly and patiently. Close your eyes. Listen to some flowing New Age or symphonic music. Just be certain the music has no lyrics to distract you.
- It is not necessary—and in fact, it is not even desirable—for you to concentrate on your hand and what it is doing. If you do not wish to keep your eyes closed during the experiment, you may even read a book, just to keep your conscious thoughts occupied.
- See to it that no direct light shines on the paper. Shield it with a piece of cardboard or something similiar.
- Chances are, in the beginning, you will merely produce nervous squiggles without any meaning. But sooner or later, messages will come through.
- It usually takes three or four sittings before the first intelligent results are achieved. Be patient. And don't prolong your sittings unduly, even after you have begun receiving meaningful messages.

Crystal Gazing

Claudia M. of Arizona told us that she had achieved excellent results in making spirit contact by the age-old method of crystal gazing.

- If you don't want to buy a crystal ball, you can use a glass filled with ordinary tap or spring water. Or get a large piece of natural, clear quartz crystal from a rock shop.
- Whatever you use, I suggest that you place it on some dark or black material to eliminate glare or reflections.
- Make your mind a blank. Gaze—don't stare—steadily at the crystal, blinking as seldom as possible. Don't extend your steady gaze for more than five minutes at a time. If your eyes have begun to water, this may be taken as an indication that your time limit has been reached. You should then end your experimentation.
- Sooner or later, if you are in tune with this particular method of establishing spirit contact, your crystal will cloud over. When this passes, you may perceive small figures moving about in the crystal itself. It's a lot like watching miniature motion pictures or a miniature television set.
- As you keep watching, certain scenes will be acted out before your eyes. Of course these pictures are not really appearing in the crystal, but are merely projected there by your subconscious mind.
- If you are unable to see anything in the crystal, you can try to train your ability by closing your

eyes for a few minutes and thinking intensely of someone you know well who has crossed over. Then open your eyes and try to see the person in the crystal.

- Remember that not everyone is successful with this technique, so don't be too disappointed if you are among those who cannot develop this specific gift.

Gathering Compatible Members for Group Sittings

Experienced individuals in this area of spiritual development state that once those seeking spirit communication have begun to produce results in their experiments, it is advisable to give up their solitary sittings and to work with one or more other persons. Not only does this considerably lessen the danger of fatigue or boredom, which cause beginners to give up too early, but it's undeniable that two or three people, even during this period of preliminary training, can accomplish more than the single experimenter.

But as Meredith F. of New York cautions, "You must be certain that you pick like-minded individuals to participate in your development sessions. For what would seem obvious reasons, you would not be likely to ask any friends who are hard-nosed skeptics, who would be likely to belittle the entire project.

"At the other end of the pole, neither should you invite those friends who are 'true believers' and who are likely to hear a supernatural signal in every click of the thermostat. It would be most desirable to choose individuals who have a strong interest in psychic development, a good deal of patience, and a pretty good sense of balance."

A Simple Exercise in Telepathy

Appoint one of your group to be the sender (or transmitter) and another the receiver. If a third or fourth member is in your group, let them be the observer and the recorder, alternating these roles among you.

Let us say that you begin by assuming the role of the sender. Seat yourself at a table, brightly lighted by a lamp placed somewhat behind you and shining directly on a piece of paper in front of you. Your face should be turned toward the place where the receiver is seated, some distance away, with his or her back to you.

On the piece of paper in front of you, draw a simple figure, such as a circle, a cross, a triangle, and so forth. For your early experiments it is wise to agree beforehand on four or five such basic designs to be transmitted.

After drawing the figure, focus your attention on it. Concentrate on it for one minute. Then, mentally, *will* the recipient to receive the impression that you are transmitting.

The recipient, in turn, tries to keep his or her mind a blank. If the recipient is also seated at a table with a piece of paper and a pen or pencil, he or she may sketch the figure that has been mentally received from you, the transmitter. Once the impression is received, the recipient should draw it without hesitation, announcing when he or she has done so.

After some practice, the results you will achieve will be rather amazing. You will find that the number of correct impressions received will figure out to be much higher than they would be if they were mere guesses. You will see them stretch far beyond the law of probability and chance.

THE SPIRIT CIRCLE

According to those who have successfully achieved spirit communication, once a group has begun to work well together it is time to form the Spirit Circle.

"It must be made very clear that only those who are strongly intent upon establishing spirit communication should ever participate in your Circle," Robert H. said. "Séances should never be intended to be a matter of an evening's fun and entertainment.

"While there are Circles designed for research and scientific exploration, the more successful groups are composed of men and women who care about one another, who are in harmonious spiritual accord, and who are serious about receiving communication from the other side. It has long been noted that sympathy, seriousness of purpose, harmony, and patience are prerequisites for establishing spirit contact."

How Many Sitters Should Form a Circle?

Meredith F. said that the number of people in a Circle is a matter of individual preference: "Two people can produce excellent results if their psychic talents have been sufficiently developed. Through generations of experimentation, it has been set forward that four to six members constitute a desirable number for a Spirit Circle. Eight sitters seem to be the maximum number for the preservation of harmony and the elimination of discord."

Where Should the Circle Meet?

Dwight N. of Ohio told us that private Circles usually meet in the home of one of the sitters. "The room set aside for the séance should be medium-sized, quiet, and so far as possible, removed from street noises and other disturbances. It should be without a telephone, for nothing can be more disruptive to spirit contact than the ringing of the telephone bell.

"The room should be well aired before the séance begins. It should be comfortably warm, but not overheated. Smoking should be banned during the session. The consumption of alcoholic beverages before and during the séance should definitely be forbidden."

When Is the Best Time to Meet?

There seems to be a general consensus that the best time for a Spirit Circle to meet is sometime in the evening after dinner.

"You should choose a convenient hour when each one of your sitters has had an opportunity to permit the day with all of its worries and responsibilities to have receded a bit into the background," Robert H. said. "It is important that you sit regularly and always at the same time and place. Twice a week is the maximum number of séances for your Circle. A once a week meeting would be preferable."

Donna J. pointed out that experience has shown that dry weather is best for the production of spirit phenomena and that dampness or rain often hinder communication. "On the other hand," she said, "a sudden thunderstorm is very often conducive to the production of most unusual manifestations."

Some General Rules for the Spirit Circle

- Each individual séance should last no longer than an hour. In the beginning of your sittings, it would be best to limit the sessions to about half an hour.
- It must be understood from the very beginning that each person in the Circle must agree to sit regularly and patiently for an absolute *minimum* of twelve séances. When you have completed the last session in the first cycle, you may permit each individual to make his or her own decision whether or not to continue to study with you.
- Never restrict those members of the Circle who become skeptical or bored with the proceedings. You should replace them as soon as possible with new sitters.
- The first time your Circle meets, you would be wise to select a leader to be in charge of the proceedings, to ask the questions as soon as a spirit communicator manifests, and to time the length of the sittings. It must be agreed by all sitters that each member will obey the orders of the leader and abide always by his or her arrangements.
- At the same time, appoint a recording secretary, who will keep notes regarding each session and who will be certain that appropriate background music is provided.
- The leader of the Circle should assign seats

around the séance table, and once a seat has been assigned to a specific member, it should be retained during the entire cycle of sittings—unless unforeseen developments should make a change advisable.

- Séances are by no means required to be conducted in complete darkness, but neither must any direct light shine upon the séance table. Some circles prefer sitting in darkness until the first unmistakable phenomena occur. From that point on, a dim light is used in the room.
- A calm state of mind must be preserved by all sitters. It isn't necessary to be overly serious or to be gloomy. Just be open-minded and relaxed.
- Intense concentration should not be attempted. Tension, excitement, fear, or nervousness can be as great a hindrance to the proceedings as arrogance, skepticism, and levity.
- Be prepared to wait patiently for what may occur.
- Don't be overly critical of what may manifest in the early stages. It is best in the beginning of your sessions to accept what occurs, rather than to make immediate assessments and attempts to interpret.
- Don't expect miracles, the levitation of one of the sitters, or dramatic psychokinetic manifestations. This is real life. Your séance room has not been equipped with Hollywood-type special effects.

Should One of Your Circle Serve as a Medium?

"If a group of like-minded folks come together for a séance sitting," Robert H. said, "it may be that all of them have mediumistic abilities. Since none of them probably wish to develop into a professional medium, it may be unimportant which one of them serves as the medium for their Circle.

"Let me say this, though. I would suggest that by the time the Circle arrives at the more complex experiments, the question of who is the best medium among them will have been answered in a dozen different ways. And then, very naturally, the less mediumistic of the Circle will serve the principal medium as 'batteries,' thus enabling the Circle to produce increasingly impressive phenomena."

What If You Should Go into a Trance?

"Trance is a completely natural and normal state," Meredith F. said. "It comes about in psychically gifted persons in order to facilitate their communications with the world of spirit."

Since entranced people remember little or nothing of what takes place or what they may say, it is important that the recorder of the Circle keep careful written accounts of what has been uttered. Memory should never be relied upon.

"If I am serving as the medium in our Spirit Circle," Meredith F. explained, "I sit quietly holding hands with persons on either side of me. They, in turn, are holding hands with whomever is beside them, thus forming a circle around the table. I remain very quiet, listening to the restful music that we always play during our sessions. I take a few deep breaths, holding them comfortably for a count of three. I wait patiently as images begin to form in my mind, then I call out, in a quiet voice, whatever letters, words, symbols, or impressions are beginning to come to me.

"My depth of trance becomes deeper and deeper with each word or image that comes to me—and then I'm deep into trance and letting whatever, or whoever, come through me. I just let go, because I know that our Circle recorder will get everything down so that we can all examine my utterances after the session."

Establishing Spirit Contact

"When you begin to receive spirit communications, you should always be cordial to the entities," Dwight N. said. "I think it is a good idea to prepare questions beforehand that you wish to ask. And when the answers do come, do not flatly contradict them and do not become argumentative and say that such things are wrong or impossible. Later, when contact is firmly established, it will become possible to question the spirits and to ask them more completely to define matters."

"Remember, all conversation with the spirit communicators should be carried on through the person that you have chosen to be the leader of the séance," Donna J. emphasized. "It is really important to adhere to this rule in order to prevent mixups and misunderstandings."

Meredith F. advised the novice Circle members not to set out to achieve any particular kind of spirit manifestation. "Take whatever comes and go from there. The messages that you will achieve will vary greatly in value and in content. Sometimes they will be absolutely startling, sometimes trifling, sometimes obviously transmitted in an attitude of teasing."

"The amount of time that may elapse before the first phenomenon occurs and the transmission of messages that can be substantiated and proved will probably vary from session to session," Donna J. said.

"Sometimes very meaningful manifestations and messages will begin just as soon as the lights are dimmed and the Circle closed. During other sittings, you might not receive anything of any particular value. What you have to bear in mind at all times is that your results will get better and better and gain in importance from sitting to sitting. With the necessary patience and perseverance, some results will be absolutely certain to come through to you."

Receiving Direct Spirit Messages

As Robert H. commented, by the time that you and your Circle have reached the point where spirit messages may be received with reasonable expectation, it will have been definitely decided who among your group is the most gifted medium.

"At that point," Robert said, "the medium should occupy a chair set a bit apart from the other sitters, who will now arrange themselves in a semicircle in front of him or her. No hand chain is formed at this stage unless the sitters prefer to link up."

Donna J. outlined a procedure followed in her Spirit Circle.

> The usual meditative background music should be played, and all lights should be extinguished. Everyone should sit quietly or converse in very low tones. Direct-voice séances are best held in complete darkness. If the Circle decides some illu-

mination is preferred, select a colored bulb or cover the bulb with a colored cloth.

The medium should allow himself or herself to begin to enter the trance state. The Circle must remain patient and contemplative.

After a while, a whisper may be heard near the ear of one of the sitters. As soon as this occurs, the conversation and the music should stop. Expectant silence should prevail.

Sitters who find themselves addressed by the voices should attempt to identify the spirit speakers. If one should hear the voice of a stranger, it is now permissable to insist upon positive identification.

YOUR PERSONAL PROGRAM OF SPIRITUAL PREPARATION

If you should decide to seek spirit communication, then we earnestly advise you to prepare yourself for such contact with a period of self-examination, prayer, and the reading of inspirational literature. You must also remember our warning regarding spirit parasites, those negative entities that may masquerade as your deceased loved ones as a means of deceiving you and seizing control over your body, mind, and spirit.

Do Not Become Vulnerable to Spiritual Parasites

Generally, these parasites of the soul cannot achieve power over humans unless they are somehow invited into the person's private space—or unless they are attracted to a human aura by that person's negativity or vulnerability.

Men and women are especially susceptible to such spirit invasion when they are abusing alcohol or drugs and their normal boundaries of control have been removed. By the same token, those who practice meditation and who enter trance states without the proper spiritual protection may also find themselves beset by spirit parasites.

Never enter meditation or a trance state with the sole thought of obtaining ego aggrandizement. Selfish motivation may risk your becoming easily affected by those spirits who have become entrapped in their own discordant vibrations.

Remember Always to Summon Your Angel Guide

Whenever you explore the spiritual world, practice a firm sort of mind control so that you will interact only with those spiritual entities in the higher planes of loving and harmonious vibrations.

Remember always to ask your spirit guardian and guide to shepherd you through a meditative state and never fail to place the Golden Circle of Angelic Light and Protection around you.

A Prayer for Protection from Negative Entities

Beloved Angel Guide, establish your protective light energies around me.

Erect a shield of love about me that is invincible, all powerful, and impenetrable.

Keep me absolutely protected from all things that are not of the Light.

Keep me immune from all negative vibrations.

Surround me with the perfect love of the Father-Mother-Creator Spirit.

While on Earth, We Are Closer to the Lower Spirit Realms

When you seek contact with spirit intelligences, remember always that our physical earthplane reality is closer to the realm of the lower, more chaotic, frequencies than it is to the dimension of the most harmonious. Because we exist in a material world, the efforts of our psyches will always contain more of the lower vibratory realm than of the higher planes.

Preparing Yourself for Communication with Enlightened Beings

Prepare yourself for communication with an enlightened spirit being from the higher spiritual worlds by bathing yourself in a wondrous expression of unconditional love.

Visualize your angelic spirit guardian moving a soft, violet light all over your body in a wave of warmth. See this heavenly light touching every part of your body. Feel it interacting with each cell.

Say inwardly or aloud to your angelic guide:

Beloved Angel Guide, assist me in calling upon the highest of energies.

Activate the God-spark within me.

Provoke the law of harmony within me so that I may never stray from the God-Light.

Permit the heavenly Light to move around and through me.

Allow the transforming energy to purify me and to remove all impure desires, anger, wrongdoing, and improper actions from my spirit.

Keep this Holy Light bright within me.

Replace all chaotic vibrations around me and in me with the pure Light of the Father-Mother-Creator Spirit.

How to Transform the Negativity of a Spirit Parasite

If you should meet a spirit parasite, you will feel at once a prickling sensation that will seem to crawl all over your body. You will experience a mounting sense of terror or a distinct sensation of unease, depending upon the strength of the discordant vibrations emanating from the spirit.

If you should establish contact with a negative, deceptive spirit being, utter prayers and blessings of love at once. Fill your entire essence with unconditional love for all things—including the manifesting spirit.

Understand that the lower spiritual planes may shelter all manner of discordant spirits. Be aware of the fact that these deceptive spirits will continue their negative ways beyond physical death, and they will often attempt to influence the minds, and thereby the lives, of those who will receive them.

If you should ever sense the presence of negative entities in your environment, practice this exercise.

- Bend your elbows and lift your hands, palms outward to the level of your chest. Take a comfortably deep breath, then emit the universal sound of elevated vibration, "om," in a long drawn-out chant, holding the sound just as long as you can: "oooommm." Repeat this until you are able to feel the energy tingling the palms of your hands.
- Once you begin to feel more positive, bring your palms toward one another until you are able to feel the energy of the love and life force as a palpable "substance" between them. Focus upon this energy. Visualize it moving upward from your palms to your fingers. Feel it moving up your arms, your shoulders, your neck, your face. Image within your mind the energy of the force feeding new life, new energy to your entire physical being.
- Utter the universal sound of "om" once again. Visualize the energy moving up to the crown chakra at the top of your head, then cascading down in sparks of golden light, as if you were being enveloped by the downward pouring of a spiritual Roman candle.
- Impress upon your consciousness that those sparks of heavenly love represent new, positive energy that is descending around your body, mind, and spirit and forming a vital protective shield against all discordant and negative spirit entities.

If you are still feeling at a low energy level after your confrontation with a discordant entity and you feel the need of some instant strength, ask your heavenly spirit guide in this manner:

Beloved Angel Guide, charge me with your great strength.

Charge me with your light and your love.

Charge me as if I were a battery, totally susceptible to your energy.

Charge each of my vital body functions with strength and energy.

Keep me ever sensitive to your guidance and your direction.

Remember that when you vibrate with the highest energy of Divine Love, when your purpose is harmonious with that of the angels, you will be able to make contact with those entities who exist in the realm of highest vibrations. You will not have to fear encountering the discordant parasites of the soul, for you will only receive meaningful, inspirational contact with spirit beings from the realm of the highest order.

CHAPTER NINE

Dreams, Visions, and Voices from the Next World

Evelyn Burns told us that her dear husband, Oliver, had been dead for nearly a year when she had a dream that precipitated a beautiful mystical connection with his spirit.

"I was feeling very low, in the very depths of despair," she said. "I missed Oliver so much. My life no longer seemed to have any purpose or meaning. Our only son lived in Germany at that time. He had come home for the funeral, but his work made it difficult to visit the States often. I had really begun to feel so overcome by loneliness that I would often be seized by spasms of uncontrolled weeping. I truly began to yearn to see my own life come to an end."

In her dream that night, Evelyn perceived herself

walking with Oliver beside a stretch of beach near La Jolla, California. It had been one of their favorite getaway places.

"Oliver had died at the age of sixty-eight after a long illness," Evelyn said. "He had always been a very strong and robust man, and he so hated being an invalid. In my dream, he was as he appeared in his early forties, filled with health and vigor."

Although Oliver had written her beautiful love poems and never forgot an anniversary, birthday, or holiday, he had not been a particularly demonstrative man when it came to expressing his deep emotional feelings.

"You know," Evelyn explained, "men of his generation were not encouraged to express their emotions. Although he would write me lovely poems, when he held me in his arms when we were alone, he would often become somewhat cold, even distant, as if he were uncertain how to please me or to truly express his love for me.

"On one level, his strange aloofness during times when he should have been warm and intimate had always troubled me. But at the same time, I knew that, in his own way, Oliver did love me."

In the dream, Evelyn confided, Oliver was quite romantic and began to demonstrate a passion that perhaps both of them wished had manifested during his lifetime. Her husband kissed her, embraced her warmly, and confessed that he had never really shown her just how much he had loved her.

"If only I had the chance to tell you just how very much you have always meant to me," Oliver said. "If only I were there to take you in my arms just once more."

Evelyn awakened with tears in her eyes. The dream had seemed so real. Now she truly felt as though she were all alone in the world.

Suddenly, she sensed a presence at her bedside. "I looked up to see a dimly lighted outline of a form that I knew to be my husband's. I could almost, but not quite, distinguish his features."

Evelyn whispered Oliver's name as she watched the illuminated form begin to move over her own body.

"The glowing mistlike image began to lower itself to me, and I felt the most incredible sensation as Oliver's spirit body blended with my physical body. Never before on the physical/material plane had I felt so at one with him. That night we truly became one spiritual entity of love." The sense of total unity with her husband's spirit lasted for what seemed to Evelyn to be at least an hour.

After the experience had ended, she said that she was blessed with a wonderful peace, and she drifted into a deep and dreamless sleep. She told us that she never again has felt loneliness or despair after the visitation of Oliver's spirit.

"Oliver returned that night to prove to me that he truly loved me and that we will always be one throughout eternity," she said, concluding her report.

Her Deceased Husband Wouldn't Allow Her to Pass

In this next fascinating account of a dream expression of the Next World, Heaven is symbolically portrayed as a beautiful, mystical silver city that rises out of the ocean. Although our respondent had the dream nearly four decades ago, it left an indelible impression on her psyche.

P.P.L.: "I am now eighty years old, and I have never before been able to tell this dream to anyone. It occurred when I was forty-one, and I have remembered it clearly all these years.

"In my dream, Paul, my second husband, and I are driving south on the Pacific Coast Highway from Palo Alto. I am looking to my right toward the ocean and remark to Paul about the beauty of the scenery and express my wish to stop for a while.

"He pulls into a small circular parking area, and as we look toward the sea, there suddenly arises from the water a swirling silver mist that reveals a beautiful city of domes, turrets, arches, and steeples. 'Oh, how beautiful,' I say to Paul. 'Let us try to find the bridge that will take us to that beautiful city in the sea.' "

At that point in the dream, P.P.L. and her husband step out of the car and begin to follow a sidewalk that she hopes will take them to a bridge to the silver city. Suddenly, a former brother-in-law named John appears and begs her to help him, saying "Sam won't let me go past the gate."

"Sam, my first husband, had died of cancer," P.P.L. explained. "One of his brothers, John, had been so hateful to me as a bride of seventeen that Sam had forbidden him to even step foot on our property unless he was home. But now, here is John, walking along with Paul and me as we follow the sidewalk toward the towering, magical buildings.

"As we circle beneath giant redwoods, I can see Sam

standing at a sort of causeway, and I begin to walk faster. There are many people coming and passing Sam as they walk out on the causeway. What is odd is that they start to fade as they progress toward the magical city. Then I realize that I am beholding wraiths of all ages, including babies, moving toward the beautiful city in the sea. And they all look so happy."

As P.P.L., Paul, and John approach Sam, he steps forward and stretches his arms out to block their passage. Although he appears solid, when she reaches out to touch him, she cannot feel him.

"Oh, honey, how nice to see you," she addressed her late husband. "We want to go with you and the others to the beautiful city."

Sam was firm in his reply: "No, sweetheart. It's not time for you to visit the city. You go home with Paul."

P.P.L. was somewhat surprised. "Oh, do you know Paul?"

Sam told her that he did know her present husband and that it wasn't time for either of them to enter the magical city.

"I pleaded with him. I said that I really wanted to go there," she told us in her report of the dream. "And all the while people are walking by Sam and he is allowing them to pass, and they just fade away after a few more steps. But there is no way that Sam will let Paul and me pass. He just kept saying that it wasn't our time to go to the city."

Sam's brother John pushed his way up toward P.P.L. and stated his case. "Sam won't let me come in because of what I did to you. No matter how much I tell him that I'm sorry. If you don't help me, he'll never let me pass."

P.P.L. understood. "It's okay, darling," she told

Sam. "What he did to me is no longer important. Let him pass."

Upon her absolution of his brother's past wrongs, Sam put down his arms and John stepped out onto the causeway—and started disappearing.

"Sam looked at me and smiled and said, 'Go home now and be happy with Paul. And do a good job launching our kids out into the world,' " P.P.L. said. "Then he stepped out on the causeway and began to fade away. In the next few moments, everything had disappeared and I awoke."

Although it was three in the morning, she awakened Paul and told him of her remarkable dream. "However, he was not too responsive at three a.m."

When he returned home from work the next evening, Paul patiently heard the details of the dream from his wife, then asked the logical question: "This John person . . . is he ill or something?"

P.P.L. answered that the last she knew of her former brother-in-law, he was well and working in the submarine base in Sausalito.

The next evening as they were eating dinner, she received a telephone call from Tom, the older brother of Sam and John. "He called to tell me that John had been found dead in his apartment two days ago."

His Son Returned to Say He Was in a Better Place

Richard Stuart, Jr., died in 1994 after losing a painful battle with leukemia. The seven-year-old boy from Middletown, Connecticut, had also suffered from Down's syndrome, which affected his speech.

His brokenhearted father, Richard Sr., was still grieving when the boy's spirit visited him from the Next World.

Richard was awakened out of sound sleep when he heard his son ask him for juice, something that the boy did quite often.

The forty-year-old father was stunned when he saw his deceased son standing at his bedside exhibiting no signs of the diseases that had tormented him through his brief life.

And Richard, Jr., was speaking normally.

> My son assured me he was in a better place and could now do all the things he had wanted to do when he was alive. And he told me that he was watching over everyone who cared for him during his life.
>
> After he came to me, it was like having a ton of bricks lifted from my shoulders. . . . I felt rejuvenated. I was ready to conquer the world.[1]

Her Spirit Came in a Dream to Grant Forgiveness

While he was stationed in Germany in the 1970s, Stanley B. met a beautiful girl named Karla, with whom he promptly fell in love. In his opinion, she was the quintessential Nordic blonde. They were both in their early twenties, and the quaint German villages seemed made for romance. Although Stanley had decided on a career in the navy, he thought for a time that he might toss it all aside for the good life in Germany with Karla.

The two discussed marriage many times, but they

could never quite reach a firm decision as to its parameters. They each professed to be in love with the other, but whenever the topic of matrimony would surface, one or the other of them would soon torpedo it.

Once Stanley had even gone so far as to buy an engagement ring, but he never even showed it to Karla. In retrospect, he said that he guessed she would say yes and graft it to her finger forever.

When it came time for Stanley to return to the States, the two lovers were faced with the moment of truth. They spent a last weekend together in a lovely old hotel. The first night they wept in each other's arms until nearly dawn. They would be apart for the first time in two years.

At last they spoke seriously of marriage. They admitted that they could not imagine marrying anyone other than each other.

Karla suggested that they should see how they felt after Stanley returned to the United States. The absence would test their love and determine whether or not it was true.

After Stanley's return to the States, the two lovers began a passionate correspondence. He nearly wore out his thesaurus looking up synonyms for "love" and "sweetheart," and Karla exhibited such an uninhibited flair for writing love letters that Stanley told her she should become a romance novelist.

As the weeks and months went by, however, Stanley found himself concentrating more intensely on his naval career. He had new opportunities for advancement and that meant putting his spare energy into preparing for examinations, not writing love letters.

He wrote to Karla that his letters would now begin to emphasize quality, not quantity—but it wasn't long before his output had dropped from a letter a day to one a week, then to one a month.

Karla's letters continued at a more steady pace, but after a few months, she began to match his infrequent schedule.

And it was about that time that Stanley met Darcy, a navy brat whose father was a career man. The last letter that he wrote to Karla confessed that he had found someone who really understood his commitment to the sea and who would fit better into his career.

Stanley felt really bad about writing such a blunt letter to Karla, but he rationalized that an honest, clean break was the better one. He convinced himself that he had done the best thing for all concerned.

Two years passed. Stanley had reported to duty aboard a destroyer based at the Virginia Beach shipyards.

"On the evening of June 15, I had been working late in the disbursement office, preparing for payday only a few days away," Stanley said. "I had been sitting at my desk typing up the pay roster until about twelve-twenty a.m. I remember being very tired and leaning my head back against my chair to doze off for just a few minutes."

When he opened his eyes, Stanley was startled to behold the image of Karla, dressed only in red shorts and a halter. "She was crying, tears running down her cheeks. She looked just the way that she had the day we said good-bye in Germany."

Stanley was completely nonplussed. He knew that he must be dreaming, yet everything, including Karla, looked and seemed so real.

He started to ask irrelevant questions, such as how

she had managed to get on board the destroyer without security stopping her.

She ignored his questions, but spoke directly of other matters. "Stan, I am here to tell you that I understood about Darcy—and I forgive you."

Stanley remembered trying to grasp a few words that might somehow comprise a proper response.

Karla only held up her hand for silence so she might continue.

"I knew that you were right in doing what you did," she began. "I was sad, of course, but I decided that life must go on. I was about to be married myself in just a few days."

She took his hand in hers, and Stanley recalled that she held it very tightly. "I only ask one thing of you. All I want is that you will promise to remember me always with kindness."

Stanley's voice became soft, choked with emotion. "Of course. You know I will."

"We did have a wonderful love together," Karla went on. "Respect the memory of our love . . . and have a wonderful, happy life with Darcy."

Stanley nodded quietly, feeling tears fill the corners of his eyes.

Karla smiled, squeezed his hand in farewell, then faded from sight.

The next thing Stanley knew, the security watch was shaking him, wondering if he was all right.

"I mumbled something or other, then went back to work on the pay roster," Stanley said. "But whatever had occurred—dream, vision, weird fantasy—during those incredible few moments that had disrupted the flow of my normal life experience had blown me away. There was no way that I could remove the experience from my mind."

After he had worked a while longer on the pay roster, Stanley set aside his paperwork and wrote a letter to Karla.

"I wanted to know if she was all right," he said. "Maybe she was ill. Or maybe I had received some kind of premonition of something bad about to happen to her. On the other hand, maybe she had just been thinking intently of me at the time that her image had appeared in my office aboard the destroyer."

About twelve days later, Stanley received a reply from Mrs. R. G., Karla's mother, who informed him that Karla had died instantly in a head-on automobile crash early on the morning of June 16. The time of Karla's death was equivalent to about 12:20 A.M. June 15 in Virginia Beach. She had just left the house on a brief errand and was dressed only in red shorts and a halter.

"Mrs. G. told me that she had already been looking for my address to inform me of her daughter's death just as my letter arrived," Stanley said. "Only days before her death, Karla had spoken of me and how sorry she was that she had not answered my letter about my marriage to Darcy.

"Mrs. G. also verified that Karla was engaged and would have been married in just a few weeks. It seems that the bond of love that we once shared had somehow enabled Karla to bid me a tender and forgiving farewell."

Listen with Your Heart and Hear the Sounds of Eternity

Our dear friend John Harricharan, the award-winning author of *When You Can Walk on Water, Take the Boat* and *Morning Has Been All Night Coming,* shared a number of experiences of his continuing contact with the spirit of his beautiful wife Mardai, who made her transition a few years ago.

Mardai's battle with cancer had been a long and terrible one. Although she had fought bravely, she could not prevail, and John lost the light from his life one summer's day.

"We had been married for twenty years, and I had no idea how I would continue in life without Mardai. As I stood there that July day holding my two children close to me, the emptiness within me was so horrible that all I could think was, 'Is there no balm in Gilead?' "

In the days that followed, there were times when John looked around him and perceived life as a meaningless mess. But there were other times when a quiet voice would whisper in his ear that life was not as bad as it appeared. Life was much more than a short span on Earth. A lifetime was but a blink in eternity. Ever so slowly, he began to understand.

Sometimes while driving, he would look over at the empty seat beside him and wonder where Mardai had gone. "Everyone knows where the caterpillar goes—it goes into the butterfly. But who knows where the butterfly goes?"

John began to think of Mardai as a butterfly of the universe. "I would pray that her journey be a joyous one and that she would find some way of letting me know that she was fine in her world."

One day as he was thinking such thoughts, he pulled up at a red traffic light behind another car. As he waited for the light to change, he silently said,

"Mardai, if you are around, please let me know. I would feel much better."

The light changed, and as the car in front of him pulled away, John saw on the license plate MEH 711. *MEH* were Mardai's initials and *711* represented July 11, the date she died.

A calmness and a joy welled up within him, and John heard a voice in his mind say, *"I am with you."*

After that experience, John told us, many others were to follow. "They seemed to come at times when I most needed reassurance about life and its direction," he said.

"After a while it became commonplace to see Mardai's initials on billboards and license plates, and I would look at a clock for no apparent reason only to find that the time would be 7:11. I became so used to seeing such signs as these that as time went on, I began to ignore many of them for fear of becoming too dependent upon them. Yet I always found a strange, beautiful comfort in such reminders."

Sometimes, John told us, he would be thinking of Mardai, and at that very moment a song that she loved would play on the radio.

"It was as if she were saying, 'I just want you to know that I love you and am with you whenever you think of me.' "

John has often stated that it is his belief that our loved ones continue their lives in an area just beyond our physical senses.

"I feel that they reach out to help, to guide, to comfort us in a most loving way. There may be signs of their presence all around us if we but look more closely and listen more attentively."

John also believes that the bonds that exist between

those who love deeply are stronger than death itself. Perhaps, he commented, love is the greatest reality in the universe.

"Although I no longer see Mardai in her physical body nor hear her lovely musical voice, I know that she exists—and I have a notion that she is closer than I think," he said.

"Sometimes I meet her in my dreams, and at other times I feel as if she speaks to me in the quietness between my thoughts."

John's beloved father died a few years before Mardai went home to Heaven, and he continues to feel his presence as well. "Those whom we love will always be with us," he said.

John shared with us that sometimes, on a beautiful, cloudless, starry night, he sits on his porch and looks into the woods behind his house. That is when he often hears the voices of his loved ones in his heart and in the very whispering of the wind through the leaves.

He looks up into the sky and spots the second star on the belt of Orion the Hunter, and he can see Mardai smiling at him.

As he looks and listens in the quietness of his soul, John can hear Mardai say

> I have always loved you, and you will always be my joy, my pride, and my prince. I have known you from eternity, and I will be with you again one day, even as we used to be together in the life you now live.
>
> When you are sad, I feel your sorrow. When you are happy, I rejoice with you.
>
> You must finish the work that you came to

Earth to do. Time will lighten the heaviness in your heart, and then I will be able to communicate with you more clearly.

I watch over you and our children, and I know how difficult it can get at times. But you are not alone. There are others here who also watch and help. Our work on Earth was finished, so we had to go on. We are all brilliantly alive.

I visit you sometimes in your dreams. The veil that separates your reality from mine is very thin. In your quiet moments, you sometimes pierce that veil and obtain a glimpse of our reality. It is gloriously exciting where we are—and one day we shall all meet again. You have much to do before you join us, but know that we will be with you every step of the way.

My dearest John, I have always loved you, and I will love you through the Halls of Forever. When you are ready to come here, I will be the first one waiting to greet you. Live life joyously and fully.

John told us that he does strive to live life as gloriously and as fully as he can. His son and daughter are happy, and he continues to rebuild a good part of himself.

"I know that our loved ones are always with us," he said. "I know that love prevails over everything—even over death. Listen to your heart, and you will hear the sounds of eternity. You will feel the ties that bind you in an everlasting love. May your journey home to Heaven be a joyous one."

Her Deceased Husband Appeared in a Dream to Lead Her to the Hidden Mortgage Payment

In the March 1957 issue of *Fate* magazine, Mrs. Minnie Harris told how the spirit of her deceased husband returned to pay the mortgage.

The Harris family was having a tough go of things during that hard Depression year of 1932. To make matters worse, a money lender whom they had nicknamed "Old Skinflint" was demanding repayment of a loan.

John Harris had just returned from town where he had withdrawn ten crisp new one-hundred-dollar bills to pay off Old Skinflint. He was seeing to the livestock when something spooked their mule and set it to kicking wildly, knocking over pails of feed, smashing the boards of its stall. Then, tragically, one of those panicked hooves caught John in the side of his head and crushed his skull.

In the sudden tragedy of her husband's death, Minnie had forgotten all about the money for Old Skinflint until the undertaker came to remove John's body. When she went through his clothing, she was shocked to discover that the envelope containing the ten bills was missing.

Minnie's mother arrived, and the two women went over John's clothing inch by inch. When that sad task was completed, the two women searched the house, the closets, the cupboards, the dressers—even the feed bins in the barn. Minnie had complete trust in the neighbor who had helped her with John's body. She knew that their friend would not have stolen the money.

Only one explanation remained: John had hidden the money just before the flailing hooves of the mule had crushed his skull. Old Skinflint's note was due in a couple of weeks, and he would not hesitate to foreclose and take the Harris home and farm unless the money was forthcoming.

A week before the note was to be paid, Minnie received a curt, unsympathetic reminder from the moneylender that he most certainly expected the money on the appointed date, regardless of the unexpected death in the Harris family.

In frenzied desperation, Minnie looked under sacks of mash, beneath the straw in the hens' nests, in tool chests—but she could not find the one thousand dollars that would keep the moneylender from foreclosing on their farm.

Three days before the note was due, Minnie had a dream in which John came to her and tried to tell her where he had hidden the money.

"But he couldn't speak because of his broken jaw." Minnie remembered her anguish. She screamed at him as he sadly turned to leave the room. She begged him to come back and tell her where he had hidden the money.

In spite of her desperate cries, John faded into mist, and Minnie came awake in cold perspiration to find her mother shaking her.

Minnie was a bit resentful that her mother had awakened her. She was convinced that the spirit of her dead husband would have given her some clue to the whereabouts of the money if she had only been allowed to continue to dream.

The next night, Minnie sat up in bed until very late, reading the Bible, searching out all the verses that dealt with dreams and visions. When at last she fell into a fitful sleep, she saw John appear in the doorway of the bedroom and motion to her to follow him.

Minnie begged him to wait for her to get out of bed—then she was once again abruptly awakened by her mother.

On the third night, Minnie went to bed with the conviction that John would once again return and attempt to communicate with her. She pleaded with her mother not to awaken her no matter how loudly she might cry out in her sleep.

It was nearly dawn when the image of her husband appeared at her bedside. He took her hand and led her to the kitchen door.

Minnie saw that it had snowed during the night and the rising sun was painting a rosy glow over the barnyards and fields. John pointed to his footprints leading from the front door of the house to the big haystack at the corner of the barn.

Then he was transformed into a fleecy cloud, and his image melted away like a vapor before the rays of the morning sun.

Minnie found herself back in bed, the first light of dawn shining across her face. She hastily pulled on a robe and ran to the kitchen door.

The newly fallen snow was smooth and unmarked, but her memory of the dream-vision was clear. In her mind she could still see her husband's footprints zigzagging through the snow toward the haystack.

She paused only to slip on a coat and a pair of overshoes. She found the money in a tobacco tin hidden deep under the hay.

How to Recall a Dream of Spirit Communication

There may be occasions when you awaken in the night and know that you have been receiving dream teachings or spirit communication. You may feel distressed when you become aware that you seem unable to retain the full importance and meaning of the dream.

Do not permit yourself to become angry or frustrated with yourself for having permitted the lesson or communication to become lost to your waking consciousness.

Call out to your angelic spirit guide to help you to recover the full understanding of the message that an intelligence from the heavenly realm wishes you to know. Ask that when you return to sleep and to dream, you will receive the full knowledge of the dream-vision that has just been entrusted to you.

If you should not be able to recall the lesson or the communication on that particular evening, awaken the next morning with the resolution that you shall reclaim it on the next night. Prepare yourself during the day with transmissions of love to the spirit of the loved one who attempted communication during your dream. Then, just before falling asleep, call upon the loving energy of your angelic spirit guide to send its heightened awareness into your psyche.

Charge yourself with the task of bringing back anew the vital substance of the dream messages and teaching. Ask your guide to stand watch over you so that only good may enter your reception of the spirit message.

Seeking a Dream or Vision of Spirit Contact

Dreams of spirit teachings and communication are best achieved by entering the silence of meditation before retiring for the evening.

When you truly enter the higher levels of meditation, you will feel and know that you have reached vibrations of cosmic light and love. You will sense around you the presence of great master teachers and highly evolved spirit beings.

The essence of this level of awareness is the power of the light and unconditional love. And pulsating deep within such light and love is the essence of the Source of All That Is, God—the Father-Mother-Creator Spirit.

As you lie in your bed, take three comfortably deep breaths, holding each one for the count of three. Feel at one with the God-spark within you.

Visualize that God-spark igniting a golden flame of love within your heart chakra, which is one of the seven energy centers of the body in yogic and esoteric traditions.

In your mind, travel a ray of golden light from your heart to the Source of All That Is that exists in the heavenly realms. Understand that, as powerful and beautiful as the feeling of the Source is within you, your own spirit energy can only absorb an infinitesimal portion of its true majesty.

See yourself now sending a beam of your spirit essence to the Source that vibrates in the heavenly dimension.

Feel your spirit essence becoming closer to the Source. See points of violet light touching every part of your physical body as your spirit light begins to connect with the unconditional love of the heavenly realm.

Begin to sense strongly a closeness, a unity with the love within the heavenly dimension.

Concentrate for a moment on making your body as still as possible. Direct your attention to the Source and focus on the flame within your heart chakra. See clearly the ray of light that you are transmitting to the Source in the heavenly realm.

Now feel your consciousness becoming one with the energy of love that emanates from the heavenly dimension and begin to request a dream or vision of spirit contact.

Eliminate mental awareness of the physical body as much as it is possible for you to do so. Understand that your physical body is a connection only to Earth, not to the heavenly dimension.

Visualize yourself holding forth open hands, as if in supplication.

Mentally affirm the following:

> *"Source of All That Is, Father-Mother-Creator Spirit, if it is thy will and if it is for my good and my gaining, give unto me a dream or a vision of my beloved who dwell now in the heavenly realm. Grant me all that I need to know for my own higher awareness. And grant that my angelic spirit guide protects me from all negative entities here on Earth and between dimensions."*

On the day that you plan to request a particularly meaningful dream of spirit communication, it is wisest to make a direct plea for the experience immediately upon arising. Begin with your first consciousness and morning prayers to make a positive affirmation that your dream goal will be achieved.

From time to time through the day, quiet yourself, if even for a moment, and give recognition to the energy of the Father-Mother-Creator Spirit that exists both within you and without.

Visualize the God-Force as the powerful energy that ignites the golden flame of love that burns within your heart chakra. The more profoundly you can visualize this connection, the greater the results of your dream-vision.

Although intellectually we may understand that the Source of All That Is is an energy rather than some giant, anthropomorphic being, many people find that it does aid them in their visualizations and prayers to picture the God-Force as an individualized presence. While today many focus their prayers and contemplative thoughts upon an image of a glowing light being, perhaps the majority still prefer the image of a loving father or mother.

Since we humans seem to communicate more effectively with images that most resemble us, we always encourage our students to develop their own personal idea of a loving intelligence that is ready to answer their every call, that is willing to answer every request that is for their spirit's good and gaining.

Several times a day before seeking a profound dream or vision of spirit communication, give your attention to your personal image of the Source and send your love to its holy presence.

If you wish, you may verbalize your love and call the name of your angelic spirit guide or teacher to aid you in intensifying the transmission. Many students have said that they have actually felt a warmth touching the tops of their heads during their sending of love to the source.

You must remember that your motive for summoning a dream or vision of spirit communication must always be the result of a balanced desire. Your goal in achieving spirit contact should never be frivolous or based upon mere ego gratification.

When you awaken after receiving a dream or vision of spirit communication, hold the images in your mind as long as you can. It is important to do so in order to impress their energy upon earthplane reality.

Sometimes you may feel a compulsion to share the message of your dream or vision with others. Do so. In such a case, each time you share the messages with another person, you are likely to receive even more details of the communication. Your angelic spirit guide will advise you in this matter, and you will clearly know when a spirit message is intended only as your own individualized teaching and when it should not be described or shared with another.

CHAPTER TEN

Touched by Heaven's Light

G.G.S.: "This experience with the heavenly light and an angelic being happened to me when I was about nine years old. I'm forty-two now, but I remember it as clearly as if it had just occurred yesterday.

"I had lost my way in the forest around our vacation cabin in northern Minnesota. I was a cocky city kid who knew nothing about surviving the wild. I was just going to go for a walk by myself and get away from my nagging older sisters for a while. Pretty soon I thought, who needs the worn trailway. I'll branch off on my own.

"When I realized that I was lost, I became almost paralyzed with fear. All the warnings about wolves and bears came cascading down on me. Every chipmunk scampering in the leaves behind me became the paws of a grizzly bear thundering toward me, intent on swallowing me whole. It would soon be dark, and I figured that a pack of wolves would soon be closing in on me.

"As the sun was setting, I had enough common-sense to realize that I could really hurt myself wandering around in the woods after dark. I sat down and leaned back against a tree, closed my eyes, folded my hands, and really began to pray as I had never before prayed in my life. This was not some Sunday School memorized job—this was a real from-the-depths-of-despair kind of prayer.

"After a few minutes, I opened my eyes because of the incredibly bright light that was going right through my eyelids. I thought the small tree off to my right was on fire, and I jumped to my feet. Then I saw that the light was situated just in front of the tree and that it was not fire at all.

"A voice from the midst of the brilliant light called my name and told me that it was my guardian angel surrounded by God's light from Heaven. It told me not to be afraid and to stay where I was. It said it would stay with me until help came. Somehow I knew that the being speaking from within the light had always been with me and would always be around somewhere keeping an eye on me. I thought also of the story of Moses and the burning bush and the voice of the Angel of the Lord that spoke to him.

"Eventually, feeling calm, peaceful, and protected, I fell asleep. When I woke up, powerful flashlight beams were slicing through the darkness toward me. I called out, and pretty soon my father and half a dozen other men were standing around me, asking if I was all right. They said that they had found me because of the fire that I had started. They were really confused when they could find no trace of a campfire—no ashes, no soot, no burned spot, nothing."

The Blinding Light of Heavenly Illumination

The medium Deon Frey, whom we met in an earlier chapter, remembered sitting in her room one night, having been in meditation for quite some time, when all of a sudden the whole room was filled with a brilliant light.

Deon said that the light appeared to be emanating from one corner of the room, and it seemed as though she could almost make out a form within it. "The color was indescribable. It had edges of violet hue, but it was crystal white—or mother of pearl—and so bright that it could almost blind me. I had a feeling of Oneness with it, a unity. It was like being one with everything at once. I was just suddenly drawn into it. Although I heard no voice, I was filled with a knowing quality. I just knew things. It wasn't as if the light were speaking to me, but it seemed to give me direct answers to a lot of questions in my mind."

The Heavenly Light of Cosmic Consciousness

Many revelators and those who have experienced spirit visitations have mentioned a brilliant light that surrounded them at the onset of their experience. Such accounts immediately bring to mind the story of Saul, on the road to Damascus, who encounters the brilliant light that blinds him and transforms him into the apostle of Jesus we know as St. Paul.

Almost without exception, those who have experienced the sudden flooding of the brilliant heavenly light have stated that their sense of time was obscured, and while in this state of Eternal Now, they realized a sense of unity with all things.

Psychic sensitive Betty Allen told us that once, while she was seated at her typewriter, "I was bathed in a golden light. It was just like being flooded with love, and I felt like I was sitting in a beam of light.

"I realized that there was a remarkable world beyond my ordinary senses. I realized that I was a part of it, and I knew that I wasn't really struggling alone."

In his classic work, *Cosmic Consciousness,* Dr. Richard Maurice Bucke was not so presumptuous to include himself in the company of the illumined individuals whose lives he examined in his book, but he did relate—in the third person—an account of his own experience with the heavenly light.

It was, he tells us, in the early spring of his thirty-sixth year. He and two friends had spent the evening reading inspirational words from Wordsworth, Keats, and Browning, with a special emphasis on Whitman. As he rode in a hansom cab, his mind remained deeply under the influence of the "ideas, images and emotions called up by the reading and talk of the evening." He recalled that he was in a state of quiet, "almost passive enjoyment."

> All at once, without warning of any kind, he found himself wrapped around as it were by a flame-colored cloud. For an instant he thought of

fire . . . the next he knew that the light was within himself. Directly afterwards came upon him a sense of exultation, of immense joyousness accompanied or immediately followed by an intellectual illumination quite impossible to describe. Into his brain streamed one momentary lightning-flash of the Brahmic Splendor which has ever since lightened his life; upon his heart fell one drop of Brahmic Bliss, leaving thenceforward for always an aftertaste of Heaven. . . . He saw and knew that the soul of man is immortal, that the universe is so built and ordered that without any peradventure all things work together for good of each and all, that the foundation principle of this world is what we call love and that the happiness of everyone is in the long run absolutely certain. He claims that he learned more within the few seconds during which the illumination lasted than in previous months or even years of study, and that he learned much that no study could ever have taught.

His Father Appeared in Brilliant Light with an Angel Escort

R.T.W.: "I was awakened one night by a bright light shining at the foot of our bed. My wife was sound asleep, and somehow I knew that I would not be able to awaken her.

"I had to squint into the light, it was so bright. Then I saw that a human shape was beginning to form within the light. I assumed that it had to be an angel to be surrounded by such brilliant illumination. After a few more moments, another form became visible, and I was astonished to see my father standing side by side with an angelic being.

"My father told me not to be frightened, but he had asked permission to visit me to encourage me to return to college and complete the degree that I had abandoned six years before. He also asked me to be more attentive toward my stepmother and to help her make the adjustment over his sudden passing.

"When I asked Dad about the angel escort, his answer was simple: 'I was afraid I couldn't get down to Earth and back to Heaven by myself.' "

Her Spirit Manifested in the Light to Say Good-bye

For nearly two weeks after her stroke, Mrs. M. M. struggled to continue her life on the earthplane.

"My mother-in-law had always been a vigorous person, healthy and spry, until she suffered a stroke in her mid-eighties," Elaine M. said. "As she lay in a bed in the intensive care unit of the hospital, moving back and forth over a narrow line between life and death, my husband, Tom, and her other children were fearful that the stroke might leave her paralyzed or otherwise physically impaired.

"While they wanted their mother with them forever, they were stricken with even greater grief when they considered a scenario that would see their once active mother spending her last days as a virtual vegetable on a life support system."

On the fourteenth day after her stroke, the doctors informed the family that their mother was doing so well that she could be transferred from the intensive care unit into a regular room and that she could begin to receive visits from her friends.

Elaine remembered that Tom felt as though their prayers had been answered. They would have Mother M. with them for a while longer, and she would soon be able to resume her normal pattern of activities.

They had a quiet dinner at home with their two small sons, then decided to retire early for some much-needed sleep.

Elaine said that she was still operating on too much adrenaline to drop right off to sleep, so she decided that she would read in bed until she got drowsy enough to turn out the light. Tom was used to her reading in bed, so the illumination did not bother him.

"I had not read for more than fifteen or twenty minutes when I heard the two boys begin to shout and the older of our sons cry out that there was a weird light in the hallway," Elaine said.

Tom was immediately awake and the two of them watched in astonishment as a brightly glowing ball of orange-colored light, about the size of a baseball, moved up and down the hallway in a zigzag pattern. The light hovered over the heads of the two boys, then moved on to bob above Tom and Elaine.

The light became so bright that none of them could look directly at it—then it just disappeared.

"Oh, my God, Elaine," Tom said, his voice unsteady. "I know that Mama has just been here to give us a sign that she has died."

Elaine put her arm around her husband's shoulders to comfort him. Although they had just left a much-improved Mrs. M. at the hospital, she felt on a soul-level of awareness that Tom's impression of the mysterious glowing light was accurate.

"When I called the hospital, we learned that Mother had slipped into a coma just a few minutes before the manifestation of the glowing ball of light in our home," Elaine said. "She died only a few minutes later.

"Tom and I will always feel that somehow Mother was able to project her spiritual love into a glowing ball of light so she could visit us to say a last farewell before she left on the path to Heaven's eternal light."

His Mother's Illuminated Spirit Attempted to Warn Him

Two weeks before she died, Lorna Cassidy had told her son Barry about her vision of Heaven: "I saw myself walking toward beautiful green rolling meadows with the loveliest flowers imaginable. I was wearing a white, flowing robe, and I was following a path that I knew would lead me to Heaven."

The night after her funeral, Barry sat down in the old recliner chair in the living room to rest a moment before going home to his own apartment. He had just seen his father off to bed, and he decided to lean back and allow the memories of Mom to come forth unchecked.

He remembered how frightened he had been to leave her side and start his first day at school. His memory banks flooded his brain with rapidly fleeting images of bruised knees that needed Mommy's kiss so they wouldn't hurt, of putting a tooth under a pillow for the Tooth Fairy, of the best oatmeal-raisin cookies in the world.

Barry felt the tears coming as he spoke aloud to the empty room: "Oh, Mom, did you know that you were going to die? Did you know that your time to move up to a higher dimension was almost upon you?"

Yes!

The familiar voice that answered his plaintive query made his spine go rigid. "Mom?"

"That's when I saw the spirit of my mother," Barry said. "She was surrounded by this brilliant light, and she appeared as a transparent figure. She told me that she was now walking on those same green, rolling meadows that she had seen in her dream. She went on to say that where she was now, there was no pain, no dissension, no hatred—only peace, love, and tranquility.

"And then Mom said that if I wanted some peace and contentment in my earth life, I had better listen to what she had to say."

The brightly glowing image of his mother then proceeded to warn Barry not to go ahead with his divorce from his present wife in order to marry his current lover. If he should not heed her advice and if he should marry his lover, he would undergo a learning experience of utter misery.

"What is more," the spirit warned him, "she will treat you terribly, and she will divorce you within three years—and she will be merciless in the settlement."

Barry said that his mother's spirit form remained with him for at least five minutes before it faded from his sight.

To his everlasting regret, Barry managed to convince himself that the spirit visitation of his mother had only been a troubled dream brought about by grief and emotional stress.

"Mom's advice from the spirit world proved to be totally accurate. I followed through with my divorce and married my lover, who brought me to new depths of anguish and despair. We were divorced after three years of a hellishly miserable marriage."

The Heavenly Light of Her Angel Guide Returned Her to Life

Forty-year-old artist Linda Johnston was traveling on a Mississippi highway when her pickup truck was hit from behind. Her body crashed through the windshield, struck a roadside sign, then landed hard on the sun-baked pavement. In the process, she broke both legs, shattered her pelvis and right hip, and compressed three of her vertebrae.

It was during the time that her body was airborne that she knew she'd died. Linda felt her body rise and move through a spinning tunnel. She felt nothing, but she heard the last of her breath leave her body as it struck the pavement.

As she moved through the tunnel, she could see a door from which bright light issued, and she could also hear the sound of choral music. Then she saw something so incredibly bright that it took her a moment to recognize the same angel that had pulled her from in front of a moving car when she was eight and that had stood at her bedside at age twelve when she underwent an emergency appendectomy.

Linda said the angel always appears with no wings or halo and with a hood that covers its head. The glow that surrounds the being's form is so bright that she has never been able to distinguish the eyes or mouth of the angel, but she can make out the hands and arms. The brilliant illumination that seems to emanate from the angelic spirit guide itself is comprised of a white light with flecks of blue and yellow.

And always, Linda said, the angelic being's voice was very calm, distinct, soothing, and assuring. Upon hearing its words of comfort, Linda felt surrounded by love and all fear left her.

The angel pointed to its left, and Linda looked down to perceive her own lifeless body. She was lying on her back, and there was blood all around her.

It was at that point in the experience that the angel asked her if she was ready. No, she answered. She had a husband and two small kids. She had too much to do. She had to go back.

The angelic light being nodded its head, and Linda was next aware of everything going black. But the darkness lasted for only a brief period of time, and when she looked up, she saw her husband and a number of medical personnel. Her request had been granted. She was alive.

Linda Johnston spent the next fifty-eight days in the hospital. The light being visited her again four times while her shattered body was mending.

"Things were touch and go," she said, "but my angel told me not to worry. I later spent five months in a wheelchair, and the doctors told me that I would never walk again. But now I can walk with a cane. My recovery was a miracle, but then, I believe in miracles."

Linda now paints pictures based on her experiences with the brilliant angel of light.

God's Everlasting Love Shines Brighter than Gold

P.B. (mother of five, grandmother of seven, happily married for twenty-seven years): "Around the age of six or seven, I felt alone and very different from the others in my family. I was an avid reader, and I began to turn inward, imagining that I was carrying on long conversations with Jesus. One day I asked my image of Jesus, 'If gold is the root of all evil, why are the streets of Heaven paved with gold?'

"Shortly after I had posed this question, I had a series of nightly dreams or out-of-body experiences. I'm not certain which, for I suffered from asthma, and I would quit breathing for short periods of time during the night.

"In this series of dreams, on the first night, I went into a very dark tunnel. It was pitch black, and I woke up frightened and in a sweat.

"The second night, I went back into the tunnel, and it seemed not quite so dark and less frightening. It felt like I walked forever in the tunnel, but I never seemed to get anywhere.

"The third and fourth nights, just as soon as I walked into the tunnel, I zoomed up to where I had left off the night before. When I woke up, it was all still a little frightening to me, as I had never had the same dream so many nights in a row.

"On the fifth night, I saw a bright light and went toward—and into—the light. The first thing that struck me was this euphoric unconditional love and a sense of completeness that I was where I belonged.

"I sensed, more than I saw, beings crowding each other to get a look at me. I felt that these beings were family that had passed before me. I think they didn't wish to frighten me by coming too close.

"I passed through an area white and foggy, and I was met by an elder being with a white beard, who was dressed in a white, flowing robe. To my understanding, I assumed he must be St. Peter.

"He took me to a being standing to the right of a large gate. Behind this being was a beautiful green tree, possibly the Tree of Life! This being was radiating such a brilliant light that I could not see his face, but I knew that it was Jesus.

"Jesus let me know that I was not going to go through the gate, but I was to go with him. We floated to the top of a high hill. We looked down upon a very old-looking city with a temple with a golden dome in its center. The temple was shining very brightly, but surrounding the entire city was a beautiful, soft, peaceful, loving, yellowish-white, *gold* light that I knew emanated from God.

"Even though I knew my question about why the streets of Heaven seemed to be made of gold had been answered, I still wasn't terribly clear about such matters.

"It was a good thirty years later that I saw this very city on television from the very same angle. I was watching a documentary on Jerusalem and the camera was set above the ancient city looking down.

"As I remembered my dream, it came to me that Jesus had been telling me that the Light of God was brighter and more precious than all the gold in the world. God could outshine all earthly illumination and his light was worth more in our lives than mere gold."

God Is Light

Mrs. Jo Peters of Honolulu told us of a most interesting experience that her little daughter Andrea underwent in December 1971. In a matter of a few minutes, the girl came down with a fever of 106 degrees.

Jo, who had a background in nursing, psychology, and nutrition, quickly started covering Andrea with ice packs and gave her vitamin C.

"During the evening it would get down to one-oh-four," Jo said, "then it would go back up to one-oh-six. The next morning the fever was nearly gone, because I kept her in cold water."

Later that morning, Jo was holding Andrea in her arms, relieved that her fever had gone.

"All of a sudden she began to laugh, then she made a horrible face and breathed in forcefully," Jo said. "Andrea was looking up at the ceiling, and she said that she was seeing the most beautiful color. She saw the color blue, then she screamed horribly. After this terrible scream, she began to smile again and said, 'I see Jesus on the Cross.' "

Jo explained that while her children knew about Jesus, they had never emphasized the image of Jesus on the Cross.

"Andrea said that He was looking at the little animals and talking to them. Then she said, "The Light is sooo beautiful. It is gold and it is yellow. I see God. Oh, Mommy, God is Light! *God is Light!*"

Jo Peters said that neither she nor her husband had ever taught Andrea such a thing.

"I have always said that God is Love. But Andrea kept repeating over and over again that God is Light and that He is so beautiful. She is not a dramatic child and never talks expressively."

Then, all of a sudden, Andrea reached out for her and said, "Mommy, I don't want to go there, yet! Please keep me here!"

Jo said that her daughter hugged her very tightly, and then seemed to return to full conscious awareness. Whatever it had been, the experience was ended.

"I talked to her later, and she remembered the experience clearly," Jo said. "But each day it would fade away a bit in her memory. Now when I talk about it, she seems to have forgotten much of what happened. I think Andrea came close to passing on to the Next World."

When Spirit Light Meets God Light, Only Goodness Can Result

Al G. Manning is a 1950 magna cum laude graduate from UCLA with a degree in business administration. He has served in an executive capacity at two aerospace manufacturing and research firms. Al was in his middle twenties when he received a visitation from Heaven's divine light.

"It was as if a searchlight were turned on directly above my head and was shining down on me," he told us. "I was in the middle of this shaft of light. I could feel the warmth and the love. A voice spoke to me from within the stream of light, but I was not allowed to bring back any messages from the experience at that time—although for some time after the illumination, I did have the power of levitation.

"I tremendously misinterpreted the experience in the beginning," Al admitted. "I had the idea that all I had to do next was to do a little research and fill the Hollywood Bowl with a levitation demonstration. Ridiculous, but I was young. What can I say?

"But the experience with the Light did start me seriously seeking, and the inspiration of those moments has stayed with me all these years. I have touched the Light many times."

It is Al's position that the individual mystical experience is the common denominator of all religious expression and that without having touched the Divine Fire, the Light, whatever one wishes to call it, worship is only of the mind.

"Worship becomes of the whole being only when we touch the Light and feel the response of love," he said. "I sit down at my altar each morning and evening. The first thing I do is to reach up to my highest concept of God, to something greater than I, and I *expect* a response.

"No, I do not always find the room brightened and find myself bathed in light, but there is always a response. There is a *feeling,* which I do not believe is totally subjective. The energy often feels like someone shot some electricity on my head. The descriptions are difficult, because we don't have words in our language to describe them well."

Al stressed that every time he reaches for the Light—whether he is at a big business conference at somebody's board of directors meeting or driving down the street or sitting comfortably at his home altar—he expects a response.

"If I don't get one, I stop everything until I do,

because to be that far out of tune would be just chaos to me," Al explained. "Before I leave my altar, I reattune myself with the Light and send it before me."

Al said that the affirmation that he used varied somewhat, but basically, it is this:

> Now I direct the Light to go before me to make the path easy and the way straight. May the Light bring upliftment, inspiration, effectiveness, enthusiasm, and joy to everyone who comes close to my aura. I am Light going to meet Light—and only goodness can result.

In Al G. Manning's opinion, his feeling of the Light is the same as the feeding of the *mana* to the High Self by the Kahuna priests. It compares to the *samadhi* of the Hindu, the *satori* of the Zen Buddhist, or to the *Holy Spirit* of the Christian.

In his *Varieties of Religious Experience,* William James quotes Vivekananda's work on Raja Yoga, published in London in 1896, in regard to the mystical illumination known as *samadhi:*

> All the different steps in yoga are intended to bring us scientifically to the superconscious state or *Samadhi*. . . . Just as unconscious work is beneath consciousness, so there is another work which is above consciousness, and which also is not accompanied with the feeling of egoism. . . . There is no feeling of *I*, and yet the mind works desireless, free from restlessness, objectless, bodiless. Then the Truth shines in its full effulgence, and we know ourselves . . . for what we truly

> are, free, immortal, omnipotent, loosed from the finite . . . and identical with the Atman or Universal Soul.

In his *An Introduction to Zen Buddhism,* Daisetz T. Suzuki quotes Professor Nukariya's description of *satori,* the state of illumination attained by reaching a higher level of consciousness.

> It is the godly light, the inner heaven, the key to all the treasures of the mind, the focal point of thought and consciousness, the source of power and might, the seat of goodness, of justice, of sympathy, of the measure of all things. When this inmost knowledge is fully awakened, we are able to understand that each of us is identical in spirit, in being, and in nature with universal life.

A Majestic Light Being Taught Her the True Meaning of Prayer

M.J.S. wrote to tell us that she was in the worst state of anxiety and depression that she could ever recall. When she went to bed one September night, she wondered how much more she could possibly endure—and why so many burdens were being placed upon her. In addition, she wondered, as perhaps so many do, why God was picking on her. "Not that I hadn't been forewarned since childhood of God's testy disposition," M.J.S. said.

"God, as I had been taught by those in charge of my religious thought, was a distant, imposing male figure who was filled with vengeance and wrath. He was retired and living in Heaven where things were more to his liking. His only recorded messages contained barbed threats of annihilation, following his judgment on us. God seemed to me to be ancient, cranky, jealous, fierce, and demanding. I knew that God must have judged me guilty of something, but I couldn't figure out just what it was that I had done to so arouse his wrath against me."

Then, in the early, pre-dawn hours, M.J.S. was awakened by a bright light shining in her eyes. "When I opened my eyes, I saw that a sphere of light about four feet in diameter was floating in my room, about six to eight feet from my bed," she said. "It looked like luminous, wispy fog, and it was swirling within itself, very gently rotating from my right to left.

"I was immediately filled with a sense of great peace and tranquility. All of my troubled feelings immediately vanished. And then this sphere of light spoke to me."

A clear, soft male voice asked M.J.S. if she were afraid. After taking some moments to collect her mental equilibrium, she told the light being that she felt no fear.

"I was nearly overcome because he was radiating something of unspeakable beauty," she said. "I felt his light envelop me and flow through me. It was a light which was not limited by boundaries of physical matter. It was a light of great gentleness and compassion beyond words.

"I do not have the ability to express all that the Light Being brought me to feel. I was laughing and also crying. I wanted to jump up and down, yet I lay still as I could, not taking my eyes off of him. He was simply magnificent."

The Light Being said that he wished to speak of spirituality. He told M.J.S. that in terms of collective humanity, humans remained in a very primitive state. "It is time for you to evolve spiritually," he told her. "Your concept of God is primitive, and you don't even know how to pray."

M.J.S. objected, stating that many humans do quite a bit of praying.

The Light Being corrected her. "What you call prayer is more like songs of woe or the offering of excuses for your actions. You beseech God not to punish you for your misdeeds—or you beg to be forgiven for actions which you have every intention of repeating."

The brilliantly glowing entity said that begging for forgiveness was something that humans did only to assuage their personal feelings of guilt or shame. "It would be far better simply to live your lives in such a way that you will not feel the need to be asking forgiveness."

The Light Being then went on to state that humans were neither judged nor punished by the Creator Spirit. "You are loved unconditionally," he said. "The Creator Spirit is not filled with wrath and vengence as so many Earth religions have taught, but that which you call 'God' is pure love beyond comprehension. What you humans have mistaken as punishment from your fierce concept of God is nothing more than the effects of your own actions."

M.J.S. said that the Light Being placed great importance on our need to begin to understand the relationship between cause and effect, because it was through this understanding that human spiritual evolution will occur.

"When you pray," the being told M.J.S., "pray with joy. Prayer is a love song, and you have forgotten how to sing it."

At this point, M.J.S. said, the Light Being began to glow brightly. "And the light coming from him went through me—and I experienced unconditional love for the first time in my life. It was searing—and exquisite. It was as though I was being bathed in a light which entered every cell in my body and filled everything it passed through with love.

"As the light washed through me, it removed all traces of fear, anxiety, guilt, and loneliness, and I felt clean and profoundly at peace. I began vibrating, as though to the sound of light, and I suddenly became aware of each cell in my body and I felt love and compassion for them."

Open yourself and fill yourself with what comes from me!

M.J.S. did as the Light Being bade her. "Incredibly, as I allowed more of his light energy to wash through me, I felt filled—but knew that I could never truly be filled," she said. "And although he was filling my being with this incredible love, his own brilliant light was not diminishing.

"When I saw this, I knew the light was coming from a source that was endless and was equally available for all people. I knew that I was not being singled out. This same love was available for all of creation.

"And this realization only added to my elation, because there was great comfort in discovering that I was not a single entity: I was a part of all creation. I was feeling joy, relief, peace, love beyond any level I ever thought the human body was capable of achieving."

The Light Being startled M.J.S. when he suddenly asked her to think of her worst enemy. She thought such a request to be an odd one for the moment, but she did as she was asked.

"Now, project that with which you are filled toward your enemy," the Light Being commanded.

"I did this," M.J.S. said, "and saw my projection leave in the form of light. But as I was projecting this light, the illumination within me did not flicker or grow dim. I was still shining."

And then, she declared, something beautiful happened.

"As the energy that I was projecting engulfed that old enemy and flowed through her, there was an explosion of light like the reflection of the sun in a mirror, and all that I had sent out to her suddenly returned to me.

"I was already filled and glowing, but now what I had sent out had also come back and filled me even further. Again, there was no way for me to express this sensation of wild joy. I wanted to sing with the light, although I had no breath."

M.J.S. was aware that she was sitting on the edge of her bed, tears running down her face, a smile on her lips. Slowly, her breath returned.

The Light Being waited in silence as M.J.S. recovered from an experience that she will remember and follow forever. Then, very quietly, he said, "You have just prayed for the first time in your life. Teach others how to pray."

CHAPTER ELEVEN

Heavenly Memories of Life Before Life

Share the thrill of spirit-awakening as Robert Brown, author of *The Paths of Awakening*, recounts the ending of a revelatory dream, "monumental in length and complexity," for our research.

> I cried from a depth I had never known before. I cried a tribute to the releasing of ignorance. As I looked into the eyes of each person, the years and wrinkles fell away. Before me stood the people I had known in past lives. Each brilliant face smiled a little smile as I witnessed our history through their eyes.
>
> Lovers, betrayers, teachers, gurus . . . they were all there, every one of them. They radiated such

love that I simply stood and cried . . . and loved them back.

All the pieces of the puzzle came together, and I understood it. I understood it all. . . . I was aglow with a wholeness and depth of love that cannot be expressed.

I witnessed the veil of time lifted between events and watched them pool to form the state I have attained in my present life. I understand now where it is we are going, why there is pain and sorrow, why we believe in yesterday, today, and tomorrow. That I am being allowed to retain this knowledge as of late is wonderful.

What is most exciting is the fact that this same awakening lies within each of us. There never, ever could have been a better place or design in which to hide this knowledge than within ourselves. Where to begin is the hardest. The ending we already know. It's just a matter of remembering.

Centuries of Searching Reveal There Is More than One Lifetime

Author and teacher Leia Stinnett states in *Death: Our Portal to Life* that our souls live more than one lifetime. "We have to accept through all of our searching that there is more than just this experience. Our soul began as an essence of light from the Godhead, and in its creation was offered opportunities to continue to learn and to grow, to evolve as a soul, consciously in this world and in others.

"As a soul passes from this experience and returns to the world of spirit, it continues its lessons there. . . . An advanced soul can spend its time between lifetimes serving others, as a spirit guide, teacher, or as an angelic messenger."

A Clear Memory of Angrily Waking in a Baby's Body

G.M.M.: "Although my report to you may seem strange, I swear that it is true. When I was eighteen months old, I have a clear memory of 'waking up' one day feeling disoriented. I was crawling, dragging myself around on the ground, and I thought, 'How stupid!' So I stood up and began walking.

"A few days later, I had to sneak out of the house because this lady, my mother, would not let me go. It seemed to me that she was holding me prisoner for some reason. I remember this all very clearly, sneaking out the kitchen door when her back was turned.

"But I couldn't recognize where I was. There was an elementary school across the street. I could see San Diego Bay. The sky was a deep blue with powder puff white clouds scattered across it. For a minute or two I thought how nice everything looked—and then I realized, *I was back on Earth!*

"This made me very upset, and I started yelling at someone I could see above me, though I can't remember his image today. 'Why am I back? You promised me!'

"And I remember him telling me that I had misunderstood, I *had* to come back. And I kept arguing and yelling, *'No!'*

"Then, at one point, I looked down at my body, and that was when I really realized that I was a baby.

I looked up at him and started yelling again: " '*What am I doing here in this baby's body—and with diapers? No! No! You promised me!*'

"While I am carrying on this conversation in perfect English with this being, my mother inside the house is hearing me crying and screaming my head off so loud that she is thinking that something bad is happening to me. When I heard this 'lady' calling out for me, I really started begging the being to take me back with him. I pleaded with him. I didn't want to start over as a baby again. But it was a no-go.

"And as my mother found me, I turned and yelled at the being, 'And just who is this woman?' Then she picked me up and carried me back inside.

"I can remember the being giving me the final word, but I can't recall exactly what he said. Just that I was stuck back here on Earth."

G.M.M. did retain a number of paranormal abilities from his sojourn between lives. He expressed precognition and clairvoyance, and his ability to see the near future once saved his older brother's life. Then, when he was around twenty-six years old, these talents left him. He continues to study his dreams for patterns that may explain his unusual life experiences.

A Christian Pastor Has a Memory Suggestive of Reincarnation

Dr. P.B.C.: "Even though I am a Born-Again Christian as well as a minister, I try not to be judgmental. I personally believe that not all 'psychic' abilities are from the devil or are evil. What most Christians seem to forget is that the Bible speaks of the 'gifts of the Spirit.' Who are we to put limits on what these gifts might be?

"When I was thirteen years old, I had a near-death experience. All through my teenage years, as well as my twenties and most of my thirties (I am now thirty-nine), I was experiencing things that I could not explain and was frightened to share them with anyone for fear of being accused of being possessed or being labeled as crazy."

The conscientious, open-minded pastor then shared an experience that could be considered suggestive of a past-life recall.

"I was around eight or nine, home alone watching a western movie on the television. The movie was about half over when there was mention of a town having an outbreak of scarlet fever.

"At that age, I had no idea of what the disease was; however, as soon as the words were spoken, everything around me changed. I found myself in an old-fashioned bedroom. As I looked around the room, I saw a bed, and in it a little girl of about ten years of age. I also noticed that the curtains were closed, allowing in only a minimal amount of light.

"Covering the girl in bed was a large quilt. Somehow I knew that the quilt had been made especially for her and that the time period was somewhere around the middle 1800s.

"The girl had light-colored hair cut up around her shoulders and parted down the center with bangs over her forehead. She was wearing an old-fashioned, long-sleeved nightshirt, off-white or gray in color. Her head and shoulders were propped up by several pillows.

"As I was looking at her, it occurred to me that although I was seeing the bed with her in it from my outside perspective, *I was also, somehow, viewing everything through her eyes.* And everything seen through her eyes was fuzzy or blurred around the edges.

"I could also feel what the girl was experiencing. I could feel that she was hot, very hot. She was sweating so profusely that the nightshirt and bedding were sticking to her body, making her even more uncomfortable.

"All at once, everything went black. I no longer felt so very hot. And then I was looking at the television again. The movie had ended and the credits were scrolling across the screen.

"Ever since that time, whenever I hear the words 'scarlet fever,' the experience, in varying degrees, happens all over again. I would usually forget about it until it would be 'triggered' once again. When it occurred again in August 1996, something told me that it was time to write it down. In other experiences I have had involving the same girl, I have learned that her name is Dorothy, and that her mother pronounced it as 'Dor-ra-thy.' "

In a dream-vision experienced in February of 1997, Pastor P.B.C. found himself standing in a strange, brightly illuminated place.

"There was nothing else there, just the light, myself, and a tall, dark figure whose face I could not see. Then, replacing the light, there was nothing but a dark mass everywhere. Shortly thereafter, there was something like a wind blowing and the dark masses began to swirl and fold into one another.

"Then I started seeing images everywhere. Some were pleasant and beautiful—others were dark and horrible.

"Suddenly a voice inside my head started speaking. It told me that this place was called the 'Dead Zone' and that while many travelers came here, only a few remained. The voice went on to say that the main way for humans to enter this realm is when they are asleep. While their body sleeps, their essence—their lifeforce, their spirit—enters this place through a 'gateway.' Once inside, they can see and experience horrible things.

"In order to leave, they have to exit through the same gateway through which they entered. Few people have any difficulty finding the gateway, but those who cannot have lost their way back and must remain in the Dead Zone until they find it."

Could the thoughtful Pastor P.B.C. have been receiving pastlife impressions of the time when he was a young girl stricken with scarlet fever? And could his subsequent vision of the Dead Zone be symbolically descriptive of a kind of limbo region wherein certain "lost" spirits await the time when they have been reconstituted spiritually and may once again return to Earth to resume their acquisition of lessons to be learned as their souls evolve toward the Godhead?

The Angels of Destiny

"In the higher dimensions after death, the souls of human beings do much reviewing and analyzing concerning their next incarnation," inspirational author Beverly Hale Watson writes in her book, *Reincarnation: The Evolutionary Path of the Soul.*

"After a long lapse of time, one understands better his own limitations as well as the qualities he needs to develop. This brings about a greater pliability and teachableness. One does not know until he returns to the outer world whether he will benefit from the resolves made between incarnations."

Assisting the human souls in their evaluation process between lives are the Kindel, the Angels of Destiny. Beverly Hale Watson describes the Kindel as those Karmic Angels who are in charge of the working and progress of evolution itself. When a soul enters into a physical life experience, it comes with the major outline of its destiny already graphed.

According to Mrs. Watson, it is the task of the Kindel to evaluate which souls need to return to Earth. About one hundred years before the next physical incarnation, each earthbound soul will receive the exclusive attention of a Kindel, who will be in charge of that entity's complete life history and spiritual evolution.

"The Angels of Destiny work with you in between incarnations," Mrs. Watson writes. "While you may have a preference as to where and when you wish to incarnate, a great deal of what you are allowed to do hinges on your karmic needs.

"You may state your desires; however, the final guidance and decision is that of the Kindel Archangel working with you. Wherever you will gain your greatest growth and spiritual aspirations will be your destination."

Lori Jean Flory, author of *The Wisdom Teachings of Archangel Michael*, repeats the words of her principal angelic guide Daephrenocles, who states that there is a waiting period that all souls must undergo before reentry into a physical body on Earth:

> Once [the soul] has become prepared to return, it undergoes a time of counseling, of meeting with angels and guides who will have charge over one's lessons, growth, and pathway. Timing is very important, since the parents have been chosen beforehand according to the necessary group and family dynamics and it has been arranged which souls one will meet again for higher growth.
>
> Before the [soul is reborn] there may be final consultations with one's guiding angels and guides that have come along to help through this one's lifetime in service. Then the veils are drawn over the memory and a new journey begins.

Heavenly Soul Voyagers Who Return to Earth

Before he left his native Sweden to come to the United States, the contemporary mystic Olof Jonsson, the psychic-sensitive who became world famous for his participation in the Moon-to-Earth ESP experiments during the flight of Apollo 14, had placed nearly one thousand people into hypnotic trance and led them back to relive what appeared to be their former lives. In some cases, researchers were able to establish the validity of the prior existences by searching through old church records and locating deeds and birth certificates in civil record repositories.

"One time when I had a subject deep in trance," Olof told us, "I moved him from the death experience to a spiritual plateau between lives. Then I asked him how the soul progresses. He said that the soul is built around a body that later develops until the point of physical death. At that time, the soul continues its wanderings in the world of spirit.

"A span of about one hundred forty-four years passes before the soul once again takes habitation in a new body, and each soul is reborn an average of twelve times. After the final incarnation, the soul becomes a wholly spiritual entity."

When Olof asked what it was like to live in Heaven, the world of spirits, his entranced subject answered that it was wonderful, he had felt so in harmony with the Universe.

"He also informed me that each soul is reunited with his soulmate, the mate he had in his first incarnation," Olof said. "The soulmate is like one's true 'other half,' and one will be whole and happy after his final incarnation."

Based on his years of study and his own spiritual insights, Olof envisions the soul leaving the earth-plane of materialism to be very much like a voyager leaving the mainland and venturing out to sea.

"After time passes, the voyager's thoughts drift farther and farther away from his life in the old world. And after he had docked in the fascinating new world, he becomes less interested in what he has left behind him and becomes more concerned about developing the new opportunities he sees before him.

"At first, the voyager may feel a bit insecure while he is getting to know new friends and so forth, but when he has established his new home, the old mainland becomes only a part of his memory."

Then why reincarnation? Why do the heavenly voyagers come back to the mainland?

"I don't believe everyone does," Olof said. "I do not believe everyone reincarnates—or at least not so often. I think it is like planting season when the farmer puts seeds into the earth. Some of the plants grow and others do not. I think it may be the same with souls. Not all of them grow properly.

"And this is where Karma, the Divine Laws of Compensation and the Supreme Law of Spiritual Growth enter into the picture. I believe that we may all have to endure certain kinds of situations, certain kinds of sufferings, in order to learn important lessons so that our souls might advance to total harmony with the Universe."

You Must Be Born Again

From 1967 until his death in 1975, we investigated dozens of cases suggestive of reincarnation with Loring "Bill" Williams, and we taped hundreds of hours with men and women dramatically providing details of what seemed to be actual life experiences which they—or, more properly, their spiritual essences—had lived in other times.

In numerous instances we, as had Olof Jonsson, found birth certificates, land grants, property transfers, military papers, and death certificates of the actual personages whom our hypnotically regressed subjects claimed to have been in prior life experiences. We also found many individuals whose spirit memories included a life between life in Heaven. Though we were by no means dogmatic about such a finding, we found an average of approximately eighty years between lifetimes on Earth.

Williams himself had come to believe that each individual possessed several layers of consciousness. "What we call physical life is only one layer—and not necessarily the bottom one. These layers go up and up," he theorized. "I think that when people die their souls first pass to a level of consciousness that is very closely related to our physical world. On that level, souls can still see what's going on in the physical world—and in some cases may be able to make contact with people who are alive in the physical world. Such instances may explain some ghost phenomena and some spirit communication."

Bill told of one instance in his research wherein a hypnotized subject recalling the period of time soon after physical death told of attempting to contact his brother by summoning enough psychic strength to knock over a lamp. But he gave up when the cat got the blame.

"I believe that a soul remains on this lower level for varying lengths of time, depending on the manner in which he died," Bill said. "I have found that those who died an early or violent death tend to stay on this lower level longer than those who die naturally, peacefully, of old age."

Bill's research indicated that the soul entities in Heaven, the spirit world, always seemed very calm just prior to the rebirth experience.

"When Jesus said that we must be born again, he may not have been trying to be as mystical as some interpreters of the Bible suggest," Bill said. "Maybe he meant exactly what he said, 'You must be born again'—period.

"Likewise his admonition to lay up treasures in Heaven rather than on Earth certainly becomes more meaningful in the dogma of Karma, the Divine Law of Compensation—what you sow, you shall reap. The life you live on Earth becomes your treasure, and the way you live your life is what counts, not how many wordly possessions you can accumulate."

And, we agreed, when Jesus told his disciples to be perfect even as the Father in Heaven is perfect, he was referring to a spiritual progression in which one's spiritual lessons continue until the soul reaches the point where it can be absorbed into the Divine Mind.

Bill Williams often stated that his research into past lives had strengthened his belief in God. "I believe that God is a force that is in everything and a part of everything."

Determining Your Principal Mission on Earth

In the period from 1977 to 1992, when we were providing individual consultations and conducting extensive seminars and workshops across the United States and overseas, we found that one of the most common sources of frustration and unrest among our clientele and our students was an inability to determine what their mission on Earth was to be. We encountered many individuals who had quit good-paying jobs and abandoned successful careers because they were continually troubled by an inner awareness that they were not doing what they had come to Earth to do.

We share now one of several exercises that we developed to assist those troubled men and women to determine their true mission on Earth. If you have been disturbed by similar inner feelings of dissatisfaction with your present life choices and an urgency to discover what you should really be doing with your life, you might wish to experiment with the following technique.

The Relaxation Technique: You may use the relaxation technique described in Chapter Six. We will remind you that it is possible for you to read the technique, pausing now and then to contemplate the significance of your inner journey.

Better, perhaps, is the enlisting of a trusted friend or family member to read the process to you. Or, as many individuals have advised, record your own voice into a cassette and thus allow your own voice to guide you through the techniques. However or whomever, the relaxation process especially should be read in a calm and unhurried manner.

We also recommend the use of some appropriate musical background, such as symphonic or New Age music.

Once the subject is in a state of deep relaxation, proceed with the spiritual exercise.

The Spiritual Exercise: Discovering Your True Mission in Life

See before you now a magnificent Angel of Destiny. This commanding figure is robed in violet and surrounded by a halo of golden light.

Although you are aware that the Angel of Destiny has made all the correct decisions concerning your spiritual evolution, you know that you have the angel's permission to ask questions.

You have permission to ask:

- *Why* you had to come once again to put on the fleshly clothes of Earth.
- *Why* you had to come in your present life as the person you are now.
- *Why* certain individuals had to enter your life to complete work left undone, to master a lesson left unlearned.

The Angel of Destiny smiles benevolently, then bends over you and touches your shoulder. Then, gently, the magnificent angel's forefinger lightly touches your eyes, your ears, your mouth.

You know within that this touching means that you are about to see and hear a wondrous revelation that will answer your question concerning your true mission in life.

Look carefully into the eyes of the Angel of Destiny.

You may likely have seen this being in your dreams. You may have been aware of this angelic being since your earliest memories. Feel the love emanating to you from the Angel of Destiny.

You feel relaxed, at peace, and at one with the Angel of Destiny.

You are now fascinated by what the Angel of Destiny holds in its hands. It is a tiny flame, such as one you might see on a match or a candle. The flame flickers and dances. You cannot keep your eyes from it.

The flame seems to capture all of your attention, and it begins to pull you toward it. It is as if your very spirit is being pulled from your body and drawn toward the flame.

The flame is becoming brighter—brighter and

larger. You cannot take your eyes from this strange, compelling flame.

You are no longer aware of anything other than the flame. It is growing larger, larger and brighter. It is as if there is nothing else in the entire Universe but the flame—the flame, the Angel of Destiny, and you.

Now you know that this is the Divine Fire. You know now that this flame has appeared to bring you illumination.

You know that it is not really a fire, not really a flame, but a divine and holy energy—the same energy that is interwoven with all of life.

Within the Divine Fire, you now see a large crystal.

The Angel of Destiny tells you that the answers to your questions about your true mission on Earth will appear on the smooth surface of the crystal each time it rings a golden bell. The Angel of Destiny holds the golden bell in its hand. It raises the bell.

When the golden bell rings, you will see on the smooth surface of the crystal the answer to the question *Why have I come to Earth in the physical body that I now wear?*

The Angel of Destiny rings the golden bell *now*! [*Pause for thirty seconds for the answer to manifest.*]

When the golden bell rings again, you will see on the smooth surface of the crystal the answer to the question *Why have I come together again with certain individuals to complete lessons or tasks left undone?*

The Angel of Destiny rings the golden bell *now*! [*Pause thirty seconds for the answer to manifest.*]

When the golden bell rings again, you will see on the smooth surface of the crystal the answer to the question *What mission am I to accomplish in this lifetime to aid my soul's evolution?*

The Angel of Destiny rings the golden bell *now*! [Pause for thirty seconds for the answer to manifest.]

And now the Angel of Destiny says that it is time for you to return to Earth time, back to human time, back to your present life experience, back to the performance of your mission.

You will remember all that you need to know for your good and your gaining.

You will be strengthened to face the challenges and the learning experiences of life.

You are now awakening, surrounded by light and by unconditional love. You feel very, very good in mind, body, and spirit. You feel better than you have in weeks, months, years.

You will awaken fully at the count of five.

CHAPTER TWELVE

A Glimpse Inside Heaven's Gates

Dr. D.P.K. said that while attending the funeral of Dr. A. C., a colleague whom he had known for over thirty years, he actually saw his friend's soul ascending to Heaven.

Dr. K. knew well that his friend's life had been one of kindness and service. He had been a sincere, practicing Catholic and had often worked in various free clinics in the city. As a colleague, he had always given unselfishly of his time and energy. Dr. C. had never married, and he had lived as strict a celibate life as any priest.

"I was thinking of my dear friend's many years of devotion to his faith and to his fellow man, when I thought that I perceived a vapor or a mist immediately beside his casket," Dr. D.P.K. said. "To be frank, I at first thought it to be a trick of the altar candles' flames reflecting off my eyeglasses. But as my attention remained focused on the mist, I was astonished to see that it gradually took on the image of Dr. C.

"I looked around me at others seated in my pew and nearby, but I saw no immediate sign that any of the other mourners were perceiving the wondrous sight which I was privileged to behold."

Dr. K. thought of his beloved grandmother with her old country perception who, when he was just a small boy, had declared that he had been born with "second sight." He acknowledged that throughout his childhood and young adulthood, he had often "seen" or "known" things before others appeared to be aware of them. He also recalled his grandmother's folklore that the soul remained near the body until after the funeral services were completed.

"While all of these recollections were swirling around inside my brain, I was startled to suddenly behold a group of white-robed children materialize in front of Dr. C.'s casket," he said. "They carried small baskets of what appeared to be flowers woven of mingled sunbeams and roses. I wondered if they were angelic beings or the spirits of children who had passed to the other side under Dr. C.'s tender and loving ministrations."

Moments later, Dr. K. saw a number of white-robed spirits materialize behind the image of his friend.

"I was able to recognize many of these spirits as deceased friends and family members of Dr. C.'s. It seemed apparent to me that these beloved ones had come to welcome their relative and friend inside Heaven's gates."

Dr. K. went on to state that almost at the very moment that the priest had completed the funeral service, a very beautiful angel, robed in the purest white, approached the newly liberated spirit of Dr. C.

"This magnificent angelic messenger bore in its hands a lovely wreath, the center of which supported a large white flower," Dr. K. said. "With this floral diadem, the angel crowned the spirit body of my dear friend, Dr. A. C."

Within the next few moments, the spirit image of Dr. C., together with the angels and the attending spirits, floated toward the large stained glass window at the side of the altar.

"For a small period in our earth time—I cannot guess how long—I was blessed to receive a glimpse of my friend returning to our true home in Heaven," Dr. D.P.K. testified.

"I saw the angelic and spirit entourage accompany Dr. C. to the beautiful pearl-white gate of an awesomely beautiful city that seemed formed of shining crystal. I saw the towering gates swing open to admit my dear friend—and then the vision faded from my view."

After the funeral service, as Dr. K. was leaving the church, he overheard one of Dr. C.'s nieces asking her small son why he had begun to giggle and become restless toward the end of the ceremony. "Oh, Mommy," the child said, smiling, "I'm sorry I laughed out loud. But I just loved it so much when the little angels came in with all the flowers for Uncle A."

In Heaven, It's What You Are that Really Counts

In 1932, Arthur Yensen had a near-death experience as the result of an automobile accident. In his book *I Saw Heaven,* which he published in 1955, he tells of his soul leaving the physical body through the top of his head and soaring to a "bright, new beautiful world." For a matter of only a few seconds, he could somehow perceive both Earth and the Next World, then he stood in a glory that could only belong to Heaven.

Yensen encountered numerous "heaven-people" who explained the wonders of Heaven. All the while he walked about Heaven, he kept noticing that the landscape was becoming more and more familiar. He could not shake the feeling that he had been there before.

"Then," he writes, "with a sudden burst of joy, I realized that this was my real home! Back on Earth I had been a visitor, a misfit, and a homesick stranger. With a sigh of relief, I said to myself, 'Thank God, I'm back again. This time I'll stay!' "

It was not yet to be. Against his protests, Yensen was told that he must return to Earth. Although he screamed and carried on "like a kid having a tantrum," his protestations did no good. He was told that he still had important work to do on Earth and that he must return and do it. When his mission was completed, then he could return to Heaven—and stay there.

Yensen did return with some interesting and valuable lessons to share with his fellow humans, however. Among them was the answer to his question of what people might do while they are living that will make things better for them when they die. According to a wise, elderly resident of Heaven:

> All you can do is to develop along the lines of unselfish love. People don't come here because of their good deeds or because they believe in this or that, but because they fit in here and they belong. Good deeds are the natural result of being good, and bad deeds are the natural result of being bad. Each carries its own reward and punishment. It's what you are that counts!

A Vision of Heaven Altered Some Long-Held Beliefs

A deeply religious fundamentalist Christian said that he received a preview of Heaven that shook some of his previously held belief concepts.

One night the Angel of the Lord lifted his soul to a beautiful place in Heaven where he was permitted to view the most awesome sights that he could ever have imagined. Then, as remarkable as it seemed, he was allowed to witness legions of angels at their work of sorting the souls of those who had recently entered the Next World.

The Angel of the Lord informed him that a pure belief and faith in God were basic requirements for the soul to enter Heaven. But, he was told to his astonishment, *not just those labeled Christian could enter Heaven.*

There were good teachings in other religions as well, and there were many who believed in God and kept the commandments besides Christians. While most of the teachings of fundamental Christianity were good, humankind, in its ignorance, had abused and misused many of its principles. As startling as it was to his former beliefs, he was shown that it was a *defiance* of God and that which is good that separated the souls at the appointed time, rather than adherence to a particular religious creed.

The revelator stated that he had been and will continue to be a fundamentalist Christian. "But," he added, "my view of what is fundamentally real has changed."

A Visit to Heaven Healed Her Crushed Skull

When L. B.'s horse stepped into a gopher hole as she was riding on the back portion of the ranch, the first prayer that came to her mind was, "Please, Dear God, don't let his legs break!"

"My stepsister and I had been looking for some underweight cows when she spotted them at a distance and we decided to race," L. B. said in her account to us. "I had just got up speed when the stallion that I had been training stepped in that gopher hole. I saw the ground racing up toward me . . . then I lost all conscious awareness and everything went black."

The next thing L. B. knew, she was floating in a gray, cloudy tunnel toward a white light. Then she was in a half-sitting position and was looking at an entity who she thought must surely be God himself.

"He was sitting on a white throne, clothed in white robes, and there was a brilliant—but not blinding—pure white light in front of his face."

As she lay there before the brilliant heavenly throne, L. B. was aware of three beings behind her, working on the back of her head. When she tried to turn around to see them, one of them told her, "Lie still. Don't turn around. You're not supposed to know what we look like."

L. B. did as she was instructed and decided to enjoy the reality of Heaven. "The atmosphere there was one of indescribably joyous love, peace, and contentment—and everything made perfect sense. I wanted to stay there, and I begged the Creator to allow me to remain. I think he was about to let me when the three beings said they were finished and they left."

As L. B. remained before the heavenly throne, the brilliant being showed her the planet Earth, "as if from an orbit, but much farther away."

L. B. asked, "What about Earth? What's going to happen to it?"

The light being answered her by saying, "That's why you have to go back."

L. B. remembered saying, "Okay," and then she was back in her body, lying on the ground.

As she slowly returned to full consciousness, she saw her employer, the ranch owner, stepping out of his pickup. As he ran toward her, L. B. started to get to her feet.

"He looked surprised to see me awake," she recalled. "I told him that I just had a slight headache and had a little dizziness. There was no blood or bruising on me, just some dust. I was more concerned about my horse, and I was relieved to see that his legs were all right."

The ranch owner helped her to a cold drink of

fresh spring water. L. B. checked out her horse to see for herself that he was fine, then she saddled up to ride back after the cattle—though she was still filled with a longing for the heavenly kingdom of love, peace, and contentment and found it a bit difficult to concentrate on rounding up cows.

Later, her stepsister told her that after the horse had gone knee-deep in the gopher hole, L. B. had flipped over the stallion's head and landed hard on the ground. Then the horse had rolled over on top of her, pushing the saddle horn into the back of her head.

When her stepsister had ridden back to the barn to get help, L. B.'s head had looked caved-in and crushed so bad that she thought L. B. must surely be dead.

According to L. B.: "This whole experience has left me totally inspired with love, faith, and trust in our infinite Creator—and now I have no fear of dying. I guess my fear of death has left me because now I know what awaits me in Heaven."

A Meditation to Alleviate the Fear of Death

It may well be that most people fear death because it is the ultimate voyage into the unknown.

A recently published booklet entitled *Beings of All Directions: Messages and Meditations* by Liberty Anderson and Wybrechtje Smit contains an effective meditation that has been provided by the authors to help people overcome their fear of death or any other troublesome facet of the unknown.

"The root of fear is fear," Anderson and Smit state

simply enough. "Fear of the great unknown, which is not unknown. The unknown relates to the future, and the future does not exist since all time is *now.*"

They recommend embracing the fear and using it as a driving force versus a paralyzing force. Release the fear of the unknown, they say, live mindfully, live in each and every moment, and trust that the Universe will offer only that which you are prepared to face.

Fear, they affirm, interferes with self-realization. "Fear is related to the ego, which is part of the mind. Fear is control, control of self and others. Fear is lack of control, lack of control of self and others. The only control one has is how to deal with the present, so let go of the fear—because it is an illusion."

Anderson and Smit urge those struggling with fears of death or other apprehensions to face them, embrace them, and let them go. "Make a conscious decision to live in love, not in fear. Love and fear cannot coexist. The choice is yours."

The authors suggest that you might be guided to use sound and color during the following meditation. Experiment, they say, be playful, and use discernment.

The Meditation

Take a few moments to focus on your breathing. Breathe *in* unconditional love. Breathe *out* fear.

As you let go of fear, replace it with Love. Universal Energy is Unconditional Love. Set your intent to spin all chakras/energy centers in your body. The gravitational force thus created will attract Universal Energy/Unconditional Love.

Visualize this Unconditional Love entering your body with the breath and through the chakras.

Now, focus your intent to the energy flowing

through the meridians (grid systems) of the body and connecting with the grid systems of the Earth and the Universe.

Take a few moments to experience your connectedness to the Earth and Universe.

When you are ready, return your focus to your breathing and your bodily sensations. Slowly open your eyes, and reorient yourself to your environment. Remember to drink plenty of water after each meditation.

Exactly Where Is Heaven?

In her book, *Your Passport to Heaven,* Diane Tessman, head of the Starlite Mystic Center, answers that age-old question by acknowledging that, according to all existing evidence, there is every reason to believe that when we die our soul will travel to a place, a region, a level of consciousness that befits the manner in which we lived our life on Earth. But, she qualifies, according to her channeled information, Heaven is not one single place.

> Heaven is a series of spiritual zones that are literally the way you believe and wish them to be. There are a multitude of heavens each with their own individual characteristics. In essence, the Heaven we go to is a place that is exactly what we deserve, because our minds have created its existence through our deeds and efforts while on the physical plane.

Diane cautions us not to be quick to judge such a belief concept as heresy. "Remember that after his resurrection, Jesus said that He was going to Heaven to prepare a place for us, and that in His Father's house there were *'many mansions.'* Jesus never said that there was only one Heaven. He, in fact, indicated that there were at least several dwelling places where we would go to join the Almighty."

Diane also comments upon those who have returned to consciousness and life after surviving near-death experiences. "It has become evident that as a well-meaning person you will find Heaven to be a beautiful place where goodness and peace abide always."

Just as the material world has its solid walls, streets, trees, and so forth and is solid because the human mind/spirit has solidified its reality in order to find direction and meaning, so, she maintains, will the dimension of Heaven where one will go be a solid place as well.

"Heaven is literally a higher level of consciousness; a complete and real dimension for your consciousness to dwell upon. . . . Whatever level of awareness you have progressed to, this is exactly the zone your soul will inhabit in the afterworld.

"Briefly, Heaven is exactly what you think it is! It will be real and solid for you in exactly the dimension your spirit perceives and deserves."

Heavenly Levels of Soul Progress

Lori Jean Flory has relayed information from her angelic guide Daephrenocles that explains that a soul who has just made the transition from the physical body will travel through levels of dimensional, vibrational frequences that become more and more light.

> The farther that one is away from the third-dimensional pull of Earth, traversing at a high speed through the tunnel of light, moving home to the heavenly realms of the Light, the faster one moves toward the Light. [The spirit] can feel the vibrational shift occur as each dimension is traversed, and it becomes lighter and lighter until it is once again home in the realms of light.

The great psychical researcher Frederic W.H. Myers, whom we quoted earlier in this book, passed to the Next World in 1901. After his arrival on the other side, he is said to have communicated a series of messages to various mediums that dealt with the heavenly environment. According to the spirit of Myers, the soul experienced seven planes of existence, each one preparing the entity for the higher level:

- The Earth Plane of physical, three-dimensional existence
- The Intermediate Plane, wherein the spirit undergoes a Life Review after physical death
- The Plane of Illusion, a dimension of total mind
- The Plane of Color, a new level of consciousness for the spirit
- The Plane of Flame, in which the spirit achieves freedom from our solar system
- The Plane of Light, the final step in the spirit's evolution
- Timelessness, living in eternity with the Godhead

The spirit entity Portia, communicating through Liz "Liberty" Anderson, also states that the newly released soul must travel through various heavenly levels:

> Yes, there are certain levels, as you call them, that [spirits] must travel through, depending where their final destination is to be. There are levels of consciousness surrounding all planetary spheres. Many of these are traversed without the conscious knowledge of the departing soul. You travel in *merkabah* [defined in the *Keys of Enoch* as a vehicle of Divine Light] and therefore knowledge of the other spheres is not conscious, *per se*, but on a higher level you know where you are.
>
> There are seven levels of consciousness surrounding your planet and within each another seven levels of "beingness." Wheels within wheels, level within level. These are often referred to as the seven mansion worlds. Remember, there are worlds within worlds—and yours is not the exception.

Heaven Is Our Home

We human beings are more things than we can imagine. More processes take place within us than we know.

We are all multidimensional beings, comfortable in many dimensions of reality—and while today we are transitory citizens of Earth, our inner knowing continually reminds us that our true home is in Heaven.

The ancient alchemist's goal was not simply the transmutation of base metals into gold. That legendary much-sought-after process really served as a metaphor for the desired transmutation of the alchemist's base, material self into a purer being of higher consciousness.

We should all strive to become spiritual alchemists, concerned always with the process of transforming our physical mundane selves into the beings of light who make Heaven their permanent residence.

Although Earth is a lovely oasis in space that provides us with the building blocks of our physical existence, it is we ourselves who must work toward bringing our spiritual selves to heavenly perfection. Through our individual processes of spiritual alchemy, we must strive to make the impure into the pure. And because all potentialities are inherent within each of us, what we awaken within us will manifest and come forth.

Only the soul lives eternally. Our soul will endure while our body decays, just as a seed must rot if it is to bear fruit.

Decay has been called the midwife of great things. It brings about the birth and rebirth of forms a thousand times removed. It has been said that this process is the highest and the greatest mystery of God.

There is nothing in Heaven or in Earth that is not also in our immortal souls. All the forces of Heaven operate in us and through us. In the soul essence of each of us is God, who is also in Heaven.

We must honor all people equally, bearing in mind the soul essence that is in us is also in all others. And until we make our final transition to the Next World, where else can Heaven be found if not in each other?

References and Resources

Chapter One: Heaven Is Our Home

1. Source for the statement comes from Roper Starch Worldwide for *Worth*. Anne R. Carey and Kay Worthington for *USA Today*, October 24–26, 1997.

2. Miller, Leslie. "More Report Mystical Experiences." *USA Today*, January 12, 1994.

3. Sheler, Jeffrey L. "Heaven in the Age of Reason." *U.S. News & World Report*, March 31, 1997.

4. *ibid.*

Dr. Bruce Goldberg may be contacted at 4300 Natoma Avenue, Woodland Hills, CA 91364. 800-527-6248.

To obtain a copy of the *Steiger Questionnaire of Paranormal, Mystical, and UFO Experiences* send a stamped, self-addressed envelope to Timewalker Productions, P.O. Box 434, Forest City, IA 50436.

Recommended Reading

McDannell, Collen & Lang, Bernhard. *Heaven—A History*. Vintage Books: New York, 1990.

Steinour, Harold. *Exploring the Unseen World*. Citadel Press: New York, 1959.

Sullivan, Lawrence E. (Editor). *Death, Afterlife, and the Soul*. Macmillan: New York, 1987, 1989.

Swedenborg, Emanuel (Translated by John C. Ager; Introduction by Helen Keller). *Heaven and Its Wonders and Hell*. Citadel Press: New York, 1965.

Chapter Two: Out-of-Body Visits to the Other Side

Lori Jean Flory may be contacted at Touch of Wings Publishing, PO Box 1328, Conifer, CO 80433.

For more information about Leia Stinnett's books and classes, write to her at 813 W. University Avenue, #112, Flagstaff, AZ 86001.

Contact Diane Tessman, Starlite Mystic Center, Box 352, St. Ansgar, IA 50472.

Recommended Reading

Atwater, P.M.H. *Beyond the Light*. Birch Lane Press: New York, 1994.

Moody, Jr., Raymond A. *Life After Life*. Mocking Bird Books: Covington, GA, 1977.

Morse, Melvin with Paul Perry. *Closer to the Light: Learning from the Near-Death Experiences of Children*. Villard Books: New York, 1990.

Ring, Kenneth. *Life at Death*. Coward, McCann & Geoghegan: New York, 1980.

Steiger, Brad. *One with the Light.* Signet: New York, 1994.

———and Sherry Hansen Steiger. *Children of the Light.* Signet, 1995.

Chapter Three: Angelic Beings Who Guide Spirits Home

Kay L. Barrett may be reached at the Sevenfold Peace Foundation, 215 Lake Trail Drive, Double Oak, TX 75067

Recommended Reading

Denning, Hazel M. *True Hauntings: Spirits with a Purpose.* Llewellyn: St. Paul, 1996.

Flory, Lori Jean. *The Wisdom Teachings of Archangel Michael.* Signet: New York, 1997.

Steiger, Brad. *Angels of Love.* Pinnacle Books: New York, 1995.

———and Sherry Hansen Steiger. *Angels Over Their Shoulders: Children's Encounters with Heavenly Beings.* Fawcett Columbine: New York, 1995.

Chapter Four: Loved Ones Who Left Heaven for a Final Farewell

Liz Smith Anderson, also known as "Liberty," may be contacted at 2926 Forest Hills Circle, Rock Hill, SC 29732-9418.

1. Flammarion, Camille. *Death and Its Mystery After Death.* The Century Company: New York and London, 1923.

2. Dreifus, Claudia. "At Home with Streisand:

Love Soft as an Easy Chair (Cue the Violins)." *The New York Times*, November 11, 1997.

3. "Jaclyn Smith: How Granddad's Ghost Changed My Life!" *Examiner*, November 3, 1992.

4. Mullins, Joe. "The Ghost of My Dead Father Saved My Life." *National Enquirer*, October 8, 1991.

5. Smith, Virginia. "Exclusive Interview: Susan Lucci." *Examiner*, December 4, 1990.

6. Anderson, Liz Smith. *Death: Our Portal to Life!* Sevenfold Peace Foundation: Double Oak, TX, 1997.

7. Flory, Lori Jean. *Death: Our Portal to Life!* Sevenfold Peace Foundation: Double Oak, TX, 1997.

Recommended Reading

Baird, A.T. (Editor). *One Hundred Cases for Survival After Death.* Bernard Ackerman: New York, 1944.

Flammarion, Camille. *Death and Its Mystery After Death.* The Century Company: New York and London, 1923.

Jeffrey, Grant R. *Heaven: The Last Frontier.* Bantam Books: New York, 1991.

Sherman, Harold. *You Live After Death.* Fawcett: New York, 1972.

Smith, Alson J. *Immortality: The Scientific Evidence.* Prentice Hall: New York, 1954.

Chapter Five: The Mystery of Mediumship: Talking to Heaven's Inhabitants

Irene F. Hughes may be contacted at The Golden Path, 500 N. Michigan Avenue, #1040, Chicago, IL 60611.

Recommended Reading

Borgia, Anthony. *Life in the World Unseen.* Odhams Press: Long Acre, London, 1954.

Gibbes, E.B. (Compiler from the unpublished scripts of Geraldine Cummins) *They Survive.* Rider & Company: New York & London, *circa* 1943.

Sherman, Harold. *The Dead Are Alive and Do Communicate with You.* Amherst Press: Amherst, Wisconsin, 1981.

Steiger, Brad. *Know the Future Today: The Amazing Prophecies of Irene Hughes.* Paperback Library: New York, 1970.

Chapter Six: Guardian Angels and Spirit Guides: Heaven's Personal Messengers

Carrington, Hereward. *The Case for Psychic Survival.* Citadel Press: New York, 1957.

Recommended Reading

Borgia, Anthony. *More About Life in the World Unseen.* Odhams Press: Long Acre, London, 1956.

Hastings, Arthur. *With the Tongues of Men and Angels.* Holt, Rinehart and Winston: Fort Worth, 1991.

Steiger, Brad. *Guardian Angels and Spirit Guides.* Plume Books: New York, 1995.

———and Sherry Hansen Steiger. *Angels Around the World.* Fawcett Columbine: New York, 1996.

Chapter Seven: Station H-E-A-V-E-N Calling Earth: The Enigma of Electronic Voice Communication

1. As quoted in *Your Passport to Heaven* by Diane

Tessman and Timothy Green Beckley, Inner Light: New Brunswick, NJ, 1998.
2. *ibid.*
3. Sterner, Kay. A *Psychic Explores the Unseen World.* California Parapsychology Foundation: Lemon Grove, CA, 1984.
4. Estep, Sarah Wilson. *Voice of Eternity.* Fawcett Gold Medal: New York, 1988.
5. *ibid.*
6. *ibid.*
7. Tessman & Beckley. *Your Passport to Heaven.*
8. *ibid.*
9. Spaeth, Frank. "Electronic Communication with the Great Beyond: An Interview with Mark Macy." *Fate,* February 1997.

Recommended Reading

Estep, Sarah Wilson. *Voice of Eternity.* Fawcett Gold Medal: New York, 1988.

Raudive, Konstanin (Translated by Nadia Fowler; edited by Joyce Morton). *Breakthrough.* Taplinger: New York, 1971.

Uphoff, Walter and Mary Jo. *New Psychic Frontiers: Your Key to New Worlds.* Colin Smythe Limited: Gerrards Cross, Buck, England, 1975.

Chapter Eight: Receiving Messages from Those Spirits Who Dwell in Heaven's Harbor

1. Quote from George Lindsay Johnson. See Recommended Reading for this chapter.

Recommended Reading

Crookall, Robert. *Intimations of Immortality.* James Clarke: London, 1965.

Johnson, George Lindsay. *Does Man Survive?* Harper & Brothers: New York and London, 1936.

Loehr, Franklin. *Diary After Death.* Religious Research Frontiers: Los Angeles, 1976.

Van Dusen, Wilson. *The Natural Depth in Man.* Harper & Row: New York, 1972.

Chapter Nine: Dreams, Visions, and Voices from the Next World

Stuart, Richard. "My Little Boy Visited Me from Heaven." *Examiner*, November 15, 1994.

John Harricharan may be contacted at 2130 Mark Hall Court, Marietta, GA 30062.

Recommended Reading

Steiger, Sherry & Brad. *The Teaching Power of Dreams.* Whitford Press: West Chester, PA, 1990.

Van Dusen, Wilson. *The Presence of Other Worlds.* Harper & Row: New York, 1974.

Chapter Ten: Touched by Heaven's Light

Johnston, Linda. "My Guardian Angel Guided Me Back to the Land of the Living." *Examiner.* June 28, 1994.

Recommended Reading

Goldberg, Bruce. *Soul Healing.* Llewellyn Publications: St. Paul, 1996.

Steiger, Sherry Hansen. *The Power of Prayer to Heal and Transform Your Life.* Signet Visions: New York, 1997.

Steiger, Brad. *The Healing Power of Love.* Whitford Press: West Chester, PA, 1988.

———. *Exploring the Power Within.* Whitford Press: West Chester, PA, 1989.

Chapter Eleven: Heavenly Memories of Life Before Life

For information about the very useful booklet *Reincarnation: Evolutionary Path of the Soul,* write to Beverly Hale Watson, Sevenfold Peace Foundation, 215 Lake Trail Drive, Double Oak, TX 75067.

Recommended Reading

Binder, Bettye B. *Discovering Your Past Lives and Other Dimensions.* PO Box 7781, Culver City, CA 90233-7781

Cerminara, Gina. *Many Mansions.* William Morrow: New York, 1950

Steiger, Brad. *Returning from the Light.* Signet: New York, 1996.

———. *You Will Live Again.* Confucian Press: New York, 1978; Blue Dolphin: Grass Valley, CA, 1996.

Sutphen, Richard. *You Were Born Again to Be Together.* Pocket Books: New York, 1976.

Whitton, Joel L. & Joe Fisher. *Life Between Life.* Doubleday: New York, 1986.

Chapter Twelve: A Glimpse Inside Heaven's Gates

For information about the booklet of messages and

meditations *Beings of All Directions,* write to Liberty Anderson, 2926 Forest Hill Circle, Rock Hill, SC 29732-9418.

Death: Our Portal to Life is a compendium of the thoughts of five popular contemporary spiritual teachers about life after death. Included are the comments and channeled teachings of Liz Smith Anderson, Kay L. Barrett, Gina Fenske, Lori Jean Flory, and Leia Stinnet. For information, write to Sevenfold Peace Foundation, 215 Lake Trail Drive, Double Oak, TX 75067.

Your Passport to Heaven by Diane Tessman and Timothy Green Beckley may be ordered directly from Inner Light Publications, Box 753, New Brunswick, NJ 08903.